I0652017

William Wickliffe Johnson

Sketches of the late depression

Its cause, effect and lessons

William Wickliffe Johnson

Sketches of the late depression
Its cause, effect and lessons

ISBN/EAN: 9783744723497

Printed in Europe, USA, Canada, Australia, Japan

Cover: Foto ©Andreas Hilbeck / pixelio.de

More available books at **www.hansebooks.com**

SKETCHES

OF THE

LATE DEPRESSION;

ITS CAUSE, EFFECT AND LESSONS.

WITH

A Synoptical Review of Leading Trades

DURING THE

PAST DECADE.

———————

BY

WILLIAM WICKLIFFE JOHNSON,

Manager for Dun, Wiman & Co.,

MONTREAL.

———————

J. THEO. ROBINSON, Publisher.

1882.

CONTENTS.

———•———

(OVER.)

PREFACE.

—•◦•—

Ordinarily, the writing up of prosaic commercial axioms and histories requires little introduction; the work proceeds in a groove of its own, the phrases made common by usage, the customs in vogue among merchants, and the conditions surrounding trade situations tend to make a compilation of this character mechanical, and create but small necessity for a preface.

I have endeavoured, however, to place some old but wholesome truths in as strong a light as is possible for me to reflect, and my object has been to emphasize their meaning and value.

My belief that morality goes hand in hand with success in business, that extremely valuable lessons can be learned during a period of adversity—so well learned that they will never be forgotten in the flush of better years,—together with other points which it seems to me are seldom thoroughly considered, will be illustrated in the succeeding sketches, and, if my effort serves to remind merchants that there is a higher, yet accessible plane of action for the class to reach in their dealings with each other,—a line of business morale the exercise of which may cause fewer regrets when opportunities for reform become less frequent, I shall have attained the object which is paramount in writing this book.

W. W. J.

Montreal, April, 1882.

CHIEF CAUSES OF THE DEPRESSION.

The inauguration of our recent protracted and exceptionally severe period of stagnation, disaster, and general shrinkage in commerce may be chronicled as dating from the spring of 1874. Its sure approach, however, was shadowed forth during the previous two years,—to those who closely studied the logic of events, and kept alive to the conditions creating these.

The downfall of several houses of the mushroom type of growth, of weak and uncertain antecedent record, with little claim to consideration in any sense, yet who had managed to work up large turnovers of business through the overweening credit-confidence of the time, was the earliest result of an almost unparalleled inflation. These failures were followed by the stoppage of a few sounder interests, and by the attempted contraction of business in more conservative quarters, until the advent of an extended term of depression became fully patent.

In the bright light afforded by calm reflection in these latter years, it seems incredible from many points of view, that dispensers of credit in the money centres, possessing, as many of them did, a comprehensive knowledge of the Dominion's capacity respecting the proportion of imports to exports, and a close count of population and consequent ratio of supply and demand, should have been caught with unfurled sails in the wildest adverse gale which ever swept the commercial interests of our country. But once committed as we were, the actual force and severity of the situation tended for a long time thereafter to keep alive elements antagonistic in character—a natural outcome of our surroundings in 1874. The general desire to make poor ventures *pay out* to the best advantage, the scramble for security as well as continued accommodation, the difficulty of getting discount limits down to a normal point, the poor eventual realization of long-nursed assets, and the shifts and expedients resorted to in the attempt to stave off the inevitable day of settlement, only resulted in a prolongation of the trouble, and final greater loss ensued to all, save to those few who had not departed from the business principles of the preceding generation.

The effects of these trade disturbances were, from first to last, most acutely felt in the Province of Quebec, though the depresssion was general. The Maritime Provinces also felt distress seriously, but it attacked their interests in alternate years, and their worst periods did not run into each other so closely as was the case in the former Province. Their troubles were the result of more exceptional causes—such as the spasmodic action of the West India interest, mining paralyzation and losses, serious fires and subsequent overbuilding—while upon the Province of Quebec—at its metropolis—fell the brunt of the effect of local troubles at *all* points throughout the country, as well as those peculiar to its own boundaries. Among the latter may be classed its weak and partial agricultural development, its stationary mining interests, its loss of a large revenue from lumber production—which in better times found its chief channels to be those leading through Montreal and Quebec—and its grossly overdone state of business in all branches. Its chief cities by natural causes were made the centres of losses occurring through failures in every part of the Dominion, in proportion as the merchants of these cities reached out into every Province to find customers. Throughout three-fourths of the decade ending with 1880, the pro-rata amount of actual loss thus fathered by this Province was—it is safe to estimate—three dollars to one sustained by any other trade centre.

The result of this undermining of strength at the end of 1880, is made clear by the record of casualties during the time quoted. From 1872 to the end of 1880, *one hundred and forty-nine wholesalers and manufacturers were swept entirely out of existence in this unfortunate Province*, while ninety-two additional houses had failed, but continued business with an impairment average of capital and turnover of about 50 per cent. During the same period three banks were forced to retire from business, and three reduced their capital largely. In the above recapitulation of the embarrassments of the era, only the larger concerns are enumerated, whose existence was largely dependent upon continued confidence, and the vitality created by a sounder state of affairs ; the other Provinces show a much better record, the casualities in the same class of houses being not over two-thirds in number, and representing not quite five-eights of the same liability. Adding to this gloomy history the actual numerical record proportion of other smaller unfortunates, as well as the count of all cases of failure in other Provinces, we have the fearful ratio for the two darkest years of the decade, of one failure in every twenty-eight, and one in every twenty-nine traders respectively.

While the commercial interests of Canada then were subjected by local causes to this extensive purging and reactionary effect, other countries were passing through the throes of serious and general disturbance. The great Republic laying to the south, with its enormous vitality and self-contained strength, found a general revival of trade impossible for nearly five years, and as a consequence drew upon Canadian lumbermen for but meagre requirements in the way of sawn stuff, its building interests being clogged and demoralized. The depressed state of affairs in the old country also operated against any increase in the demand for our square timber and other products, we had no help from any quarter to an appreciable extent, in the way of gain through commercial interchange or demand ; we were simply forced to undergo the process of gradual elimination of weak elements within our own boundaries, and through concentration at home, work out the problem which pointedly presented itself for solution in 1874.

Among the chief direct causes which steadily led up to a crippled condition of the countries energies then, were first : the encouragement extended, through credit being cheap, to enterprises which were already overdone, or which were comparatively untried. This state of things was in turn easily referable for explanation to the fact that we had too much banking capital seeking employment, and to the immense importations of 1872, 1873, 1874 and 1875. During two of these years our imports rolled up the annual amount of $127,000,000 ; an increase since 1871 of $41,000,000, for the respective years, while the exports during the same two years were only an average of $89,000,000—an advance of but $15,000,000 in the same length of time. This large excess of importation was caused by the wonderful readiness of English merchants to enlarge the credit facilities of small jobbers here, who really possessed but little general aptitude for business, and were known—in many cases—to wield insufficient capital. All houses, however, shared, more or less, in being tempted to load up with stocks in undue proportion to the actual necessities of the country, and this pressure of goods led quite naturally to desperate measures for relief, and provision against the dates upon which old country acceptances matured, and to the fostering of the "support account" system. This method of unloading surplus stocks was not entirely new, but had never proved successful, and for very good reasons, for those in charge of these "support branches" were in the main mere *figure heads*. They owned very little of the capital at stake, and, through the exigencies of the city wholesaler—their chief creditor— were often forced to realize at *any* price in order to provide him with fresh paper, which, in turn, had to be discounted at ruinous rates, if accepted at bank. Not only were these weak branches newly established throughout the country, but the evil was extended to many country dealers of sounder character. These, attracted by the generous, rose-coloured inducements presented by commercial travellers, bought far more largely than ever before, and found that though the assets were representatives of value, their realization was more uncertain of accomplishment in a given time, than were the certain and inevitable dates of the maturity of corresponding liability. Renewals then became the order of the day, with their eventual loss of interest and attendant anxiety. Business, under these circumstances could not be made profitable, unless a country merchant found himself commanding a wide and healthy district where competition had not yet succeeded in paralyzing his trade. These vantage points were soon discovered after 1873, then, between the "support account" dealer, and the insolvent estate realization of some unfortunate *confrere* in his immediate vicinity, the legitimate merchant found his hands tied, and was in very many cases forced to live upon the substance accumulated by former years of close attention to business and self-denial.

The *terms upon which goods were largely sold* during a greater part of the last ten years has also contributed indirectly to depress and handicap our merchants as well as manufacturers. The plan of "dating forward" of merchandize obligations, by its tempting but illusory promise of ease, was the motor by which the "support account" system was endowed with life, and it led to the continuance, if not to the inauguration, of this mischievous feature of modern business. The English merchant has, over and over again, sold goods to Canadian importers, upon practically, a nine month's credit, and renewals in some cases have lengthened out the time to twelve months before actual, final realization by the English merchant, or his banker, was accomplished. Following this lead, the Canadian manufacturer marks out the same line of procedure, and after one or two seasons finds himself loaded up with a lot of goods he ought never to have made, but which he has counted upon disposing of in the same unsound manner. His banking facilities— never as good as those of the wholesaler, because of his locked-up capital, and the early effect upon his business of a bad agricultural year, over-production, labour troubles, &c.,—are now curtailed, and he inevitably suffers a resulting shrinkage of surplus and vitality. This, because he went beyond the natural principles governing the safe-conduct of his peculiarly sensitive line of business, and declined to stop manufacturing until he could place his products where and when they were actually needed and could be paid for within legitimate dates.

A cause which intensified existing troubles had its origin in the very lenient treatment extended to farmers by general store merchants in nearly every agricultural district. It has grown to be a very common occurrence for grain-growing, and even for general produce raisers to expect from their local merchants a credit of months in advance of the dates upon which their crops can be marketed. In many cases, country dealers have foreseen the pernicious effects of this practice, when made the rule instead of the exception, they have also been quite aware of the fact that should they take firm stand upon the point, and either refuse to entertain such an unsound and hazardous mode of continuing an account, or endeavour to hedge by limiting terms, or insisting upon collateral in the shape of chattel mortgages, they would soon find their business reduced to a minimum. Their old time customers, whose business was valuable until it became inoculated with this weakness, would go over to "support account" stores or to other dealers whose ruling passion impelled them to accept any overtures in the hope of being able to run up large turnovers. These latter merchants *must* please their city backers with large weekly returns of so-called sales, and thus create for themselves a new lease of life as country managers for their ambitious and needy patrons.

These evil features of modern business have been, and still are well-nigh unlimited in their decidedly bad and unwholesome effect. The farmer is tempted aside from the path in which alone success is won by his class; he not only gives rein to unnecessary expenditure, when goods can so easily be got, but he immediately and voluntarily shoulders a mountain of liability in the shape of interest. Than this, nothing is so insidious in its grówth and disastrous when it is opposed to the small margin of gain afforded the farmer in a bad year; or when through city speculation, the prices of his product is beaten down to less than the crop can be grown for, even by a *well-to-do* farmer with no shackles about him in the way of debt.

The country merchant in turn finds his business abnormally swelled, the second and third years of such dealing telling fearfully upon net results, though the first promised great things perhaps. His anxiety now commences; the original credit has grown with each season; he cannot bring his customer up to sharp terms, but must go with him and face the ever-growing exhibit of unrealizable outstandings. He has ceased to feel the independence of old, he renews in the city, and his interest account eats up all he might have made had he worked upon a sounder policy. He will not face the exigencies he has himself created, and call his creditors together. No! this is the very last thing the *modern merchant feels called upon to do;* but he continues with many a shift destructive of his manhood, and only leading him deeper into the mire, until he is just in the position, that when called upon to oblige his city creditor by going upon accommodation paper to ease the latter, he is his slave sufficiently to do it, and without in many cases the slightest hesitation. Unfortunately, such has been the record of many of this class during the last eight years, and the cause is to be found in the strange laxity of credit conditions.

The city wholesaler, in due course, must get relief. He makes all he can of the comparatively few good country marks still upon his books;

their paper it is which gives him countenance at his bank, and with it, if he has learned the lessons of *modern finance*, he slides in under cover, such paper as is not at once known to be of the " kite" order. His props, however, gradually drop away as his demoralization becomes manifest. The "official assignees," under the Act of 1875, get hold of past due obligations, and a writ is served by which he is placed where he ought to have been months before, *i.e.*, the insolvent stage. Thus we see the outcome of the credit system, as practised for so many years in our country. Beginning with the farmer, who has been allowed, not only to pile up a big advance credit upon the strength of his coming crop, but in some cases has actually kept his country storekeeper out of money for several seasons upon an old account, until he could get better prices for his *old* grain, the evil spreads in all directions, the lead is toward sharp dealing, the life is sapped from each who participate in this triangular duel, the outrage upon sound trade principles is complete.

The advantages of a *practical business training* for young merchants has not been sufficiently considered, a thorough knowledge of the general trade conditions of their country is seldom acquired by them, a niche is found for them, and they embark, their only experience being of a theoretical character. The homeliness of business detail, and the dull routine of practical application should never, they argue, be forced upon *them*, for are not their positions made for them by some grubbing father—who never made money as rapidly as they expect to do, and who was never as much of a gentleman as are they. It might be very well for the last generation to train for the slow gains then possible, but results in latter days must come more quickly, and as detail knowledge becomes distasteful, it is supplanted by *speculation*. Gains may accrue, but are seldom enduring ones ; inherited capital is lost ; kind but weak fathers are ruined, and the modern scion *then* begins in some subordinate position, the learning of the true business alphabet.

There are other causes which lead up to commercial disaster ; these are more fully treated in a subsequent sketch, it would be out of place in this chapter to recapitulate them, but the careful attention of the reader is invited to their perusal in due course.

MORALITY IN BUSINESS.

"He who by the card of the world's opinion steers his course, shall harbour in no safe port."

"The thoughtful man of business, whatever his religious belief, does not fail to perceive that there is commercial, as well as spiritual danger in everything which unsettles the confidence of man in man, and tends to overthrow that faith in right and truth which must be the foundation of all legitimate transactions. Were this belief not generally accepted, commerce would inevitably become a mere contest between unscrupulous knaves, amongst whom honour would be a synonym for expediency, truth for a clever concealment of deception, and apparent honesty a cloak against the discovery of fraud."

It was a beautiful custom—that of the old Holland merchants of a century ago, when they labelled their ledgers in gilt type—" with God ;" the interpretation being that their acts with their fellows could be safely left to His inspection. In our dealings with each other, we are not always provided with a touchstone by which we can distinguish the true from the false, but it is certain that without trust in, and reliance upon man's fine and inner sense of honour, no general business can be for any length of time successfully done. Men may become warped in their judgment of right and wrong, circumstances may arise which are closely associated with self-interest, and prevent the correct perception of truth and honour. But the majority of business men, as they sit in their offices during a pause in the day's busy whirl, or whenever a quiet hour of reflection comes to them, recognize their dependence upon commercial honour and sincerity, for *very life*, in a financial sense. More than this, the evidence of experienced and right-thinking men, after a battle of years with the world, is to the effect, that *naturally* mankind is honest, that purity is preferred, if not yearned for by their brothers, that their general intention is to acquire a good reputation, and that they mostly desire to practice the golden rule which really binds men together. That cases of fraud occur is true, yet these are always made more prominent than are the numberless instances of devotion to principle ; the countless, though often unnoticed examples and sacrifices in the cause of right. The depression from which our country is now freshly emerging, is so close to us in the immediate past, that we all can, without much effort, recall individual cases of deception and resulting disappointment, even among those whom we have thought bound by every instinct of honour and sentiment to keep faith with us. Such experience it is which causes the iron of general distrust to enter our souls, and by its sharp reaction to paralyze and deaden our belief in, and sympathy for others. Though natural, perhaps, this judgment of men and motives is most unsound, and always assists during a period of commercial trial, in bringing about an intensified, if not a chronic state of doubt and fear, and a consequent increase of disaster.

Saddled with such a disproportionate weight of trade interests as has been our country during eight years of the last decade, what wonder is it that instances of sharp dealing have resulted? With such pressure upon trade situations as to cause a failure in every twenty-eight merchants, is it wonderful that dark-hued cases, and breaches of faith arise in our retrospect of the era? Men have been cornered as they never were before; heretofore profitable interests have suffered the most extreme and unlooked for shrinkages; everything has conspired to drive merchants into desperate resort and expedient, and human nature unfortified by long and careful moral training, has at intervals succumbed. There is, however, a more cheering side to this mental review of the period. How many actual cases of dishonesty can we enumerate? How great a proportion of disaster has been characterized by fraud? Is not the record comparatively an excellent one? Decidedly it is! and in common justice to humanity let us also, as recollections crowd fast upon us, keep clear and sweet the events of the past, where traders have been *honestly* unfortunate. Where they have presented clean showings to their creditors, in which no preferences were prominent, for years living as closely and as prudently as though they were employes instead of principals—with all the anxieties of their business to carry. Whose misfortunes culminated not so much through fault of their own, as through other causes forced upon them by modern innovations in the way of illegitimate " support account " competitors; easy and most absurd compositions—

granted to sharper *confreres*, as well as causes of minor significance, but all tending to destroy the conditions of healthy trade. To such men as these, the stoppage of payment is a fearful thing to face, yet history furnishes very many names who have thus stopped, and in time to prevent the annihilation of their estates, though they *might* have gone on indefinitely, upon their old and good records.

There did indeed exist, in the period referred to, a few men in each large centre, desirous of emulating Wall Street's boldest spirits, having but little stake at risk, protected by the laws of the country and born upon its soil, but not *of* it in heart. If they committed its fair name by notorious land operations, and by cheeky, dishonest insurance, brokerage or other schemes, alike disreputable, did any one of them gain by their manipulations of property which was never theirs? Did public opinion render their continuance with us possible? No! One by one they were forced to forego their intentions upon the Government, corporate or individual purse, and in other places far distant, are to-day, it may be, realizing that money honestly, though slowly earned, gives peace and enjoyment in far greater measure than when acquired under cover of glowing prospectuses or other advertisements having at their backs no merit, commercial soundness or common honesty. As the world grows older, such men are likely to become fewer, for as a rule they have brains enough to see that year by year, their prospects for gain in the old forbidden paths become more uncertain and remote. Our rapid advancement in civilization and general knowledge, the recognized value of a stern morality in all business interchange, and the appreciation extended by means of a wider education to straightforward dealing—all these are paving the way for an exodus of *sharp* men, and will leave no tenable ground for the creation of so-called interests, in whose platform the planks of merit and honesty of purpose are absent.

The present age will not tolerate such playing upon its welfare, and will resent with disgust the moves of the jugglers who at intervals, and brief ones, may appear upon its stage; the curtain is descending upon the scenes where they were central figures, and adventurers generally are fast becoming aware of this.

There is, however, a pretty numerous class of traders who are inclined to practice *small* shuffles or "tricks of trade." These little divergencies from the beaten path of mercantile integrity, are often more annoying and demoralizing in general effect, than are the grander pieces of rascality perpetrated by the class above referred to. Men have been known to expend more brain power in accomplishing a small sharp trick, whereby they have got the "best" of a confrere, than would be necessary in making ten times the same actual gain in a perfectly honest and easy transaction. They have created life-long enmities, simply because they have shown that it was possible for a human form to possess so small a soul. These tricks have in most cases been early taught them by their seniors, who defeat their own object by their windy advertisements of wares they know to be worthless, by the adulteration of goods, the imitations of well-established trade marks, in brief, the thousand and one small traps set for the customer, who would prove a valuable one if treated with ordinary fairness, but who resents an *imposition*, be it ever so slight. A well-known writer says : " If every lie told in the shops, across mahogany and show case, by buyers and sellers, were nailed like base coin to the counter, there would be no room for the display of goods. The half truths told, and the whole truth suppressed, are humiliating enough, and it is considered no mean compliment to *some* business men to say that they are sharp at a bargain ; " yet this sharpness is only, in many cases, the warp of a mind trained to ingenious lying.

The rivalry between houses in any given line of trade is often intense. If one practises trade "dodges," the other seems to reason that he must follow suit, but neither realize that the advantage gained is but transient. The contest at stretching of consciences may be exciting, but is pursued at great hazard, and is simply scorned by that public whose credulity they hope to trade upon. At best, a gain is made which is lost in turn ; the traders ears are filled with the unpleasant comments of his customers, and if he possesses either pride or dignity, he experiences in time a degree of abasement which surprises himself. All subterfuges in trade recoil upon their authors, without, in the large majority of instances, adding any substantial gain. In fact, those traders who have indulged in systematic misrepresentation, have often made the earliest and very worst failures, while they carry into every local surrounding and into their homes, the bad moral influence of their shop life. They create an antagonism against themselves ; they cannot fill the ordinary offices of life, or become leaders of any movement, without undergoing the strictures of their victims, as well as those of their competing brethren. They place themselves under a disadvantage in all respects, and in the few isolated cases where they manage to accumulate any great financial strength, often become their own "nemesis," and throw their fortunes away in some effort to obtain popularity, honour or increased wealth—a result which no one looks for when their life of supposed safe, though sharp dealing is considered, but which is often witnessed in any considerable trade centre.

Every individual life has its influence, and business men with a large staff of employes, find themselves in a most responsible position as regards the moral conduct of their business. Many reason that their duty ends with ordinary civility and prompt payment of wages to those assisting them. This is altogether too easy a creed, for if they are the means by which a new crop of future sharp dealing shopkeepers are turned out upon the commercial world—the fatal education to which they invite their juniors, in their early and imitative years, is to be laid at their doors. Business dealing, if characterized by frankness and sincerity, *is benefitted grandly*. No one can act dishonestly long without more or less of humiliating discovery ; for "where truth is not, nature will always be striving to show herself, and will assuredly betray the trickster by her presence," and at, for him, inopportune times.

> ...." To thine own self be true,
> And it must follow, as the night the day,
> Thou canst not then be false to any man."

There are no neutral, though there may be many unfinished characters. Like the phosphorescent wake of a vessel, our course through the seas of life may irradiate and adorn our passage, or diffuse a baneful influence at each step. The effect of good example may be slow in its silent operation, but it is none the less sure in working out inevitable good, and each day's hours and minutes make up a gain or a loss to our weak natures. There are very *few* natures who persistently remain blind to the force of consistent good example, and there are still fewer instances where earnest *frankness* fails to win the day. It begets the admiration of rogues—as much as it certainly secures for itself strong adherents among others ; wherever it shows its invincible power for good, it knits business men together as nothing else will ; it is a power in itself, and is adored as it deserves wherever it is seen. Can it not be practised by all, when its exercise creates and multiplies its ever-growing power as a factor between us all ? Is not its encouragement feasible ? If, in isolated cases, its exhibition has exposed us to a disadvantage, it has indirectly won a fresh ally, for the person gaining by our unarmed condition, has felt its beauty even as he secured the mean advantage ; has felt that it is a stronger friend and backer than he can well afford to kill, and upon another occasion will generally be found ready and quick to forego the pettiness of his earlier and unappreciative act. Reservations, or conceal-ment of motives, where they inspire us to act at the cost of another's peace of mind, or to prevent and hinder his exercise of one of the first principles of pure and successful business, cannot be too thoroughly deprecated. There will usually be no need of openly *resenting* these attacks upon our frank overtures. This course would naturally harden the offender. Leave him to himself ; he will the quicker see the ugliness of his offence. A well-known writer says : "There are men who do everything by indirection ; who meet one as warily as if words were traps and pitfalls ; who manage a friendly interview as a general would a campaign ; and if they make the first demonstration, we are naturally placed upon guard. We unconsciously become wary and distrustful. They plant distrust and secretiveness, and they produce in us after their kind. No man can be treated frankly in this world unless he himself be frank. If we would win confidence to ourselves, we must put confidence in others. The soul is like a mirror, reflecting that which stands before it. Frankness begets frankness, just as naturally and as certainly, under the proper conditions, as like produces like in the animal and vegetable kingdom ;" and if its use makes business easier, is it not well to encourage it by every means in our power, when the opportunity is nearly always at hand.

In concluding this sketch, it may not be inappropriate to allude briefly to the vital need of *sympathy* by us all in our business trials. Generally speaking we are too full of our own affairs to appreciate justly the circumstances of hardship which environ many of our kind. A warm word, an expression of kindly regard or a thoughtful suggestion may, however, often be gratefully received, and the care which inspires it go home with telling effect to the heart which is as warm as our own, though it may have become encrusted with a sense of isolation, and have endured for years the indifference of its kind. But few men have not a spot which can be touched by timely sympathy and evidence of feeling. Every man, to be successful, has an object for which he is striving, and, *disappointment in obtaining it*, is the cause of his antagonistic attitude when approached. His troubles sour him, but continued kindness of word and act will tell, and must certainly inspire him with hope and new confidence to fight his battles. Then in turn he will be the willing medium by which other souls reach the light.

> " For what are men better than sheep or goats,
> That nourish a blind life within the brain,
> If, knowing God, they lift not hands of help
> Both for themselves and those whom they call friend ? "

Sympathy will work wonders, and when we see an opportunity to exercise it, we should strive to avoid the wearing doubt, which will sometimes intrude as to the unfortunate one's *motives*. The judgment of the world is often grievously astray. " Rather give twenty rogues credit for being honest men, than wrong one honest man by pronouncing him a rogue." Never impute evil meaning where a more charitable construction is possible, or the evil you long to see eradicated from among your fellows is sure to be increased.

CAUSES OF DISASTER.

"If a man look sharp and attentively, he shall see fortune: for, though she be blind, she is not invisible."

"Imprudence is *the* fault peculiar to men.   You injure yourself: why blame fortune for it?"

A few months prior to Lord Beaconsfield's fatal illness, he invited Sir George Elliott to his residence, when it is said that these two men, each the artificer of his own fortune, and each eminently qualified to speak of success in life, began to moralize upon the attributes which led to such success.   The mutual comparison of notes during this interview is said to have resulted in the immediate underlining of the following commonplace, but necessary qualities, *i. e.,* self help, industry and energy, determination and talent; and these were supplemented by first, *a lively sense of personal honor* ; secondly, *tact, and unfailing serenity of temper ;* and thirdly, *the happy art of inspiring and retaining friendship.*   These are the true key notes of the situation, and though a few other common necessities, such as adequate capital, proper location, &c., may be quoted by many who do not entirely appreciate the significance of the former qualities, these, nevertheless, must be present in some degree to ensure success.

While, then, business safety is attained by the exercise of less than a dozen leading concomitants, or important rules, it is endangered by hundreds of weaknesses.   The record of the last quarter of a century shews that not more than ten in one hundred merchants have been uniformly successful, and if the business lives of each of the ten be closely scanned, it will be proven that fully one-third of these have, through some imprudence or lack of judgment, laid themselves open to severe loss at one time or another, and if at the end of a long lifetime they are placed upon the meagre muster roll of sound business men, they are virtually undeserving of the title.

During the present generation, a class of unfortunates born to wealth and ignorance of the value of money, has had its rise and fall. Rocket like in their advent, the declension of this grade of traders has been as rapid. Believing that the *sang bleu* of *family* in their veins, coupled with the hereditary prestige of gold, ought to save them from the coarse, common drudgery apparent all around them, they were not able to avoid the conclusion perhaps natural to them—that in some indefinite manner they ought to live, despite the usual conditions which go to make up a successful business occupation. They have been tempted into undertakings, whose traps and pitfalls were so well covered, that their untrained minds could not tear away the disguise, and when operating for themselves alone, have found that they were mere children in the art of making money ; then, after seeing their inherited capital steadily dwindle away, they have found that the same drudgery and practical application to business which they originally scorned, would have indeed been their best education, and in turning their backs upon it, have, as it were, turned from their best friend.

Trained to habits of luxury, and regarding the possession of money as a birthright, the unfortunate of this class is poor indeed when trouble overtakes him. His position then is more defenceless than that of any other trader, and his recovery far more slow of accomplishment.

Many merchants find to-day that they are not worth the actual surplus they had in 1873 ; it consequently behooves them to study the question of *expense* limitation, for their current gains are made smaller by reason of a reduced business, and not only this, but marginal profits are generally cut finer.

Much of the distress of the past decade is directly chargeable to the fact that *private expenditure* has been kept up in a ruinous proportion to the actual income from gains. Even where such income has not existed at all, the households of traders have been maintained at as high rates as when their businesses were in a sounder condition. Creditors have eventually paid the livings of scores of merchants, not but that the latter *meant* to reduce their private outgoes, but because they found it the last thing possible of accomplishment. Having a certain social status to keep intact, subscriptions to scores of charities to keep alive, &c., &c., the luckless trader has in hundreds of cases found in his yearly balances ominous figures arrayed against him in his private account, until out of mere dread of the exhibit, he has passed one, two and more years, without exercising the moral courage necessary to get out such balances. This respite from facing the actual knowledge of his absorption of capital, has, probably never in one single case, caused any reduction of expenditure, but it has lulled and blunted his sense of ultimate danger, given a wrong impression to all about him, and has led him into living a double life. However foreign to his nature and inclination this unnatural phase of his career may be, having once entered it, he cannot usually recede, nor refuse to practice its easy philosophy. Each year he hopes for, and perhaps *confidently expects* better returns from his business, but during a depression such as the one from which we are freshly emerging, losses by bad debts, shrinkages of outside assets, declining values of inside stocks, and curtailment of turnovers, preclude the possibility of obtaining relief from his regular trade, and he is stranded among the shoals of bankruptcy, with an estate shewing a poor dividend at best, and which, through the costly working, and absurd application of the Insolvent Act of 1875, fritters away all but a trifling percentage.

He has undone the work of a lifetime, and does he obtain any reward for the sacrifice ? No ! His family are called suddenly to face a far deeper humiliation than would have been incurred by them had they set a smaller value upon the claims of society, when opposed to righteous economy. His creditors do not feel like extending a settlement to a man who formerly made it his boast that *his* counting-house, at least, was free from the charge of reckless book-keeping, yet who in turn refuted all his professions of excellence in this regard ; and even if a composition is at last obtained, it is at so high a rate, and upon such sharp terms, that he is well nigh paralyzed by the consciousness of the load he is forced to shoulder. For him a weary future stretches forth, enlivened by no satisfying remembrances, but rendered more distressing by the retrospect of opportunities lost.

It is true, that here and there a merchant in this sad plight has been enabled to make a good turn upon his assets, after they have been bought in for him by an obliging third party, and while he has been kept from a discharge by indignant creditors; but this in no way affects the fact that he has lost the advantage for future business, which he might have retained by a more careful and correct course. He is virtually shelved, and if he be of middle age or beyond it, realizes that his status will never be regained in its entirety.

Much has been said and written illustrative of the effect of *intemperance* upon business interests, but too much emphasis cannot be used in depicting its fatal influence. As a cause of ruin, it stands first and foremost; there is no limit to its baneful ravages, and the day can come none too soon when, through a wider education, the outcry of popular sentiment and woeful experience, a stern legislation shall deal with this pest of commercial and social life, and drive it from the fair face of our country. In the meantime, however, we all can *begin* to work its extinction; and one of the first steps to take, perhaps, is to make the votaries of drink—from this time forth, so far as our influence can be felt—conscious of our disgust and lack of faith in them. Let the expression of our *distrust* of them as *business men*, our unwillingness to place our goods and interests in their hands, or to associate with them in any way, shame them into reform. We are quick to withdraw our deposits from a shaking bank, why should we jeopardize our goods by continuing an account doomed to ruin? Let us distrust even the *moderate* drinker. He may be, by natural accident, made strong enough to withstand the wear of mind and body superinduced by this fearful habit, but it takes him away from business at the very time we want to deal with him, and his example fastens the habit upon our best friends and others. What are his deserts? Does he not form the very centre and nucleus of temptation? Then why countenance him any more than you would a traitor to all that is good. The influence of such a creature as this extends itself far more widely than does that of a man who goes to extremes. In reply to warning after warning, young men point to the moderate drinker, who has been known to them since they were children, as a successful man, ready, in a way, to encourage moral works, and to discharge the duties of his life in a regular manner, and reason that they also possess a strong head, and can draw the line, &c., &c.

Allusion has been made to the *loss of time* occasioned by the habit of drinking. It is a well-known fact among regular business men, in a wholesale way, that more business can be done, and to better advantage, during the first half of the day, than afterward. The rush occurs between ten and two o'clock, ordinarily. The merchant comes down in the morning, anxious to carry into effect certain combinations which he has industriously elaborated during the afternoon or evening of the preceding day ; and it is between the hours named that they naturally culminate in transactions. The moderate drinker cannot pass eleven o'clock without some stimulus, and it follows that, if he be a merchant, he fritters away the next hour in the chaff this habit begets, for he has plenty of imitators, and in many cases old friends in trade, who, as regularly as the hour comes, accompany him "round the corner." If twitted upon this peculiar habit, these moderate drinkers will tell you that they often accomplish business during these trips, that it leads to negotiations of immense importance, &c., &c. But all these excuses can be discounted until but a shred of the heresy is left. The circumstances which surround them at the bar, render it *impossible* to dwell upon subjects foreign to the matter directly in hand, and if, in a few cases a bargain is closed, it is often re-opened, if not entirely cancelled, by wordy disputes as to the connection of the conversation while the contracting parties stood, glass in hand.

Want of *method and regularity* often causes much shrinkage and disadvantage, and coupled with *want of concentration*, are enough in themselves to effect disaster. "There may be much diligence and faith and zeal, without order, but there can be only partial success." Method is all important ; whether in the counting-room or the goods department, business works with far less friction, if the work dovetails well, if the grooves are prepared, and the hours set for the machinery to move. Confusion is destined to cripple and destroy, while order allied to concentration, greatly increases the *power to make a profit*, and to enable the profit to be calculated when it is made. Frequent trial balances in the counting-room, as well as close departmentizing of stock in the warehouse, are two of the strongest aids to success. Avoid spasmodic, and consequent ill-directed attempt to incorporate these virtues in your business management ; let both be effected in a regular manner, at regular dates, and make them as much a feature of your business as the regularity of your payments.

Irresolution upon matters small or great should be sedulously guarded against. If yielded to in early years, it becomes chronic, is always a disadvantage, and an enemy to success. Addison says: "irresolution on the schemes of life, and inconstancy in pursuing them, are the greatest causes of our disquiet and unhappiness." Guard against precipitancy, but educate a feeling of reliance upon personal judgement, dispose of the matter in hand promptly, go to work upon the perplexing subject earnestly, taking for your guide the well-tried trade maxims of centuries. If there be anything rotten in the transaction at hand, discard the idea of doing the business. Drop it from your mind without further loss of time, and *never* allow yourself to regret that you did not enter upon it ; in any case, get rid of the matter, or it will hamper your every movement. Decision is a quality which every successful trader has found a strong friend ; its constant practice is imperatively necessary ; it is found side by side with the highest virtues possessed by money-makers.

Next to intemperance, the fiend of *speculation* has, probably, created more wide-spread distress than has any business failing. Its victims come upon the stage of every decade in an ever recurring procession. Nothing is more tempting than easy gain to those who delve away at business life in narrow pathways, where profits are close, and where, by natural causes, the future holds forth no solid hope of more rapid acquisitions. These are the lambs who go forth to sacrifice when tempted into speculation. Their means fail them at the very times when they would otherwise have the advantage, in the conspiracy to crush them. But few men gain in this desperate struggle who are weak in point of funds for immediate action : they are handicapped beyond redemption. For these, it is a case of loss every time, comparatively speaking, and it is this weakness that the leaders of the speculative movement in hand thrive upon.

There are probably no keener regrets experienced in commercial disaster than those felt by the small operator who has thrown away his limited but snug capital in speculation. It is unlike any other loss ; no remnant of satisfaction remains to the loser ; his trouble comes suddenly, and overwhelms him with a sense of annihilation; he has no recourse, nor does he get the smallest percentage of a saving from the wreck, in many cases, while his agony of mind from the first day of his newly created liability, astonishes and unfits him for exertion in any other interest he may have on hand.

Money made quickly, goes as quickly. This is something of a change from the old maxim, but it cannot be said that money made by speculation is made easily. Ah, no ! the anxiety and fear—necessary concomitants to the process—are dire in their effects, and age the operator far more quickly than will any other undertaking. The man of larger resources, however, finds that one successful transaction has harnessed him to a life of excitement from which he may long to, but cannot fly. His life is a repetition of losses as well as gains ; he does not find satisfaction in money made in this manner—if he have a soul—and the money does not stay with him. The majority of cases go to prove that the average speculator does not gain permanently. Any one of us can mark the record of friend or neighbor, in case after case for a number of years, and where they were decidedly speculative, the result has justified this statement. It is well that it is so, and that being illegitimate in a general sense, and full of distress to others, it carries with it punishment in proportion to its so-called gains.

The *lust for political prominence* has in our country often deprived a good business of its head, and caused some serious financial difficulties. This evil will remedy itself in time. No more thankless race can well be run ; a paltry pre-eminence among our fellows, won at the expense of a commercial reputation, will not, as our country grows larger, be considered an equivalent for what is thus resigned in its favor. "No trade in the world is so laborious and costly as that of getting oneself a great man," nor is there one which so poorly repays the head and heart for the labor expended.

Losses through endorsation of a friend or relative's paper have, during the late depression, helped to swell the list of unfortunate business men. This practice, condemned from time immemorial, claims its victims yet. . It is encouraging, however, to be able to testify that these breaches of common prudence have been fewer in number than one would expect to find chronicled, all things considered. So well is the danger of this fault known, and so quickly is the desperate condition of one who asks this "favor" understood, that it is getting to be considered by many an insult for their *friend* to prefer the request. The mental sickness following a loss of this kind is more intense than that resulting from most other losses; it is not so wide spread in its evil, but it is more poignant, and, so far as it goes, it is a cancer upon commerce, for it does much to extinguish *confidence*—that vital spark of trade.

It has been truly said that few men possess a genius so commanding that they can attain eminence, unless a subject suited to their talents presents itself, and opportunities occur for its developement. No man is born wise. Few men can successfully grapple with many interests. A business, congenial in its natnre with our tastes, is the first thing to be sought; an intimate knowledge of its detail routine should then be acquired, not less by the principal than by his staff. Give talent full play, but fortify it with practical application and general management. Earnestness will win, but if early effort be slow in producing results, remember that "All things come to him who waits." In this lays the philosophy of business life.

THE GROWTH AND FOSTERING OF TRADE,

"The trade of nations, as of individuals, must grow in proportion to the acquisition of knowledge and the accumulation of capital."

IN 1850 the total imports of our country—then composed of the two Provinces of Upper and Lower Canada—amounted to $29,454,141, while the exports were $22,109,877. The growth of commerce up to 1856 was steady, and ran up in that year a total import of $68,323,717, against a total export of $51,644,428. The depression of 1857–8 then brought down the figures to $49,763,427 of imports, and $41,207,529 of exports. In 1859 an improvement of trade set in, and continued until 1864, when there was a temporary break in the current of business, but a rally took place immediately, continuing steadily, until in 1867 the imports rolled up over $70,000,000, the exports in that year being about $10,000,000 less than those figures. On the first of July of that year, the Act of Confederation came into force, and the four Provinces of Upper and Lower Canada, Nova Scotia and New Brunswick were joined under the name of the Dominion of Canada. This occurred amid great rejoicing, and commerce grew apace until in 1873 the imports amounted to over $127,000,000, and the exports to $89,000,000. These proportions were maintained through the following year, but during 1874 it became apparent that trade had been grossly overdone, and an unparalleled reaction set in, carrying the Dominion's business rapidly down, until in 1879 the imports were $81,964,427, and the exports $71,491,255. During 1880, the effects of this wholesome decrease began to manifest themselves; much of the rotten elements of the then business situation had been eliminated; contraction had resulted in natural recuperation, and, aided by a tariff of far greater protective power than was formerly politic, the trade of our country threw off the incubus which had for so long handicapped it, and commerce strengthened at once. A most decided impetus was given to manufacturing interests of all kinds where the products were staples, the developement of the cotton goods interest being especially notable. This latter industry had been well nigh paralyzed during the depression, as it had to encounter a spirited competition with the States, and was not sufficiently protected, but under the new tariff it was fostered to such a degree that company after company was formed to extend the manufacture, until it began to be almost universally believed that the combined output of these factories would soon more than cover the demand. This fear, however, has not been realized, for though the new tariff of 1879 has proved to be inimical in some of its features, to the good of the whole country, it certainly has benefitted other interests, and among them the manufacture of cottons, and trade centres being freed from the enormous pressure of foreign goods, have been able to absorb every yard manufactured at home.

While, then, home production is being fostered by the natural force of the present economic trade conditions to a large degree, and in many leading interests, our exports are steadily gaining in their percentages over former years; the produce of our forests, fields, animals, fisheries, oils, &c., is being sent away in round amount, and as the outside world has also generally shaken off the embargoes upon its business, created by the wide-spread expansion and over production of seven years ago, we are getting better returns for our produce, and may now be regarded as in our proper and normal condition. It is true that fears have been felt that the activity of trade and the advance in values of goods could not be maintained, but a little thought will dispel these doubts, for unless inordinate speculation begins at an early date to rule our interests, there is too much pure blood in the veins of our commerce to admit of serious reaction. Payments from the country were never, in the palmiest days of the past, received in so large a percentage; renewals, when asked, are for meagre sums, as a rule, and are exceptional at that. This certainly denotes smaller stocks, and successful realization of outstandings, old lock ups removed, depression sores cleansed, and confidence restored. With these features at our backs, in our agricultural districts, it would seem to be plain that we have health just where we want it.

That the situation is open to a change in the course of time is true. Rash ventures will be made, long credits courted, stocks enlarged; but before serious trouble again threatens our country, the present conditions will have to be largely done away with, and the train of circumstances which create commercial disaster set in motion. The successive failures of the crops may accelerate its speed, or disastrous fires may give it impetus, but with a fair degree of immunity from these evils, the prime causes of a national depression would appear to be left far behind us.

Returning to the growth of trade as shewn by the relative proportions of import and export interests, it may be said that our country now, and for the second year in her history, is meeting her import drain of money by pushing out her exports in a normal and healthy manner. It is impossible to estimate how far the *profits* upon the interchange of commodities may adjust the difference or create a real gain, but the figures for the fiscal year ending 30th June, 1881, should encourage us all greatly, as they shew that we are at last realizing a balance of trade in our favor. We imported during this period $85,516,798 of dutiable goods, and exported to the value of $98,290,823.

Perhaps the most significant exhibit of the comparative growth of business during the past Fall over that of the preceding year, is to be found in the Bank Governmental Returns for these periods. The busiest month of the year throughout banking circles is September. During this month in the present year, the note circulation of banks in the Provinces of Quebec and Ontario, is reported at $28,675,553, as against $22,000,000 for September, 1880, while the aggregate discounts representing bona fide business, amounted to $108,064,744 for September, 1881, or $18,000,000 more than was reported for that month in 1880. Unsecured discounts have sensibly decreased, through more speedy concentration of all the uncertain elements which were during former years prominent in our business situation, and bank capital is now finding safe and certain employment, though the business to which it is devoted is still open to some competition.

There is, however, another phase of the Dominion's situation to consider. It is the drain of interest upon the public debt, a probability of this debt being increased through the vast undertakings of the present era, and a consequent growing cause which may absorb all the temporary advantage gained by a " trade balance" in our favor ; to this may be added the weight of foreign capital loaned in this country, secured upon property, the sum withdrawn by foreign Insurance Companies, and effect of the fluctuations of our carrying trade profits. A close estimate upon the foreign debt of our country, places it at in the neighborhood of $137,024,582. This would entail an interest liability of some $6,000,000, which *always* matures, and must be met, whether or no we, as a country, are offsetting it by a corresponding revenue. The current fiscal estimate of revenue, however, from Customs, Excise, &c., though the precise figures are not obtained, is a very satisfactory one, the receipts being about $29,000,000, and the expenditure some $25,500,000. The character of many of our leading undertakings is sound, and beyond the ever present danger of an unwise expansion, no fear of a chronic state of distress in our financial administration of ways and means is to be apprehended.

The official return of the Dominion's liabilities and assets upon June 30th, 1880, is as follows :—

LIABILITIES.

Loans payable in London	$137,024,582	53
Loans payable in Canada	36,649,346	60
Total Funded and Unfunded Debt	$173,673,929	13

MISCELLANEOUS.

Trust Funds at 6 per cent	1,178,410	58
Trust Funds at 5 per cent	5,715,012	54
Miscellaneous	5,864,516	07
Provinces of Ontario and Quebec	10,841,820	64
" Nova Scotia, 5 per cent	40,394	26
" New Brunswick, "		
" British Columbia, "	500,382	53
" Manitoba, "	393,060	89
" Prince Edw. Island, "	793,386	12
Pacific Railway Deposit Account		

BANKING ACCOUNTS.

Miscellaneous	124,410	56
Total	$199,125,323	32

ASSETS.

Sinking Fund on account of various Loans................. $9,747,372 58
Sundry Investments, bearing 3½ to 6 per cent............ 5,932,433 66

MISCELLANEOUS.

Province of Canada Debt, at 5 per cent..................... 37,225 09
New Brunswick Debt... 22,233 76
Provincial Accounts 13,432,094 61
Nova Scotia Suspense Account................................ 43,064 53
New Brunswick   do. 474 06
Miscellaneous   do. 1,032,434 66
Cash.. 7,339,770 41
Issue Account and Specie Reserve........................... 2,755,257 52
Financial Agents 822,003 84
Silver Coinage Account... 78,139 43
Miscellaneous Banking Account.............................. 940,347 87
To Balance.. 156,942,471 30

$199,125,323 32

Our Maritime Provinces are not behind in the general progress toward solid and steady improvement. They represent a good proportion of manufacturing interests, when their extent of territory is considered. Their trade relations with the West Indies, Great Britain and elsewhere, are permanent, and their mining interests are promising well in the main. It is true that the gold districts of Nova Scotia have not yet reached the highest state of developement, but new aids in the way of capital and fresh energy will set this all right. Their coal deposits continue seemingly inexhaustible, and there is wealth in the prosecution of their fisheries. Their export of products of the sea to the West Indies is an immense item in the aggregate of their annual turnover, codfish and lobster outgoes being heavy, while their shipping interest, doing business as it does, with healthy foreign countries, furnishes them with an element of strength which cannot easily become demoralized.

The ship builders of Maitland, Noel, Kingsport and Hantsport, as well as other points, have this summer added over 20,000 tons of shipping to their Province, among the vessels built being the largest barque ever sent from the stocks in Nova Scotia, with a measurement of 1,530 tons, while several ships have been built to carry from 2,000 to 2,500 tons.

The coal mines of Cape Breton have this year been worked to great advantage. It is estimated that the export will exceed the largest on record. Among the chief mines are the " Sydney," belonging to the General Mining Association, the " Bridgeport," " Reserve," " Little Glace Bay," " Caledonia," " Block House," " Gowrie," and " Lingan " mines. In most of these mines the daily output is excellent, and necessitates the total employment of over 1,000 cutters.

New Brunswick has its iron mines at different points, those at Woodstock having been most largely worked and smelted. Another metal found in large quantities in this Province is manganese, while gypsum, limestone, marble, &c., are obtained in considerable quantities.

Among the mining industries of the Dominion, those of phosphates are now attracting great attention. This interest was partially developed in 1877, and the first sale of Government phosphate lands occurred in July, 1878, at public auction, the average price realized being at rate of two dollars per acre, and the sale netted the Government some $30,000. The industry suffered a relapse, however, soon after this, and remained stagnant until the return of a livelier market abroad, and the infusion of new confidence consequent upon the lifting of the veil of depression. The importance of the phosphate mining industry is steadily assuming greater proportions, and it is now recognized as a most significant factor in our mining wealth. New enterprises, individual and associate, are opening up the townships of Templeton, Wakefield, Portland, Buckingham and Derry, and other older established plants are being worked up to a very profitable point. It is said that the mineral averages at the rate of 75 to 77 per cent. to the ton in several of the townships named. The Buckingham Mining Company have obtained from about one thousand acres, some five thousand tons of ore, paying in the neighborhood of 75 per cent., the product going to the old country. The Laurentian Mining Company took one thousand tons of ore from fourteen hundred acres in one year, while the total output of the townships named has aggregated about eight thousand tons per annum. The present year will probably see this doubled.

Gold is found in Nova Scotia, where it was discovered in 1860, by John G. Pulsiver. The return for the first year of working (1861) being $116,800. In fourteen years' working, a result of about $5,000,000 was obtained. The interest has been retarded by a lack of enthusiasm, energy and capital, but now bids fair to be prosecuted with more vigor. Gold is also found in Beauce and Compton counties, Quebec ; asbestos in Megantic and Wolf counties ; iron in Ottawa, Montcalm, St. Maurice, Champlain, Charlebois and Saguenay counties ; copper in Bagot, Megantic and Sherbrooke ; mica in Megantic, Berthier and Ottawa, and galena in Ottawa, Gaspé and Rimouski counties. All these interests need energetic developement, and will, in time, command for themselves a greater prominence.

At Capelton, Quebec, we have the splendid enterprise of the Orford Nickel and Copper Company, which was inaugurated about two years since. Its management is an excellent one ; the copper deposits are large, and the sulphur from its pyrites formation can be utilized as sulphuric acid. The prospects of the Company are bright, and the addition of this interest fortifies our mining industries greatly.

Through sections of Renfrew, notably in the Township of McNab, hematite iron ore is being found in splendid paying quantities, also in Madoc, Marmora, Elzevir, Belmont, &c., while magnetic iron ore—the most valuable of iron deposits—is found in good quantities in the Laurentian Range, in South Crosbie, &c.

A new interest—that of beet root sugar manufacture—is assuming definite shape in the Province of Quebec. The chief centres already selected are at Coaticook, West Farnham and Berthier, the company at the former place being already in active operation. It is also proposed to locate factories at Arthabaskaville and at Beauharnois. Contracts are being successfully made with farmers in each locality, by the terms of which they are bound to prepare and cultivate a certain number of acres, the manufacturers to pay them from four dollars to five dollars per ton for the beets. The idea has taken well with a number of our capitalists, and in the case of the former factories, the interest is likely to be pushed forward to results rapidly. The chief difficulty in the way lies with the farmers, many of whom, having experimented to a certain extent, think that the work, care and uncertainty involved in getting a good yield from their lands is disproportionate to the returns they can get, but in the majority of cases the land has not been properly prepared ; mistakes have been made in the handling of the young plants, either through want of attention in weeding or in thinning ; and during the spring of the present year, many were tempted to abandon the cause on account of the general disappointment resulting from damage by the exceptionally late frosts. With proper methods of cultivation, however, it is believed by the best authorities that the growing of this vegetable can be made a paying industry, as it would seem to simply resolve itself into a question of good or poor cultivation. The interest has made money for its promoters in Germany and France for many years, and as the management of the industry here is in the hands, to a great extent, of practical foremen from the countries mentioned, it is but fair to suppose that they have taken into account the difference of the climate and other drawbacks, if any exist. It is to be hoped that those growers who have been most successful with their trial crops, will inspire others to new effort, and as our *habitants* get educated to the proper tillage of the root, the product will be sufficient to keep several large companies at work without a break. Labor can be got very cheaply for the light work of thinning and weeding the growth, and from many points of view the new industry seems feasible.

It is now safe to state that our manufacturing industries are rapidly acquiring the importance which by right belongs to them. For years, and notably in the Province of Quebec, these valuable factors to the country's growth have been overshadowed and paralyzed through a number of causes. Their proper encouragement cannot be too earnestly advocated, for they are the means by which much of a small country's capital is retained, and their promotion keeps its population within its own borders. Many new interests have sprung up at different points, notably at Hamilton, Montreal, Toronto, and in the Eastern Townships. Old and fossilized industries have been rejuvenated and once more put into working shape.

We are getting to feel a confidence in our own artisans, and to recognize how much our apathy in the past has cost us.

Briefly, we possess within ourselves the elements of success. Canada has unfortunately been a country of partial developement in many avenues of industry. Dormant possibilities should be aroused, and small results added to with each year. This can be done by energy and determination, and in proportion to the exercise of these qualities, success will come. Every advantage offered by our surroundings should be made the most of; we can, if we will, work up to a state of progress, the maintenance of which will grow easier as the years succeed each other.

Care upon all sides among our kings of finance and general business, with close criticism of proposed new accounts, should still be exercised; for while the debt-paying power of thousands of traders has been wonderfully increased by the revival of nearly every interest, it should be remembered that there are many whose business condition one year ago was weak and very uncertain, and it cannot be asssumed that the condition of this latter class has been transformed from chronic insecurity to entire safety, by the magic of a year's renewed confidence and better business. A large number of traders certainly have, through the contraction of the past, found themselves in just the right position to rebuild rapidly with the return of prosperity. But there is still a round number who have been unable, through the force of limited scope and means, to participate to any considerable extent in the gains of the last two seasons.

Our exporters and importers can, however, draw nearer together, in a sense. Let them regulate their sales and purchases so as to enlarge our commercial relations with other countries, and thus draw to our doors nations who would otherwise remain strangers, and in ignorance of what we have to offer them. We can, to a certain extent, buy of such ports as will give us export business, and this will naturally advertise our claims, and lead up to a better knowledge of our producing ability.

Insolvent Acts, &c.

After a lapse of several years, an Insolvent Act was again introduced in 1864, in the Provinces of Ontario and Quebec. To this law an Amendment Act (29 Vict., c. 18), was passed in 1865.

The Provinces of Nova Scotia and New Brunswick having subsequently united themselves in confederation with those of Ontario and Quebec, under the name of the Dominion of Canada, it was deemed advisable, by legislature in 1869, to establish a uniform Insolvent law for the guidance of the whole. This Act was in turn succeeded by the Insolvent Act of 1875, the latter being framed largely upon the preceding Acts, but differing from them upon the following material points:—

1. The provision for voluntary assignments was omitted altogether from the Act of 1875.

2. A new provision was introduced respecting the discharge of insolvents, and to the following effect—sec. 58, Act of 1875—"Whenever it appears that the estate of the insolvent has not paid, or is not likely to realize for the creditors, a dividend of thirty-three cents in the dollar, on the unsecured claims, and sufficient account is not given for the deficiency, the Court or Judge may, in its or his discretion, suspend or refuse altogether the discharge of the insolvent." This section was new in practice here. The English Act of 1869 provided that the debtor must pay ten shillings in the pound before he could be released against the wishes of his creditors.

3. The foregoing necessary rate of dividend was, by an amendment in 1877, raised to fifty cents in the dollar.

4. Under the Act of 1869, the interim assignee prepared statements of the insolvent's affairs. Under the Act of 1875, the insolvent himself had to prepare these, and deliver them to the assignee. *Vide* sec. 17, Act

of 1875 : " The insolvent shall, within ten days of the date of the assignment, or from the date of the service of the writ of attachment, or if the same be contested within ten days of the date of the judgment rejecting the petition to have it quashed, furnish the assignee with a correct statement (Form F.) of all his liabilities direct and indirect, contingent or otherwise, indicating the nature and amount thereof, together with the names, additions, and residences of his creditors, and the securities held by them, in so far as may be known to him. The insolvent shall also furnish, within the same delay, a statement of all the property and assets vested in the assignee by the deed of assignment, or by the writ or writs of attachment issued against him, and such statements shall in all cases include a full, clear, and specific account of the causes to which he attributes his insolvency, and the deficiency of his assets to meet his liabilities. The insolvent may, at any time, correct or supplement the statements so made by him of his liabilities, of his property and assets." This amendment thus assumed that the assignee would permit the insolvent to have the necessary access to the accounts of the estate.

5. The appointment of official assignees under the Act of 1869 was vested in Boards of Trade. The Act of 1875 changed this, and vested the appointment in the Government. Sec. 27, Act 1875 : " The Governor in Council may appoint, in the several Provinces of Canada, except in the Province of Quebec, one or more persons to be official assignees, or joint assignees, in and for every county ; and in the Province of Quebec such appointment of official assignees or joint official assignees shall be made in and for each judicial district of the Province, except that in each of the judicial districts of Quebec, Montreal, and St. Francis, respectively, such appointment may be made either for the whole district, or for one or more electoral districts in the same. And the word ' district ' shall mean either a judicial or an electoral district, as the context may require."

6. Stringent provisions respecting the duties and remuneration of assignees were enacted by the amendments of 1875. So rigid were these that they defeated their object in many cases. Section 41, Act 1875, required that each assignee should in every case keep a register shewing the name of each insolvent with whose estate he had to deal, his residence, place and nature of business, dates of assignment and attachment writ,

amount of liabilities, amount of claims proved, amount of composition dividends, whether a discharge was obtained within a year or not, amount of dividends remaining unpaid after three months from date of declaration of last dividend, &c. This register to be open to the inspection of the public, at the office of the assignee, the latter, as soon as he takes charge of an estate, to open a separate book for each estate, shewing a debtor and creditor account of all his receipts and disbursements. In all cases where the assignee was not official, but appointed by creditors, he was required to deposit said book in the office of the official assignee of the county or district, after the winding up of each estate by him. Every assignee, under this Act, was required also, after obtaining his discharge as such, but being allowed thirty days in which to do so, to pay over to the Receiver General all moneys belonging to the estate, and then in his hands, which were not absolutely required by the working or application of the Act, accompanying such payment with a sworn statement of such moneys, under a penalty of *ten dollars per day for each day of delay* in thus accounting for his charge. Sec. 43 provides that the assignee shall be entitled to a commission of five per cent. on the amount realized not exceeding $1,000. A further sum of two-and-a-half per cent. on the amount realized in excess of $1,000, and not exceeding $5,000, and a further sum of one-and-a-quarter per cent. on the amount realized in excess of $5,000, which said commission was to be in lieu of all fees and charges, for all his services and disbursements in relation to the estate, exclusive of actual expenses in going to seize or sell, and of disbursements necessarily made in the care and removal of property. No assignee could employ any legal counsel without the consent of the inspectors, or of the creditors. If acting without such consent, he could not collect the expense from the estate. And when superseded by an assignee appointed by the creditors, his remuneration was to be fixed upon by Court or Judge, taxed by the proper officer, and then became the first charge upon the estate. Sec. 45 required the assignee to deposit all sums of money in his hands and belonging to each estate, whenever such sums should aggregate $100. A separate deposit account to be kept for each estate, the interest accruing upon such deposits to be regularly divided among the creditors, in addition to the dividends of the principal ; and in cases where this was omitted by the assignee, he was to forfeit and pay to the estate a sum equal to three times the amount of such interest. It is hardly necessary to say that owing to the make up of some estates, the natural conditions surrounding their realization, and the misapprehension of the provisions of the Act, &c., these requirements became in some cases almost a dead letter.

7. The Act of 1875 restricted the sale of real estate in the Province of Quebec only, to a sale by public auction. Sec. 75, Act 1875 : " The assignee may sell the real estate of the insolvent, but only after advertisement thereof for a period of two months, and in the same manner as is required for the actual advertisement of sales of real estate by the Sheriff in the District, or place where such real estate is situate, and to such further extent as the assignee deems expedient, provided that the period of advertisement may be shortened to not less than one month by the creditors, with the approbation of the Judge. But in the Province of Quebec, such abridgement shall not take place without the consent of the hypothecary creditors upon such real estate, if any there be ; and if the price offered for any real estate at any public sale duly advertised as aforesaid, is more than ten per cent. less than the value set upon it by a resolution of the creditors, or by the inspectors and the assignee, the sale may be adjourned for a period not exceeding one month, when, after such notice as the inspectors and assignee may deem proper to give, the sale shall be continued, commencing at the last bid offered on the previous day when the property was put up at auction, and if no higher bid be then offered, the property shall be adjudged to the person who made the such last bid. Provided that with the consent of the hypothecary or privileged creditors, or where there are no hypothecary or privileged creditors, with the approbation of the general creditors or of the inspectors, the assignee may postpone the sale to such time as may be deemed most advantageous for the estate, and whenever the sale shall have been so postponed beyond one month, the last bidder shall be discharged from any obligation under the bid he may have made on the previous day when the property was offered for sale by auction." The provisions in this section for adjournment of sale were new over the Act of 1869, sec. 47. By that Act the

assignee might withdraw the property if he thought the amount offered was too small, selling subsequently under such directions as he received from the creditors.

The time and manner of advertising the sales of real estate by the Sheriff in Ontario, requires that the notice of sale be published in the *Ontario Gazette.* In Quebec it must be advertised in the *Official Gazette* and in one English and one French newspaper, and in addition be announced at the church door of the parish where the land lies. The mortgagee of an insolvent is not obliged by this Act to await the disposal of the estate by the assignee, but may exercise his power of sale under the mortgage and rank upon the estate for any deficiency.

Sec. 76, Act 1875, provides that " all sales of real estate so made by the assignee, shall vest in the purchasers all the legal and equitable estate of the insolvent therein, and the conveyance may be made in the 'Form N.' But in the Province of Quebec such sale shall in all respects have the same effect as to mortgages, hypothecs, or privileges then existing thereon, as if the same had been made by a sheriff under a writ of execution issued in the ordinary course, but shall have no other, greater or less, effect than such sheriff's sale. And in the Province of Quebec the title conveyed by such sale shall have an equal validity with a title created by a sheriff's sale; and the deed of such sale which the assignee executes (Form N) shall, in the Province of Quebec, have the same effect as a sheriff's deed. But the assignee may grant such terms of credit as he may deem expedient, and as may be approved by the creditors, or by the inspectors, for any part of the purchase money, except that no credit shall be given in the Province of Quebec for any part of the purchase money coming to any hypothecary or privileged creditor, without the consent of such creditor, and the assignee shall be entitled to reserve a special hypothec or mortgage by the deed of sale as security for the payment of such part of the purchase money as shall be unpaid; and such deed may be executed before witnesses or notaries, according to the exigency of the law of the place where the real estate sold is situate." This section is somewhat similar to the 48th section of the Act of 1869. The words " or by the inspectors" are not, however, in that Act section.

The purchaser under the above section will take the same title that the insolvent had at the date of the assignment, or at the time the writ of attachment was placed in the assignee's hands.

8. Under the Act of 1869, proceedings in cases of contestation of claims were to be heard in the first place before the assignee. This was changed by the Act of 1875, and the proceedings were carried on from the first in Court, *vide* sec. 93 to 95, Act of 1875. " It shall be the duty of the inspectors to examine, with the assignee, the claims made against the estate, and also each dividend sheet, before the expiration of the delay within which the same may be objected to, and to instruct the assignee as to which claims or collocations should be contested by and on behalf of the estate, whereupon contestation shall be entered and made in the name of the assignee, or of the inspectors, or of some individual creditors consenting thereto, and shall be tried and determined by the Court or Judge. The cost of such contestation, unless recovered from the adverse party, shall be paid out of the funds belonging to the estate." By the 72nd section of the Act of 1869, the contestation was tried and contested before the assignee in the first instance, from whose award there was an appeal to the judge.

Section 94, Act 1875, provides : " If it appears to the assignee, on his examination of the books of the insolvent, or otherwise, that the insolvent has creditors who have not taken the proceedings requisite to entitle them to be collocated, it shall be his duty to reserve dividends for such creditors according to the nature of their claims, and to notify them of such reserve, which notification may be by letter through the post, addressed to such creditors' residences, as nearly as the same can be ascertained by the assignee, and if such creditors do not file their claims and apply for such dividends, previous to the declaration of the last dividend of the estate, the dividends reserved for them shall form part of such last dividend." This section is a re-enactment of the 69th section of the Act of 1869, but it should not be construed into meaning that if the creditor does not demand his dividend, as well as file his claim, he will be deprived of it, for that would place this class of creditors in a different position from others. But the filing of the claim was to be held as an application for a dividend under this clause, and if the claimant did not appear, and afterward claim the amount awarded him, the rule as to unclaimed dividends must be followed.

Section 95, Act 1875, provides : " If any claim be objected to at any time, or if any dividend be objected to within the said period of eight days, or if any dispute arises between the creditors or the insolvent, or between him and any creditor, as to the amount of the claim of any creditor, or as to the ranking privilege of the claim of any creditor upon such dividend sheet, the objection shall be filed in writing by or before the assignee, who shall make a record thereof, and the grounds of objections shall be distinctly stated in such writing, and the party objecting shall also file, at the same time, the evidence of previous service of a copy thereof on the claimant; and the claimant shall have three days thereafter to answer the same, which time may, however, be enlarged by the judge, with a like delay to the contestant to reply, and upon the completion of an issue upon such objection, the assignee shall transmit to the clerk of the court the dividend sheet, or a copy thereof, with all the papers and documents relating to such objection or contestation. And any party to it may fix a day—of which two days' notice shall be given to the adverse party, for proceeding to take evidence thereon before the judge, and shall thereafter proceed thereon from day to day until the evidence shall have been closed, the case heard, and the judgment rendered, which judgment shall be final, unless appealed from in the manner hereinafter provided. The proceedings on the said objection or contestation shall form part of the records of the Court, and the judgment shall be made executory as to any condemnation for costs, in the same manner as any ordinary judgment of the Court."

This changes the conditions of the Act of 1869 in so far as the time for objecting to a dividend goes.   Under that Act it was to be done after the last day of the publication of advertisement, instead of eight days as above.

9. By the Act of 1875, provision was introduced for proceedings in cases of insolvent incorporated companies, and the Act was applied to them, subject to some modifications, which, however, at the time, seemed

to cover all necessary points fully. These provisions to apply to such incorporate estates as were not specially excepted in the first section of said Act. See sec. 147, Act of 1875.

In nearly all other points the differences between the Acts of 1869 and 1875 were mere detail.

The Insolvent Act of 1875 was intended to protect the creditors of an insolvent from the weaknesses patent in the Act of 1869. A vast amount of brain labor was involved in its framing. The amendments were chosen only after great research, and contrast of cause and effect, yet, as has been said, its very detail, its stringent and labored provisions, when applied to practice in the rush and whirl of disaster experienced after 1875, defeated its praiseworthy intent, and rendered its cumbrous amendments inoperative in spirit. It is even a fact that the majority of assignees—and it must be said that some leading ones are included in this statement—did not fully comprehend all the technicalities embodied in this Act until near the abolition of it ; and a still more direct statement can be made, that a considerable number *never* understood its provisions and their application, nor would they had it lived for another decade.

That its general effect was adverse to the interests of creditors need scarcely be emphasized here. All large houses doing a general business have fully appreciated this fact. Whether it be possible to construct an Act which shall comprehend the most advantageous manner of handling, and the just distribution of assets, is a problem which the future alone can determine.

The creation of a fifty per cent. limit of discharge from insolvency was a well meaning attempt in the interests of creditors, and a check against fraud, as well as a supposed bar to the continuance in business of worthless, incapable traders, but it signally failed to effect the good which was prophesied for it. The outcome of this provision shows it to have been of little protection generally, for at an estimate, twice as many insolvents obtained compositions under the Act of 1875, at less rates than the limit, than was the case under the administration of the Act of 1869. Many houses doing large businesses, whose turnovers were largely maintained by the nursing and encouragement of weak accounts, whose management was of the happy-go-lucky style, but whose margins were naturally good, and who were regularly found to be large creditors in many cases of insolvency, would influence a settlement in short order, with the certainty of getting the continued trade of the discharged insolvent. In other words, would concede him a surplushe should not have had, and keep the account alive until they had realized a greater gain than the amount they had written off upon the original stake. With them, it was the all absorbing desire to get business; it became simply a speculation as to the results at the end of each year, but it was their policy in trade, and in many cases their influence at a creditor's meeting could not be overcome. Again, the Courts granted discharges under the Act of 1875 in many cases too easily, trusting too much to the shewings made by the assignee in the case, or interpreting the Act too liberally, and though in other instances, judges adhered more closely to the actual letter of the provisions, discharges were still obtained which, in the opinion of merchants knowing well the merits of the insolvent, were undeserved by him. Thus, while the right of the insolvent to make a voluntary assignment to some favored creditor was taken away by the Act, the exercise of friendly influence was still rendered possible, and cases of unmerited lenience frequently occurred. It is the experience of many merchants, that under the Act of 1869, fewer cases of actual fraud occurred. It must, however, be reasoned that it was more easily understood, and that neither it, or any other Act, was ever called upon in our country to provide against the overwhelming mass of exigencies, want of precedent and widespread trouble, which the Act of 1875 had to elucidate and adjust.

A very weak feature of this Act was the scope it gave to the *appointment of assignees.* In no particular did its provisions react so unfavorably as in this. It fostered the creation of a number of assignees whose record, or whose general qualifications made them most unlikely officers to carry out the meaning of the Act. It is owing to these that a great part of the obloquy—which unfortunately attaches to this well-meant Act—is expressed. Some of the most illiterate men sprang into a position in which they were autocrats, and wielded their temporary facilities with a sharp eye to the accumulation of fees, but an almost utter disregard of the interests committed to their care. Occasionally one would, as a natural consequence, levant, then it would be found that his securities amounted to nothing, or had never been soundly deposited, while his books would be found utterly inadequate to the requirements of his office. Any new Act must limit assignees in point of number, and guard against the appointment of unfit candidates, for it has passed into history that the reckless creation and inefficiency of many assignees, under the Act of 1875, led up to the loosest interpretation of its provisions and practice, in many cases.

Fortunately, the prosperity of our country has been of steady growth since the abolition of the late Act, and the need of a new bankrupt law has not been generally felt. As time goes on, however, it will be found necessary to enact one, as the existing differences between the Provincial common laws are great, and to the average merchant present an almost hopelessly tangled web of contradictions. At any rate, a simple enactment providing for the distribution of assets, and regulating or determining of the validity of claims, ought to be made, and at once. In the Province of Quebec the old Roman law does, it is true, pretty well protect the average creditor, the whole property of the insolvent being a pledge for creditors, and, with the exception of a few legal preferences, all his estate is well and equitably distributed. But in Ontario, that worst feature and relic of old times—the *chattel mortgage*—still is prevalent in use, and the debtor can run up a credit upon a mere wreck, which is apparently sound and active, and of which he has the sole manipulation, until his chief creditor chooses to register his mortgage and foreclose. That the law should continue to recognize these unjust mortgage preferences at all, is one of the surprising features of modern times. In the Maritime Provinces much the same kind of preference exists, only it is known under the name of *a bill of sale*. It is quite as efficient as the chattel mortgage for the purposes intended, however. Such preferences cannot be otherwise than unjust and injurious to the creditor who may reside at a distance, and who must trust largely to the good faith of his customer.

Whatever law be enacted, it should be simple, and intended for the whole country. Equitable distribution, a sharper method of testing claims and assigning them their proper places, the character and record of the insolvent—all these can be made the prime features of a new

general law. Officers can be appointed, who, by reason of special qualifications, are peculiarly fitted for their duties, and should be paid *regular
salaries* instead of fees. Throw aside much of the expensive machinery
of the Courts ; do away with the delays between meetings ; after time is
given, all creditors at a distance to name a representative who shall
regularly act for them in each case ; let the sale of assets take place
expeditiously, where goods are at all perishable, and where they are not,
let practical trustees, who are fully competent in the line of goods at stake,
assist the salaried officer in naming the first period in the season when
the best prices can be obtained, and when that time comes proceed to a
realization. Even if expedition should result in a somewhat lower
percentage in case of some sales, any loss in this way would be nominal,
when compared with the loss through shrinkage caused by holding the
assets, and by the routine fees obtained by assignees under the old regime.

While there have been but few and scattered examples since the
abolition of the late Act, which have indicated the real need of new legislation upon the matter, it is assumed by many, who forecast the future
pretty soundly, that the absence of a law is beginning to injure our credit
in markets upon which we depend for fine stuffs, and indispensable neces-
saries of many kinds. The first significant coloring to this effect, was
recognized upon the recent occasion of the Right Hon. Sir John A.
Macdonald's visit to the old country, when a deputation, representing
the leading wholesale houses in London and large sellers in Canada,
called upon him in order to present the following memorial, which was
influentially signed by houses in London, Manchester and Liverpool :—

To the RIGHT HON. SIR JOHN A. MACDONALD,

Premier of the Dominion of Canada :

The undersigned merchants of the United Kingdom, being largely
interested in the commercial prosperity of the Dominion of Canada,
beg respectfully to call the attention of the Government to the following
facts :—

1. That since the repeal of the Insolvent Act of 1875, it has become
impossible for creditors to ascertain their real position and powers with

regard to insolvent debtors, the most eminent commercial lawyers having been unable to give authoritative advice upon the subject, owing to the confused state of the law, differing as it does in the different Provinces.

2. That it follows that creditors—especially those at a distance—are practically at the mercy of the dishonest debtor, experience having shewn that there is no available means of preventing a debtor from assigning all his assets, by preferential payments or bills of sale, to favored creditors, and leaving the rest without remedy.

3. That the continuance of such a state of things, however its real tendency may be disguised by the present prosperity of the Dominion, is entirely fatal to that confident expectation of fair treatment which is at the basis of all trade, and must, in the end, most seriously *impair the commercial credit* of the Dominion, to the great injury of the common interests of the country. Your petitioners would therefore pray you to introduce into the Canadian Parliament, or to favor the introduction of a Bill which should, at the least, make such preferences by an insolvent debtor impossible, and should provide for the expeditious, cheap and equitable distribution of assets in all cases when a trader is unable to meet his lawful engagements. And your petitioners would express their hope, that a means may be found to make it to the interest of the debtor in all cases to place himself unreservedly in the hands of the general body of creditors, as soon as he finds himself insolvent. And your petitioners will ever pray.

Mr. Samuel Morley, M.P., who introduced the deputation, read letters from the Manchester and Liverpool Chambers of Commerce, strongly supporting the memorial, and pointed out the need, on behalf of Canadian as well as English creditors, of some arrangement which should deprive the dishonest debtor of his present facilities for assigning his whole estate to particular creditors, and, in illustration, mentioned a case where a debtor had used the threat of a preferential assignment to force his creditors to accept a composition.

In reply, Sir John pointed out that, "in addition to the great and essential difficulties of the subject of bankruptcy, there were in Canada special difficulties arising from the concurrent powers of the Dominion and Provincial Legislatures. He himself voted for the continuance of the Act of 1875, but there was too strong a feeling against it in the Canadian Parliament. It was considered that the facility of discharge under it was demoralizing the traders of the country. The Legislatures are exceedingly anxious to protect the honest trader, and every effort will be made to enact such prohibitions as will prevent fraudulent preferences of any kind. But the practical difficulty is, that, though the Dominion Legislature is competent to deal with insolvency and bankruptcy in general, it is doubtful if a partial measure, directed only against such preferences, would not belong to the Provincial Legislatures, and before proposing any Bill covering the whole ground, the Canadian Government desires to wait and see the result of the legislation now expected from the Imperial Parliament."

While we are really prosperous, then, it is likely that our traders will not be curtailed at points where credit is of the first importance to them; but should a change occur, renewals be asked, stocks get heavy, payments come in slowly, a fire devastate closely-settled sections, or a crop or two turn out badly, it is evident that supplies of goods might, and probably would, be delayed or curtailed greatly. Where distrust exists, it is said that a profitable interchange of commodities is impossible.

That our country is geographically in a difficult position to execute a law which possesses harsh or extreme features in its make, is certain. If pressed, a debtor may, if lacking principle, suddenly vanish over the border, and, by his absence, render as good realization of his remaining assets much more uncertain, than if he could be encouraged to stay and assist in the handling—particularly of his outstandings. But as has been suggested, it *is* possible to frame a simple Act, which, while it gives the weak-minded debtor a reason for remaining at his post, will make the distribution of assets all over the country quite equitable, and comparatively inexpensive through its expeditious action. It is as certain as that the sun rises, that before another period of commercial depression occurs, a simple yet comprehensive Insolvent Act will be an imperative necessity.

Grain, Produce and Shipping Interests.

With the exception of the tropics, wheat is grown in nearly all sections of the globe. But though most countries raising it, generally speaking, produce enough for home wants, few, comparatively, have a surplus to export. The United States is the largest wheat growing, wheat consuming and wheat exporting country in the world. From competent authority it is learned that the yield of that country has reached as high as 480,000,000 bushels in a year. The same authority shows that, allowing five bushels per capita for home consumption, there is then left 230,000,000 bushels for export—less the amount required for seed. During the fiscal year ending June 30th, 1880, the United States exported 153,752,800 bushels of wheat and 6,011,400 barrels of wheat flour. This flour was equal to 30,570,000 bushels of wheat, thus giving a total for that year of 184,322,800 bushels. This return is, then, a fair average for that country, although for the year ending 1881 the growth will appear at considerably smaller figures, owing largely to the June drouth in the South-Western and Western States. The State of California is said to raise about one-ninth of the total crop.

Of foreign countries, France leads with a crop of 300,000,000 in her best years. France is therefore generally depended upon to relieve the wants of less favored countries, and in some years can export 100,000,000 bushels of surplus grain. Russia follows hard upon France, and has yielded as much as 240,000,000 bushels. Germany, Spain, Italy, Austria-Hungary, and the United Kingdom are the next heaviest producers, the maximum crop in these countries being about the same through a number of years, and may be quoted at in the vicinity of 110,000,000 to 120,000,000 bushels. It is to be regretted that no close or very authentic statistics are officially compiled for the Dominion of Canada as to its total yield, but estimates place the growth for 1880 at 35,000,000 bushels, and for 1881 at 45,000,000 bushels, the exports being some 20,000,000 bushels for 1880 and for 1881. Australasia, as per the Sydney *Trade Review*, has had an excellent season, Victoria producing 9,719,000 bushels, South Australia, 8,606,000 bushels, and New Zealand, 8,147,000 bushels, the average yield per acre being—Victoria, 9.95, South Australia, 4.96, and New Zealand, 25.07 bushels. New Zealand is also by far the largest grower of oats and of barley. Manitoba has this year grown about 3,000,000 bushels of wheat, the yield being from 30 to 35 bushels per acre.

While the crop in the Dominion has this year been the largest for some twenty years, that of the States has fallen off greatly, owing to the drouth. In Britain the crop has been seriously damaged by the continued wet weather, and may be called a failure. France is below the average, and is now a buyer, as is also Austria, but Southern Russia has a good crop. The shortage in the States was also aggravated by heavy falls of rain after the cutting of the grain and before it could be got in.

The *Mark Lane Express*, in its review of the British grain trade during the last week in August, states: "The past week brought general disaster and ruin to the harvest. The series of intermittent storms culminated on Thursday in a general thunderstorm with a deluging rainfall. To adequately estimate the damage, we must remember that the downpour of rain was on sheaves which had been repeatedly wetted and dried, or upon standing grain which is literally eaten up by mildew. In the flooded districts the disaster is complete. Unthatched ricks have everywhere suffered from Thursday's deluge. The position of the harvest has materially affected trade, and rates improved a shilling on Wednesday and a further shilling on Friday. The advance, which would have amounted to several shillings had Thursday's weather continued, was checked by Thursday's sunshine. An advance in the Provinces amounted to a shilling more than in London. Of the few samples of the new crop offering, nearly all had sprouted, the earliest parcels being the best. The stocks on either side of the Atlantic being in strong hands, the supply here cannot exceed the demand until growers in America forward a new crop in sufficient bulk to overpower the Atlantic speculators. Fifteen cargoes arrived off coast, of which three were sold. Values are unchanged since Friday. The forwarding business has been considerable. The floating bulk has been increased by 309,000 quarters. For barley, values were checked, being ruled by maize, which was cheaper. Oats are at a standstill, foreign growths being cheaper. The sales of English wheat during the week were 12,671 qrs., at 51s. 10d. per qr., against 12,229 qrs., at 44s., for the corresponding week last year. There were renewed storms of rain and wind in various parts of Great Britain on Sunday night and Monday morning, and the destruction of crops in Ireland has been very great." The following is a summary of the agricultural returns of Great Britain as to acreage during the past three seasons :—

	WHEAT.	BARLEY.	OATS.
	ACRES.	ACRES.	ACRES.
1879	2,890,244	2,667,176	2,656,628
1880	2,909,438	2,467,441	2,796,905
1881	2,806,057	2,442,405	2 901,135

	POTATOES.	HOPS.
	ACRES.	ACRES.
1879	541,344	67,671
1880	550,932	66,705
1881	579,431	65,128

The present year opened with fair prices, or about $1.15 for spring wheat, in Montreal. The market continued at nominal rates until June, the drouth in the South-Western States then began to force prices upward, as also did the effect of the continuous wet weather in England. Prices ran rapidly up until they reached their highest point about the end of September, selling at an advance on $1.46 in Chicago. The market subsequently turned, and declined in all some twenty cents. There is no doubt that the rise witnessed during the summer was upon an artificial basis, to a certain extent. That there was sufficient in the situation to aid a "bull" movement is true, and that there is, at date of this sketch, December 1st, 1881, reason to believe that rates will be pretty well maintained until we ascertain the outlook for the next harvest, but it is a close question if there be ground upon which to inaugurate another rapid advance in the near future.

The United Kingdom is invariably a heavy buyer of wheat, and during this and the next quarter will be in the leading markets with a still heavier demand to satisfy. She looks principally to the United States, France, Russia, Germany, Canada and Australia, for supplies, the leading competitors in supply usually being the first two named, though this year France will be unable to supply any requirements from abroad. For the decades ending with 1870 and 1880, the proportions of wheat imported into the United Kingdom from the United States and Russia are reported to have been as follows :—

From the United States........per cent...1870...27·1......1880...47·8
From Russia..................... " ...1870...26·6......1880...20·4
From all other sources......... " ...1870...46·3......1880...31·8

While the detail percentages from other countries are not closely obtainable, it is fair to assume that a greater part of the remaining percentage came from France, Canada, &c. In 1861 to 1864, inclusive, the United States contributed from 34 to 39 per cent. of the foreign wheat imported into the United Kingdom. In 1865 the quantity from that part of the world suddenly dropped to five-and-a-half per cent., and in 1866 it was still less. It then increased its percentage from 1867, when it was 12, to 40 per cent. in 1870. In 1871 it fell to 34, and in 1872 to 21 per cent., but the proportion for 1873 was over double that of 1872, and in 1880 the percentage actually reached 65.4, while Russia contributed only five and a half in 1880, and never more than 42 per cent., which was reached in 1872.

The grain shipments for the port of Montreal, from January 1st of the present year, to November 1st, amount to 13,306,635 bushels. For the same period in 1880 the figures were 20,444,045 bushels. This exhibit shows a loss to the port of 7,137,410 bushels during 1881. The exports of flour were 557,000 barrels against 667,000 last year. These returns are, as a consequence, somewhat discouraging to the shipping interest of the port, but as the situation is an abnormal one, the conditions are likely to change with the advent of another season. Influences have been at work which will not probably be felt in such degree another year. The cheapness of Railway rates to the seaboard have equally affected the American carrying trade and that of the Dominion; in fact, we suffer a less proportionate loss than that experienced in the United States. It is estimated that the falling off of the business upon the Erie Canal in New

York, amounts to nearly one-half as compared with the previous year. Had it not been, therefore, for the war between competing railways, our return would not have visibly decreased.

The year of 1881, then, though prosperous in nearly every other branch of business, has not come up to a good average in the shipping interest, the chief reasons for this being : 1, the low railway rates occasioned by ring and corner speculations; 2, the irregular prices through the early season for grain in Europe, and, 3, the high prices at which it was held here for a time. There was, as a result, a decrease of over an hundred sea-going vessels reported at the port of Montreal at close of navigation, as compared with 1880. Ship owners, however, do not seem to have become discouraged with the outlook, and believing that another season will set this interest right, some notable additions are to be made in lines calling at this port. Among these is the inauguration of the "White Cross Line," from Antwerp. This may be termed the pioneer direct line to this port ; its continuation is said to be guaranteed, and an additional steamer will probably be placed upon it during next season. Should a large emigration from the continent arise, a weekly line will be established. The Dominion Line are now building on the Clyde, three large iron steamships of high class—the "Sarnia," the "Oregon," and the "Vancouver." The two first will be of 4,000 tons burthen, and the latter of over 5,000 tons, these steamers being intended for first-class passenger traffic, fitted with all conveniences, and attaining great speed. The Allan Line intend building a ship of the famous "Parisian" class, but of still larger tonnage, while the business of the port will be enlarged by a French line, the "Société Postale de l'Antique," and by increased accommodation in the "Thomson" line.

Attempts have frequently been made by forwarders both in the State of New York and in Canada to obtain for themselves increased benefits from their respective Governments in the way of improved water routes and reduced tolls. In view of the opening of the enlarged Welland Canal, and in order to ascertain whether an enlargement of the St. Lawrence canals could be rendered expedient, it became necessary to analyze the probable effect of the improvements upon the "Welland." An able correspondent of the Toronto *Globe* being directed to sift the mass of evidence, *pro* and *con*, proceeded to Kingston during the last season and succeeded in eliciting some impartial and valuable information. From his reports, as well as from some deductions of the Montreal *Gazette*, both supplemented by practical trade opinions, I quote, as a net result, that while our Canadian route can retain an advantage of about two cents per bushel in the face of anything which can be essayed by the American water route short of paying forwarders a bonus to use it, ocean freights to Liverpool are generally sixpence to one shilling cheaper from New York, while marine insurance is always less, and though the tolls upon grain through the canals here might, as shippers think, be done away with, it seems to be necessary to enlarge both our carrying power and our canals. This, in a period of immunity from railway speculation and consequent rate rivalry, would encourage a cheaper rate of carriage, and secure to us our rightful share of profit from our own waterways. New craft and new transhipment facilities can be created, and our natural advantages be made the most of. Canada, as a country, has displayed great courage and energy in putting her water routes into as good a condition as they are to-day ; whether they will be utilized to the best possible advantage, depends upon the continued enterprise of her people. The Erie Canal of New York State is used to the utmost possible extent, but is still unable to carry all that presents. *We have not seen* the capacity of our canals tested as fully as it might be, were the facilities for lockage, transhipment and increased tonnage enlarged. Whatever tends to reduce the cost of transporting grain to Europe, tends to increase the profits of the Western farmer, without reducing the profits of agriculturalists near the seaboard, for the price to the producer on this continent is the price in the English markets, minus the cost of transport, &c. It is, of course, true that the English price might be to a certain extent lowered were the decrease of transportation rates to cause a much greater export of grain from this continent, but the increase of population is rapid here in proportion to the increase in older countries ; the area of land under cultivation is so large in proportion to the untilled soil, that the export of grain is hardly likely to increase so rapidly but that the English price will always practically be determined by the English production. There is this to be said, however, in favor of our situation, *i. e.*, wheat shipped from Canada is known to be in the best condition, and is sought after in old country markets eagerly. This is owing to the advantage our climate gives us, in that these shipments are less liable to damage from heat, and this advantage is even more manifest in our shipping of corn, which heats easily.

There can be no doubt that the grain carrying trade is an essential interest to our country, its incidental benefits, as an able writer puts it, are far reaching, and advantageous in a high degree. The money it scatters along our front could hardly be made up were it to be discouraged and allowed to languish, while it adds materially to the life of our general shipping interests, and keeps our large steamer lines firmly allied to us. It would be absurd to reason that anything else could do this ; we certainly cannot export *manufactured goods* in any such proportion, it is the East-ward cargo that tells in the shipping business, and if it declines we are most certainly placed at a disadvantage by the effect upon our direct import carriage.

The depression, literally, has exercised but little direct influence upon the grain interests of our country, at least it did not operate as in other lines, or with a decidedly adverse effect. The causes of disaster in this business must be traced to *speculation*, which is inseparable from its conduct, the regular *order* manner of dealing being open to a speculative coloring as well. The past three years have witnessed rises and declina-tions of values, which, in twenty-four hours, in many cases, have made it impossible for houses to forecast the results of the strictest order transac-tions, no matter how legitimately made. It is unlike any other branch of trade, it deals with stern conditions, represents cash, and must be handled as carefully.

It is pleasing to learn that a project is on foot for the establishment of a " bureau of agricultural statistics " in Ontario. It is most important that this should be done, as it may free us from the danger of sudden " corners," and relieve our farmers from the danger of manipulation by speculators. The bureau, when formed, is to cover the following heads and statistics :—1. The number of acres sown in various grains, roots, fruits and other crops. 2. The quantity produced of each article. 3. The number and description of live stock kept and raised. 4. The adaptability of certain breeds to certain localities, and cost of keeping the animals, as well as the returns from them. 5. The results of fertilizers on different soils, quantities used, and methods of cultivation employed. 6. Locality, extent and nature of the pine forests of Ontario. 7. The quantity of timber annually cut down and manufactured. 8. The kinds and quantities of sawn lumber made and sold. 9. Dairy products, their extent, yield and prices obtained. Creamery and cheese factory returns and methods. 10. Fruit culture, apple, grape, peach, strawberry growing, &c. In addition to this much needed information, it is intended to elicit general statistics with respect to grain pests, epidemic diseases of cattle, untried productions, and their suitableness to our climate, amount of exports and imports of grain, fruits, animals and other prominent interests. With a well-organized bureau of this character, it will be an easy matter to trace our progress, or retrogression, as the case may be. It is simply a question of employing the right men—such as some school master or public functionary in each township, in order to obtain returns regularly. We certainly ought to command enough intelligence in our farming districts to materially aid the representatives of such a bureau, and its object can be readily achieved by systematic and earnest endeavor.

The Cheese and Butter production of our country has steadily grown, and for several years has assumed important proportions. Commencing with 1869, we were able to export as follows :—

	BUTTER.		CHEESE.	
	QUANTITY.	VALUE.	QUANTITY.	VALUE.
1869......Lbs.	10,853,268	$2,343,270	Lbs. 4,503,370	$549,572
1870	12,259,887	2,353,570	5,827,782	674,486
1871......	15,439,266	3,065,299	8,271,439	1,109,906
1872......	19,068,348	3,612,679	16,424,025	1,840,284
1873......	15,208,633	2,808,979	19,483,211	2,280,412
1874......	12,233,046	2,620,305	24,050,982	3,523,201
1875......	9,268,044	2,337,324	32,342,030	3,886,226
1876......	12,392,367	2,579,431	35,024,090	3,751,268
1877......	15,479,550	3,224,981	37,700,921	3,897,968
1878......	13,006,626	2,382,237	38,054,294	3,997,521
1879......	14,307,977	2,101,897	46,414,035	3,790,300
1880......	18,535,362	3,058,069	40,368,678	3,893,366

Of the total export of Canadian butter during 1880, Great Britain absorbed 16,687,978 lbs., and of cheese, 39,153,726 lbs., giving us for these products, $6,528,833. During the past twelve years we exported, then, no less an amount than 168,052,374 lbs. of butter, for which we received $32,487,971, and of cheese, 308,464,917 lbs., which brought us $33,194,312.

The English market for fine butter opened in January, 1880, at 115 shillings, fell during February to 110 shillings, reacting in March, and reached in April of that year, 140 shillings. With the new season, prices gave way, until 92 shillings and sixpence was touched, in June, to be followed by a sharp advance to 120 shillings in August. Afterward, prices gradually dwindled away, and the year closed with heavy stocks on hand, and 110 shillings as the top price. Throughout the fall, demand was slow, and ran almost entirely upon the finer grades. Strong flavored, stale and medium qualities were almost driven out of the market by such substitutes as oleomargarine, butterine, &c. The stocks on hand at the end of the year aggregated 49,712 packages, as against 31,239 at the close of 1879, though but little of this was of choice or fine-conditioned quality.

Cheese in January of 1880, were worth in Britain, 66 to 68 shillings, and by the end of that month brought 72 shillings, touching in April, 78 shillings. With the opening of the new season, a sharp decline at once took place, and for a week or two in July prices ruled under 48 shillings, but values immediately stiffened, and by the end of August had again reached 68 shillings. With moderate fluctuations, that range was afterward fairly maintained, as stocks were not excessive. The year closed with 96,007 boxes on hand, as against 63,510 a year before, the latter being a very small amount as a holding at that period.

The values given to fine butter early in 1881, were, for finest creamery, 130 shillings, and for finest cheese, 66 shillings. For the first week in the year, the imports to Britain from the United States and Canada amounted to 32,302 boxes of cheese, and 2,962 packages of butter. All along, however, it was well nigh impossible to get hold of any great amount of strictly first-class or creamery makes, and the lower grades were difficult to sell. In March, a decline took place which saw the figures for choice creamery down to 110 to 112 shillings, and at the end of the month, down to 100 to 105 shillings. During May, cheese dropped some six shillings, and in June about four shillings more. In August, prices were at 54 to 56 for the finest, while butter—creamery, advanced to 120 to 126 shillings. In September, extra fine white cheese brought 61 to 63 shillings, while butter was nominal. Cheese in November brought 63 to 64 shillings for strictly choice, butter being stationary.

The manufacture of more creamery butter must be prosecuted in our country, or we shall find ourselves shut out of the old country markets, or be ranked far below the States. It is estimated that we lose one million dollars per annum from our income by sending medium grades to market, when finer makes could just as well be produced by us. It is *most important* that this should be changed. The dairy interest of a country is no secondary one, but a reputation must be made and kept. In the United States, it has recently been shown that the income from dairy products actually leads that derived either from its immense wheat export or its cotton crop, the latter no longer being " king."

Alluding briefly to our marine and general shipping history, it may be interesting to many to learn, upon the authority of Mr. Kivas Tully, C.E., that the first ship which sailed across the ocean from this continent was built at Quebec. It has been said that the Intendant Talon, before leaving Canada, in 1672, ordered a ship to be built at Anse des Meres, but the most authentic statement is to the effect that the first craft which sailed across the ocean was modelled upon the banks of the river St. Charles, in 1703. Eleven years later, in 1714, the New England colonists of Plymouth, launched the first New England built schooner which ploughed the billows en route to England. In 1722, six vessels of considerable tonnage were launched on the St. Charles, from a spot now called " Marine Hospital Cove."

The number of vessels remaining on the registry books of the Dominion, on the 31st of December, 1880, including old and new vessels, sailing vessels, steamers and barges, was 7,377, measuring 1,311,218 tons register. The number of steamers was 948, with a gross tonnage of 190,159 register, and a net tonnage of 120,141 tons. Assuming the average value to be $30 per ton, the value of the registered tonnage of the Dominion on the above date, would be $39,336,540. The number of new vessels built and registered in the Dominion, during the last year, was 271, measuring 65,441 tons, this, at $45 per ton, gives a total value of $2,944,845 for new vessels. The tonnage of Canada is distributed over the various provinces, as follows :—New Brunswick, 236,976; Nova Scotia, 550,448 ; Quebec, 333,351 ; Ontario, 137,481 ; Prince Edward Island, 45,921 ; British Columbia, 5,049 ; Manitoba, 1,992.

BANKS, BROKERS AND MONEY.

During the depression, no department of business was subjected to such a degree of close scrutiny, comment and anxious attention as that of our banking interest.

Our great discounting institutions—those most important factors in business situations—were the arbiters, and controlled the destinies of many merchants whom the advent of the darker years found in an abnormally expanded condition. The policy and management of these prominent integers, of a great whole, therefore, could not escape the closest criticism, nor fail to be the cynosure of all eyes in trade circles.

The banks always work in the closest sympathy with the varying conditions of trade. The lifetide of commerce pulsates through these natural financial arteries, and barometrically registers each day's commercial advances and retrogressions, as well as the periodical stages of stagnation and recuperation of commerce. No other medium can be found which through its channels will, with such fidelity and sensitiveness, reflect cause and effect, or determine results so decisively.

In writing up a review of the course of banking for any given period—particularly when that period covers an era of depression such as the past decade has witnessed—the tone should be dispassionate, in order to carry a lesson with it, and such this humble effort is intended to be. In recording the inception and history, in brief, of those of our standard institutions which wield the greatest branch or agency interest, some general or specific allusion to the notable events of the past ten years, and their prime causes, may be appropriate, as also the expansion and contraction of general banking interests, as historically shown, the losses sustained, remarks upon inspection, contrast of systems, weaknesses, circulation statistics and illustrations, construction of bank statements, &c. All these should be considered, together with other heads which naturally come into the subject and help to form the *tout ensemble* of our banking system.

In compiling this sketch, the author is indebted to several of our leading and most conservative bankers for information, and has been allowed by them to quote from some of their most carefully written opinions as to a few important points.

As an illustration of the growth and importance of our banking interest, it is in order to follow the record of a few of our banks—those whose interests are most closely identified with the extension of business —from their origin to the present day. Beginning with the Bank of Montreal—formerly known as the Montreal Bank—we find it holding its first meeting for organization under that name on the 7th of August, 1817. The following gentlemen were at this meeting elected to serve as directors for the ensuing year:—Messrs. John Gray, John Forsyth, George Gordon, George Moffatt, Horatio Gates, Thomas A. Turner, F. M. Ermatinger, John McTavish, Austin Cuvillier, James Leslie, Hiram Nichols, George Platt and Zabdiel Thayer. John Gray was elected President, and Thomas A. Turner, Vice-President, Mr. Robert Griffin being appointed Cashier, at a salary that was then called exceptionately extravagant, *i. e.*, £300 per annum. The capital at date of the next annual meeting, in June, 1818, being $350,000. In 1819 and 1826, a dividend of three per cent. was paid ; in 1829, a dividend of two-and-a-half per cent. accrued to shareholders ; in 1827 and 1828, no dividends were paid, but in 1832 a dividend of 7 per cent., and a bonus of 5 per cent., was paid ; in 1833, 1834 and 1835, 8 per cent. and a bonus of 6 per cent., and in 1836, 8 per cent. regular and 4 per cent. bonus was paid, on a capital of $1,000,000. From 1840 to 1845, the capital was $2,000,000, and in 1845, $3,000,000, when the circulation was $1,792,212, deposits amounted to $1,429,240, and the amount under discount to $4,925,896. At this time the Hon. Peter McGill was President, and Mr. Simpson, Cashier. In 1853, the capital was increased, and this increase was added to up to 1855, when the capital stood at $4,000,000, and the discounts amounted to $9,691,600. In 1855, Mr. David Davidson became Cashier, and under his management the bank enjoyed as much success as could be attained in those days, the value of the stock at this date ranging at from 110 to 117. In 1860, the capital was increased to $6,000,000, the business of the bank growing in proportion. Mr. King assumed the general management in 1863, and during his term of office the bank made money rapidly. Mr. King was elected to the presidency in 1872, when Mr. R. B. Angus was appointed the General Manager. In 1867, the bank paid a dividend of 10 per cent.; in 1869, 11 per cent.; in 1870, 12 per cent.; in 1871, 14 per cent., and in 1872-3, for both years, a total return of 16 per cent. to shareholders, it being made up, each of those years, of 12 per cent. regular dividend and 4 per cent. bonus. The capital was standing in 1872 at $8,000,000. In 1874, it was shown that the bank had a paid up capital of $11,885,335, the shares being worth at par $200, but held at that date at a heavy premium over that amount. At this date, Hon. David Torrance was President, George Stephen, Vice-President, and Mr. Angus, General Manager, its Directors representing old and good records as men of the highest reputations and wealth. During a portion of Mr. King's management, considerable sums were made by the bank through business with the Government, who, for a time, were needy, and whose business was necessarily profitable. He also made considerable gains for the bank at New York, and though that city passed through some severe financial tests during this period, he avoided much loss. The bank also made money in assisting other Canadian banks, and was really their banker, in some cases. It also strenuously advocated and maintained for itself a large " Rest," the amount finally achieved being nearly one half of the amount of its capital. At the general meeting of June, 1874, it was shown that the profits of the past current year were, net, $2,072,540. At this time, one of the best indications of the bank's strength, as well as the live and healthful character of its business, was to be found in the fact that it had deposits of about $11,000,000, and kept out a circulation of some $3,250,000 without difficulty. In 1875-6, the bank showed as follows for the past current year :—Capital stock paid up, $11,979,000 ; Rest or Reserve, $5,500,000 ; balance to credit of Profit and Loss, $569,000 : Notes in circulation, $3,271,000 ; Deposits, $14,622,000 ; its Loans and Discounts being $27,507,000, and its Profits Current were $1,839,000. Owing to the bank's increase of capital, and to the effects of the contraction of general trade, the annual results to shareholders began to decline gradually from 1874, the net dividend declared in that year being 15 per cent.; in 1875 and 1876 it was 14 per cent.; in 1877, 13 per cent.; in 1878, 12 per cent. ; in 1879, 10 per cent. ; and in 1880, the lowest point for many years was reached, *i. e.*, 8 per cent. Among its notable losses during the later part of the decade, may be mentioned, a defalcation at Toronto, by Mr. Barber, and the depreciation of City Passenger Railway stock, as well as some failures occurring among old and large houses. In 1877, however, the bank was carrying Deposits bearing interest to the amount of $11,214,000, and those not bearing interest, to the amount of $4,804,000, while the circulation was $3,275,508. In 1878, the Net Profits were $1,430,903, and the Interest-bearing Deposits were reduced to $9,365,867, its circulation being $3,183,000, and its discounts, $27,718,613. On the 23rd of September, 1879, Mr. C. F. Smithers, formerly the New York manager, was appointed General Manager, *vice* Mr. Angus, who had just resigned. The change was made at a time when considerable excitement prevailed in banking circles over the downfall of the Consolidated Bank, the apparent necessity of reducing the capital of two other banks, and a general uncertainty in commercial circles as to the result of the year's conditions. The appointment of Mr. Smithers, however, gave a tone to the general situation, and made all values steadier. During this year, a resolution was passed at the annual meeting that the Bank should issue a half-yearly statement regularly, which resolution was carried. The annual statement appearing in May, 1880, showed a Capital paid up of $11,999,200 ; the " Rest " had been reduced to $5,000,000, the Circulation stood at $3,601,655. Deposits bearing interest had been increased to $16,889, 347, while the discounts, notwithstanding the great contraction of business, had only shrunk to $20,561,528. Many, at this time, contended that the bank was working at a disadvantage in still maintaining so large a " Rest," but it was also conceded by shrewd heads that upon the revival of trade, the bank would be found occupying the very best vantage ground on account of the general construction of its business. In the Fall of this year, this great bank quickly felt the favoring effect of the recuperation of trade, and at its annual meeting in the Spring of 1881, showed so great an earning power as to give its shareholders a dividend for the preceding six months of 4 per cent. and a bonus of 2 per cent., following this with 5 per cent. return in the Fall, or 11 per cent. for the twelve months. In June, 1881, Mr. George Stephens resigned the Presidency, and Mr. Smithers was elected to that position, Mr. W. J. Buchanan

becoming the General Manager, Mr. A. MacNider, the Assistant General
, Manager, and Mr. E. S. Clouston the Local Manager. These promotions
were natural ones, each officer being well fitted, through long service,
for their respective positions. This great institution now has a practical
working President at its head. Finally, the history of this bank furnishes
the most conclusive proof of the capacity for, and growth of business in
our country. Its progress is clearly reflected by a glance at the following
comparison of the bank's business interests in 1850 and 1881 :—

	1850.	1881.
Capital paid up	$3,000,000	$11,999,200
Circulation	1,792,212	5,458,015
Deposits	1,429,240	20,611,209
Loans and Discounts	4,925,896	26,838,759

Of the above deposits in 1881, $12,597,289 only bear interest, and
of the Loans and Discounts, only $102,946 are not specially secured,
though all probable loss upon these is provided for. The bank has now
twenty-seven branch and agency representations in Canada, besides those
in the United States and England.

The Molsons Bank was organized in 1853. The original Directors
were William Molson, President, Hon. Jno. Molson, Thos. Molson, J. H.
R. Molson and E. Hudon. In 1857, Jno. H. R. Molson resigned, and
Thomas Workman was elected to replace him. In 1879, Mr. Workman
was elected President, and Mr. J. H. R. Molson again became a Director,
and was elected Vice-President. In 1857, the capital of the bank was
$677,118, this was increased from time to time, until in 1860 it stood at
$1,000,000. The business of the bank steadily rolled up with the exten-
sion of our country's commerce, from Discounts of $756,680 in 1857, to
$7,000,000 in 1881, the circulation of the bank in 1857 was $356,660 as
against $2,122,465 in 1881 ; deposits were $206,780 in 1857, and
$4,000,558 in 1881, exclusive of Government Deposits. In 1870,
Mr. Wm. Sache retired from the position of Cashier, and was succeeded
by Mr. F. Wolferstan Thomas, who had ample experience as Manager of
the London branch of the Bank of Montreal, and who had for years
possessed a good knowledge of bank routine duties. Under Mr. Thomas'
management, the capital of ' the Molsons ' was early increased to $1,500,000

in 1871, and to $2,000,000 in 1872, the Directorate being augmented to seven gentlemen. In 1881, those composing the Board were as follows :— Thos. Workman, President, J. H. R. Molson, Vice-President, Capt. R. W. Shepherd, Messrs. H. A. Nelson, S. H. Ewing, Miles Williams, and Hon. Senator Macpherson. The bank has sixteen branches, and is under the General Management of Mr. Thomas, assisted by James Elliot as Local Manager. The bank is in excellent condition, is well represented at its Branch and Agency points, and controls a good and profitable business. On the 30th September, 1881, the bank's capital was $2,000,000 paid-up. Its circulation, $2,122,465; Public Deposits, $4,000,558; 'Rest,' $250,000; its current Discounts, $7,012,528; Discounts, past due, secured, $70,085; and those not specially secured, $20,966. Its real estate (other than bank premises), $138,360, and its bank premises $184,000. During the year, the bank carried $110,000 to the 'Rest' account, and its earnings amounted to about eleven and a half per cent. For a period of nearly twenty years the bank paid a uniform 8 per cent. dividend, with the sole exception of one half-year during that time wherein a two and a half per cent. return was paid. When, subsequently, the failure of Jay Cooke & Co. occurred, the bank's interest in connection with that house was such as to cause a reduction of the dividend rate to 6 per cent., at which figure it has since remained, though its earnings, as will be seen, are larger by a considerable per centage than this rate might indicate.

The Bank of Toronto was organized about the year 1855, Mr. Angus Cameron being its chief promoter. A number of the Honorable Hudson's Bay Company's officials were the principal original stockholders. The original capital stock was fixed at $800,000, and remained at this figure for a number of years. But it has since been twice increased, and at present, stands at $2,000,000, with a handsome reserve of $860,000. Messrs. Gooderham & Worts, the well-known Toronto distillers, were early connected with the institution as large stockholders, and have always occupied prominent positions on the directorate. Mr. Worts is President at date. To Mr. Geo. Hague, who was one of the earliest office holders, the present substantial position of the bank is largely due. The general management of the bank has always been marked by the greatest degree of care and circumspection, the directors have not been ambitious to create an extended business, but have confined the bank's operations to a few leading centres—such as Montreal, Peterboro', Cobourg, Port Hope, Barrie, St. Catherines, and Collingwood. The rate of dividend was long maintained at 10 per cent., and the Board of Directors, it is said, were seriously contemplating an increase to 12 per cent, when the depression set in, effectually dismissing the question for the time being. The present rate of dividend is 7 per cent. ; the stock is held in high esteem, principally because its condition is so free from past due and un-secured debts, and upon account of its general healthy composition. Had it pushed its business to greater lengths, these conditions in the natural course of things would probably have become a shade less promi-nent in its history. At the annual meeting in June, 1881, the bank had a circulation of $864,364; Deposits, $3,162,293 ; " Rest," $660,000, to which may be added the Contingent fund of $200,000, its current Discounts were $5,942,630 ; Discounts overdue, secured, $18,203, while those *not specially secured were only* $3,664.

The Canadian Bank of Commerce was organized in 1867, mainly through the influence of Hon. Wm. McMaster, of Toronto, who was the first President elect, and has held the office ever since. The original capital was fixed at $1,000,000, with power to increase it to $4,000,000. So favorably was the establishment of the bank received, that at the first annual meeting in 1868, the original capital had all been subscribed and $916,000 paid in. The earning power of the bank was early developed, the first years' business resulting in an 8 per cent. dividend, and it was then decided to increase the capital to $2,000,000. The business of the bank continued to develop rapidly and profitably, until in 1870, the capital was raised to $4,000,000, and in 1871 fresh powers were obtained from Parliament whereby the capital was further increased to $6,000,000. The annual report for the year 1872 showed that of the lately raised capital, $4,800,000 was subscribed, and the " Rest " stood at $1,000,000, while in 1873, the whole capital was subscribed, and the "Rest" had been increased to $1,500,000. Up to this date dividends had been continued at the rate of 8 per cent., though the profits would have warranted a higher rate, as evidenced by the large additions carried to the " Rest," but the policy of the Directors was to strengthen the position of the bank as much as possible, and protect it from possible contingencies. Later events showed their course to have been a wise one. In 1875, the highest figures of returns were reached, the bank's profits being $742,000, and the " Rest " reaching $1,900,000, a dividend of 10 per cent. was paid in this year, being the highest paid before or since. The capital was reported as fully paid-up at this date, and the increasing business with the Western States necessitated the opening of a branch in Chicago. The following year witnessed a reduction of profits, as the force of the depression made itself felt, the gains of the bank falling off to $454,000, and a return to the old 8 per cent. dividend was made. This has not since been increased. It would have been remarkable if the bank had not felt the effects of the severe stringency, as well as the general re-action of over-strained outside business and commerce at this date. In 1878, the Directors felt it necessary to appropriate $500,000 from the " Rest " for bad and doubtful debts, leaving $1,400,000 to the credit of that account, which figures have since been maintained. During the last two years the profits have improved, reaching in 1881, $652,000, the report also showing to the credit of profit and loss and contingent accounts $319,900, independent of the large " Rest " already quoted. The history of the bank, in the face of its enterprise and large interests, has been remarkable for good management. Its original five branches, i.e., Hamilton, London, Barrie, Guelph and St. Catherines, have been largely added to, and at good points as a rule, until at date the institution has thirty-two representations at leading centres, all these are under efficient management, the Montreal branch was opened in 1870.

At the bank's annual meeting in June 1881, its Circulation was shown to be $2,685,332, its Deposits $12,755,480, of which $2,759.118 did not bear interest; its paid-up Capital was $6,000,00 ; its " Rest," $1,400,000, and its Contingent Fund, $175,000. Among its assets were its discounts, which amounted to $15,908,945, while those overdue, secured, were $133,944, and those not specially secured amouuted to $213,984. Its real estate, other than bank premises, was $130,247, and its own premises and furniture were valued at $279,376. As will be seen, the business of the bank has greatly grown, and its management evidences ability. The reduction in the value of money during the past eighteen months has not enabled the profits to bear the same proportion to the extent of the business done as in former years, but they were sufficient to warrant the payment of an 8 per cent. dividend, and after providing for all the bad and doubtful debts of the year, left a surplus of $105,819. It is an evident fact that very close attention was given by the directors to the large business of the bank, and that the funds were made as productive as possible. During the year, the unusual cheapness of money led the Board to reduce the rates of interests upon deposits, but notwithstanding this these were considerably augmented.

The Merchants Bank, a local institution, was established in Montreal in 1864 and commenced business upon a paid-up capital of $100,000, the subscribed capital being some $400,000 to $500,000. Sir Hugh Allan was President, the late E. Atwater, Vice-President, and Mr. Jackson Rae, Cashier. In 1865, the capital of the bank amounted to $537,000; in 1866, to $657,000; in 1867, to $857,000, and in 1868 to $1,475,000. During 1868, this bank absorbed and amalgamated with the suspended Commercial Bank of Canada, the capital of this latter institution was, previous to its suspension, $4,000,000. The Merchants Bank assumed its outstanding liabilities, and gave its shareholders one share of the amalgamated succession for every three shares of the old Commercial Bank. The name of the amalgamated bank then became the Merchants Bank of Canada, and its business became general throughout the country instead of remaining local. At the time of the suspension of the Commercial Bank, the Hon. Sir R. J. Cartwright, late Finance Minister, was President, and the late Mr. C. S. Ross, was Cashier. The suspension of this bank was brought about chiefly in consequence of large advances made by it to the Great Western Railway Company of Canada, to construct its Western connection, known as the Detroit and Milwaukee Railroad. There was also a considerable amount of bad business paper in its assets.

The persons chiefly prominent in bringing about the amalgamation, were the President and Cashier of the Commercial Bank, the late Hon. E. H. Holton, and Sir Hugh Allan. Mr. E. H. King, acting for the Bank of Montreal, was a competitor for the purchase of the assets of the Commercial.

The Merchants Bank, from the outset, paid a dividend of 8 per cent., which in 1874 was increased to 10 per cent., but owing to shrinkages in sundry accounts, and notably to the weakness of the Detroit and Milwaukee bonds, taken over from the Commercial Bank, it was forced to reduce its capital about one-third in 1877, Mr. Jackson Rae being succeeded by Mr. Geo. Hague as General Manager, and Hon. John Hamilton becoming President. The capital of the bank in 1871 was $5,700,000; in 1872, $6,600,000; in 1873, $7,100,000; in 1874, $7,900,000; in 1875–6, $8,100,000, and in 1877 the reduction brought it down to $6,300,000. The circulation of the bank in 1872 reached $4,500,000, the Deposits being $8,000,000. In 1875, the dividend was reduced from 10 per cent. to 8 per cent., and in 1876 to 7½ per cent., in 1877 the dividend was passed, but in the year following the pruning down of the capital resulted in a declaration of 10½ per cent., which was created by the reduction, and by the current business of part of 1877. After that date the dividend was maintained at 6 per cent. The annual statement of the bank's affairs, as presented at the regular meeting, 15th June, 1881, gave the net profits of the bank for the current year at $651,600, and profits brought forward from previous year of $4,911, from which was paid the 6 per cent. dividend, amounting to $334,787, amount written off bank premises, &c., $23,506; amount added to the "Rest," $50,000; amount transferred to contingent account, $235,953, and a balance of $12,264 was carried forward to the next year. The annual statement followed, showing the condition of the bank as below :—

LIABILITIES.

Notes in Circulation	$2,835,519	00
Deposits bearing Interest	4,816,810	48
Deposits not bearing Interest	2,858,436	03
Balances due Canadian Banks, Deposit Acc'nts.	494,010	05
Balances due Canadian Banks, Daily Exchanges	4,849	73
Balances due British Banks	35,211	84
Dividends Unclaimed	4,937	84
Dividend No. 35, Payable 1st June	168,348	10
Total Liabilities to the Public	11,218,123	07
Capital Paid-up	5,611,603	33

Rest	525,000	00
Contingent Fund..	235,000	00
Balance carried forward to Cr. Profit and Loss.	12,264	59
Total............	17,601,990	99

ASSETS.

Coin on Hand....................................	385,149	17
Dominion Notes on Hand.............................	899,660	00
Notes, &c., of other Canadian Banks..............	442,277	22
Balances due by other Can. Banks, Exchanges.	58,414	96
Balances due by U. S. Agencies and Banks......	1,715,521	61
Total Assets immediately available.................	3,501,022	96
Current Discounts, Loans and Advances..........	12,565,924	10
" " " overdue and not ⎱ specially secured................................. ⎰	226,194	66
" " " secured	117,653	31
Interest-bearing Mortgages, Bonds, &c............	264,419	19
Real Estate—Productive..............................	157,386	22
Real Estate—Unproductive............................	284,362	14
Bank Premises and Furniture.......................	470,000	00
Other Assets, not included under above heads..	15,028	41
	$17,601,990	99

At present date the Hon. John Hamilton is President, and John McLennan, Esq., M.P., Vice-President. The following Directors now form, with the President and Vice-President, the Board :—Messrs. Andrew Allan, Sir Hugh Allan, Robt. Anderson, Wm. Darling, Jonathan Hodgson, Adolph Masson, Hector Mackenzie. The bank has twenty-eight branches.

The Bank of British North America, originally a purely English institution, was established in 1836, with a nominal capital of £1,000,000. Its promoters were merchants and others in London, Eng., who were deeply interested in the commerce and prosperity of the North American Colonies, and desirous of introducing British capital for their further development Among the promoters were Alexander Gillespie, John F. Cummins, and T. Carter, the first Secretary being George de B. Attwood. Between the years 1836 and 1840, £690,000 sterling was paid-up and employed in legitimate banking business at the branches which were then opened in the provinces of Upper and Lower Canada, New Brunswick, Nova Scotia and Newfoundland. During these years the business of the bank was conducted under an Act of the Imperial Parliament, which authorized it to sue and be sued in the name of an officer in England; and similar Acts of the Legislatures of the several provinces in which the branches were situated were obtained. But considerable practical inconvenience having been experienced in conducting the bank's affairs under so many different statutes, which although like in substance, contained conflicting conditions, the Directors applied in 1840, to Her Majesty's Government for a Royal Charter of incorporation, extending over the United Kingdom and all the North American Colonies, which was granted, it was understood, after communication with the Colonial Governments. During the discussions as to the conditions on which a charter should be granted to this bank, it appeared to be the opinion of Her Majesty's Government, that a large paid-up capital afforded better security to the public, than the clause of double liability introduced into the charters of the local or Colonial banks, and the Directors were required to call up the remainder of the capital of £1,000,000 sterling, as a consideration for the grant of a charter of incorporation, whereby the shareholders are relieved from personal liability after payment of the full amount of their shares. This charter was renewed in 1859, with the consent of the several Colonial Governments, the Royal Charter expiring in 1870, together with the Joint Colonial Charter. Its powers have been renewed however, and by the terms of its present charter, it is subject to the general laws of the Dominion, with respect to banks and banking.

For thirty-two years of its existence—to 1869—the bank paid an average of £5, 13s, 9d., per cent. dividends. Since 1869, it paid 9 per cent. for three years, 7 per cent. for one year, 6 per cent. another, and now averages 5 per cent.

Since the establishment of the bank, its business has been conducted in accordance with sound principles of banking, and it has been claimed for it that it has aided in improving the system of banking in Canada, and that it has maintained the most amicable relations with the other banks in the country. Its officers have from time to time, particularly in the early history of the institution, been recruited from banks in Britain, while in after years they were very warmly welcomed upon the staff of other banks, such was the value attached to their sound training.

It brought into Canada at a crucial time, *i.e.*, the date of the Rebellion, —'37–'38—a large amount of money, and thus steadied confidence and afforded material assistance to our country at a time when everything was in chaos. Its management here together with its court of directors in England have always been ready and willing to conform strictly to the requirements of Colonial legislatures, and it has stood side by side with our greatest banking institution in many important epochs of our commercial history.

Among its original officers can be found the names of J. Lunel, S. N. Binney, Thos. Paton, Alfred Smithers, Allen Good Liston, David Davidson, C. F. Smithers, R. Cassels, W. G. Cassels, Samuel and Geo. Taylor, R. C. Ferguson and others.

The last annual statement of the bank to December 31st, 1880, is as follows :—

	£	s.	d.
Capital paid up	1,000,000	0	0
Circulation	207,990	17	8
Deposits, no Interest Paid	1,260,270	1	6
Bills Payable and other Liabilities	1,478,370	4	1
Reserve for Christmas Dividend	25,000	0	0
Undivided Net Profit	151,206	18	0
Total	£4,122,838	1	3

ASSETS.

	£	s.	d.
Specie and Cash at Bankers	609,315	17	9
Bills Receivable and other Securities	3,385,453	0	1
Investments	56,569	3	5
Bank Premises	71,500	0	0
Total	£4,122,838	1	3

Its working account for the year 1880 shows dividends paid of £50,000, against a net profit of £74,236, and an addition to its undivided net profit, as left at the end of the preceding year, of nearly £25,000. During the present year, 1881, the bank's business is believed to have been a good one, and a further strengthening of its condition is probable.

The present directors of the bank are J. H. Brodie, Jno J. Cater, Henry R. Farrar, R. H. Glyn, E. A. Hoare, H. J. B. Kendall, J. J. Kingsford, Fred Lubbock, A. H. Phillpotts, and J. Murray Robertson. These gentlemen form what is known as the "court of Directors" at London, Eng. Mr. R. R. Grindley, with a record of 28 years service, is the General Manager, and Mr. J. S. Cameron, Inspector. The local management at Montreal is in the efficient hands of Mr. J. Penfold. The institution has thirteen branches at the principal points in the Dominion, one at Victoria B. C., and agents at New York, Chicago, San Francisco and Portland, Oregon.

Alluding further to the growth of commerce, as evidenced by its reflection within the doors of our great monetary institutions, all working smoothly under the general Act, it may be interesting to glance at the following comparisons. In 1866, the number of banks in active existence in the Provinces of Ontario and Quebec was 18; in 1881, the number is 24.

```
1866...........Aggregate Capital...................... $29,634,766
1881...........      "         "     ......................  52,868,703
```

CIRCULATION.

```
1866..... ................................................... $10,920,035
1881.......................................................  24,493,258
```

DEPOSITS.

```
1866....... ..................................................  $28,750,190
1881 .......................................................  86,537,000
```

DISCOUNTS—Current.

```
1861......................................................$ 44,542,634
1881......................................................  108,064,744
```

In 1875, the figures of banking turnovers exhibited a still greater gain, but as a fair comparison these can hardly be used, for the reason that business was abnormally extended, and they could not be maintained, but in the year of 1881, the general trade situation of our two most important provinces was never in a sounder shape, and results for the succeeding year must add to, rather than take from, the totals.

The general statement of the condition and business of banks throughout the Dominion at the end of November, 1881, was as follows :—

LIABILITIES.

Capital Paid-up	$59,706,011
Circulation	33,145,292
Dominion Government Deposits	10,258,500
Provincial Government 'Deposits	1,351,493
Deposits for Security of Contracts	810,822
Public Deposits	89,566,686
Loans from banks	2,024,293
Due Banks in Canada	904,777
Due Banks in United States	155,147
Due Banks in United Kingdom	413,094
Other Liabilities	452,277
Total	$198,788,392

ASSETS.

Specie	6,463,976
Dominion Notes	9,844,910
Notes of other Banks	5,465,565
Due from Banks in Canada	3,048,460
Due from Banks in the United States	20,748,575
Due from Banks in United Kingdom	7,207,642
Government Debentures	1,099,822
Foreign Public Securities	1,721,725
Loans to Government	1,517,055
Loans on Stocks and Bonds	12,699,616
Loans to Municipal Corporations	891,145
Loans to other Corporations	7,829,074
Loans to other Banks	777,037
Discounts Current	121,822,255
Notes Overdue, unsecured	1,358,820
Other Overdue Debts, unsecured	215,658
Other Overdue Debts, secured	2,283,962

Real Estate	1,797,088
Mortgages on Real Estate	524,814
Bank Premises	3,020,352
Other Assets	2,860,505
Total	$213,198,056

Naturally, there has been considerable decrease in the note circulation from October. This is owing to the effect produced upon country trade by the closing of navigation, the realization of interest, bad roads, &c. The amount circulated has been some $5,000,000 in excess of last year, and nearly $3,000,000 more than in October 1873. This evidences still further the marked improvement in trade situations, and indicates that farmers have generally realized fair prices for their products, and have largely abandoned, as a consequence, the holding of these for higher rates, and this again improves the position of country storekeepers who have, through this realization, been able to wipe out old and rusty outstandings and to pay their city friends. The Provinces of Ontario and Quebec shew in their banking returns for the month an increase of Government deposits of $1,500,000 as a result of accumulated savings in the Government Savings Banks, and the surplus revenues of the Dominion, while debts to other banks have been discharged to the extent of $630,000. There is an increase, however, " in other liabilities " of some $283,000. Among the assets, specie and Dominion notes have increased slightly, deposits in other banks have increased, and current loans, &c., reduced, the two latter by some $1,300,000. It is too early yet to expect the large return of the output of circulation, but it is probable that by next month the autumn indebtedness will be largely settled.

Alluding briefly to the notable events which have occurred in the banking record of Ontario and Quebec during the depression, it is in order to cite these by name and endeavor to establish a cause for their troubles.

The Mechanics Bank was established at Montreal by a gentleman who transferred to it a considerable amount of paper and business, which had been held and controlled by him as a private banker. Much of this paper developed weak in character, and its effect was to handicap the bank from its commencement. Moreover, the bank management was weak in so far as close analysation of its affairs was concerned for some time, and though it endeavoured to make up for the weak class of its business by charging high rates to borrowers, the result was, inevitably—heavy losses, suspension of payment, and consequent reduction of capital stock. The bank resumed business under a change of management, but faced with the depression, it had simply no opportunity to regain strength, nor to maintain itself under the reduction of capital, &c. The finale was, that the entire capital was lost, and the shareholders called upon to pay up the double liability under the provision of the Banking Act. As the affair stood, all that was found collectable, so as to be paid over at date of this writing, December 1881, amounted to forty-five cents in the dollar. It is said, however, that the estate is likely to pay from ten to fifteen per cent. more.

The Consolidated Bank, which suspended in 1879, was the result of the union of two banks, the "City" and the "Royal Canadian." The one with widely spread connections among a second-rate class of customers, and the other with a large amount of old and weak accounts, furnished elements calculated to bring disaster whenever a commercial crisis or depression overtook the country. In addition to the natural drawbacks presented at the outset, the Cashier, as well as his Assistant, each largely on his own judgment, seem to have discounted a very large amount of worthless paper, the extent of which was concealed from the Directors, who on their part were charged with negligence in so far as to omit that close scrutiny of their subordinates' operations, which was essential to the interests of the shareholders. The condition of affairs became known to some speculators, who began to "bear" the stock, and succeeded to such an extent that depositors became alarmed and inaugurated a "run," which in a very short time withdrew several million dollars from the available resources of the bank and caused its suspension. The situation at this time was one almost of panic, and the fall of the Consolidated was not without its effect upon two other institutions, who collapsed at nearly the same time—the Ville Marie and the Exchange Banks. The Consolidated has paid its debts to the general public, but at a great loss to the shareholders, who, through the operation of the double liability upon them, have received only 26 cents in the dollar. Had the bank been taken from the weak hands which swayed its destiny, at an earlier date and before its suspension, it is believed that not over one-half its capital would have been lost.

The Metropolitan Bank never had a first-class mercantile connection, but loaned largely upon bank stocks and other securities on which it made considerable losses. It also made some large loans to land speculators which it was understood, hampered it to a certain extent. A feature of its conduct was the re-discounting of its paper, which may be made a cause for doing business beyond the means of a bank. In fact the plan, if it be made a policy, must, in a time of severe depression, result in loss. The bank did not suspend, though its capital was partially lost, and it liquidated quietly and with as little expense as possible, passing into the record of institutions for which there existed under the policy pursued, but little chance of success, taking good and bad times together.

The Exchange Bank of Canada was organized in the early part of the decade. It did a good business for several years, but had a considerable number of weak accounts, which in the later years of the depression, netted the institution much loss. It was also unfortunate enough to lose by the default of its cashier, Mr. Murray : the amount of these losses, and their culmination occurring at a time when financial distress threatened many interests, weakened public confidence in the bank and its future, and during the extreme excitement in 1879, it suspended—the Consolidated and Ville Marie Banks stopping about the same time. The suspension, however, was regarded as a mistake upon the part of its management, for the personal guarantee of its Directors could have easily carried it through. It resumed business within the time required by law, reducing its stock fifty per cent., but its assets have so much improved in value that the bank has now a " Rest " of fifty per cent upon its present capital. There was a feeling in favor of reducing the stock as above, on account of thus avoiding the necessity of waiting several years for a dividend, or until the impaired capital has regained its original size, $1,000,000. The stock is now at a good premium and pays 8 per cent. dividend. It is the only bank in Canada that pays its dividends quarterly.

The following is the bank's statement of its position on the 30th September, 1881 :—

RESOURCES

Cash and Cash Items..................................	$ 262,621	43
Loans and Discounts—Less rebate interest.......	2,591,020	80
Loans Past Due, secured............................	24,281	75
" " unsecured	2,655	23
Real Estate...	26,251	84
Bank Premises...................	100,000	00
	$3,006,831	05

LIABILITIES.

Circulation	611,028	50
Deposits and Deposit Receipts...............	1,487,364	08
Due to other Banks....................................	102,298	96
Due on Bank Premises...............................	50,000	00
Capital................................	500,000	00
Surplus................................	256,139	51
	$3,006,831,05	

The bank has branches at Aylmer, Hamilton, Park Hill, and Bedford, Thos. Craig is Cashier, M. H. Gault is President, A. W. Ogilvie and E. K. Greene, Esqrs., Directors. The Vice-Presidency was held by the late Thos. Caverhill, and the vacancy has not been filled at date of writing.

La Banque Jacques Cartier became involved through making large advances upon contracts in connection with the Northern Colonization Railroad, and also through advances to a Syndicate of land speculators. In addition to this, the Cashier was charged with irregularities, the stock was reduced 50 per cent., and the bank resumed business. The subsequent management proved unsuccessful in creating gain or increased value of the assets, and upon an examination of these by a Committee of Shareholders, a further reduction of capital was recommended and carried into effect. The capital, originally $2,000,000, now stands at $500,000, but it has a surplus of over $100,000.

La Banque Ville Marie lost one-half of its capital through incompetent management, and its stock was reduced 50 per cent. The surplus is still small—say about $20,000—but the institution is believed to be on a sound basis now, and under the present management the bank ought to do quite well.

The reduction of the capital of the Merchants Bank has already been alluded to.

During 1874-5 and 6, the expansion—caused by the ease with which credits of merchandize could be got from the old country—reached its highest point, and from the latter year sowed its dire results among our banking institutions. During these years the accounts which proved the greatest source of loss were taken, and must it be said, *encouraged* by some of our banks. The desire to pay large dividends was all-absorbing, and while there was a limit placed upon the encouragement of weak traders by some of our standard institutions, others of shorter records, with fewer precedents to guide them, and with less ability among their officers and upon their boards, pressed accomodation upon names which were absolutely decried upon street corners, and which must have failed months before, but for assistance and credit from quarters where it should have been an accepted fact that they had no chance in the future, and really had had none from their start—as merchants. Even our best banks, with all the splendid management which the contingencies of the times developed, could hardly keep pace in their apprehension of the force of declining values, with the hard but realized facts which were forced upon them between their meetings. These banks were of necessity, heavy losers; what opportunities for life had then the weaker banks whose misfortunes are so well known?

In some cases it may be that our banks to-day have not got *all* the legacies inherited from those years in the shape of overdue and unproductive assets, into a normal or satisfactory condition, nor is it to be expected, for the paralyzation was unprecedented and wide-spread. Recuperation's healthful tide is flowing, but remembrancers of the evil days still linger in present items, and, though unwelcome evidences, are valuable, for they serve to remind managers of what has been, and what may come again; they also tend to confirm our most successful bankers in their convictions, and emphasize more intensely the necessary application of these. Liberal writing down of values has relieved our banks from any fear of added loss upon most of these remaining assets, however, and they have assumed more nearly the proportions which they should occupy in a time of health and progress.

The temptation to afford support, in the hope of realizing an eventual better result has largely aggravated the weakness of very many bank assets during the depression. In no accounts more notably than in those requiring a vast outlay in plant, fixtures &c., have bank advances been so irretrievably sunk. These are the skeletons within the doors of banking houses during a time of commercial hardship, and when augmented by the effect, in a country like ours, of advances to lumber interests in which no rally is possible for a long period, unless original debt be small and other markets active; a lock up of capital and growing but unpaid interest ensues to the disadvantage of other interests, and enlarges the amount until the debt becomes of a compound character, and though secured as well as it can be, makes dividends unsound and depreciates the value of the bank's stock. The large accounts are the most fruitful in the way of mischievous results. It is costly to handle them, while their asset value is always uncertain. They absorb capital which may be more actively employed, and in eras of depression, create dissatisfaction and doubt among the ordinary shareholders, besides entailing a world of care and anxiety upon the bank executive. Many millions of money were laid away in support of these large interests during our late troubles, and it must be said that in some notable cases, it was a much mooted point as to whether the business so supported could ever pay in the end owing to the rates of interest placed upon the assistance it required. In some cases, it has been authoritively stated that the interest liability of one or more lumber manufacturers, for two or three years, was actually more than their mills could offset in *gross receipts*, owing to the stagnation and limited demand experienced in this line of business. There are many merchants as well as manufacturers whose business is turned over only at the cost of $20,000 to $30,000 per annum in interest alone, and unless they make a certain profit upon their goods they cannot hope to pay this as well as their numerous current expenses. Why cannot contentment follow concentrated operations? All interests abnormally enlarged are open to hundreds of dangers, in fact they do not on the average pay better than more modest exertions, yet they saddle the merchant with disproportionate care, and continually lead up to exigencies where the first false step results in ruin. Encouragement then should be slowly extended to very many interests such as have received it during our past dark decade. Dividends would cease to fluctuate so uncertainly, stocks maintain a more regular value, capital continue unimpaired and a bank's earning power would instantly increase with the first breath of prosperity, being unshackled with dead weight and possessing the most unbounded confidence of old and new patrons. A bank failure excites public interest quickly and leads to sharp comment, which, in its radiation lowers the *morale* of the system under which all act. Directors of other banks awaken, but old habits of ease and feelings of security blind them in some cases to a sense of their duty in its highest degree. To all these it may be well to quote the provisions of our Banking Act anew, and to remark that though the legal penalties for nonperformance of duty may not always be enforced, the time may arrive when omissions of duty may be loaded with as much reponsibility as actual commissions of acts adverse to the interests of shareholders and dangerous to those of depositors.

Sec. 10 of the Act provides " no dividend or bonus shall ever be made so as to impair the paid-up capital, and if any dividend or bonus be so made, the directors knowingly and wilfully concurring therein, shall be jointly and severally liable for the amount thereof, as a debt due by them to the bank."

Honesty, judgment and moral courage sufficient to face the position of a bank's affairs and give them to the shareholders at their true worth, can, in banking circles find a scope for exercise greater than can be discovered in any other one line of business. The interests entrusted to the management of the executive and directors of a bank, are of the first importance to otherwise unprotected and uncommercial people of all grades. The moral obligation incurred then, should be as binding as any statute or parliamentary decree.

Grades or degrees of executive ability are varied, but conduct of business as well as its results determine the manager. That sort of instinctive power to diagnose well a situation, or an offered opportunity for business may not be possessed by all, but in the banking business of the present day, the manager must have ability, and display it upon occasion, or he must lapse into mediocrity.

Quoting from an eminent authority, respecting profitable business, " It is more profitable in the end to lend money at moderate rates—according to the market at the time—when it is lent to sound people, who are doing a safe business, than to take risky transactions or deal with doubtful people, even at figures much above the current rate. It should never be forgotten that a banker, though he apparently takes the interest of a note at the time he discounts it, does not really *receive* interest until the note is paid. If, then he does not get payment of a note or debt in full, even if he should receive instalments, or a composition, to the extent of ninety cents to the dollar, he loses the whole of his interest. It is better even to lose *deposits* than to keep them at unprofitable rates." As the demand, however, for capital to use in industrial and commercial enterprises offsets the supply, and rates of interest on loans &c., advance to the old time rates of 8 and 9 per cent., banks will again be obliged to pay a larger interest on deposits, and to assume through the force of competition and large capitals some risk from which they are now free, this does not militate however against the leading principles of safe banking. No business is free from *all* reverses, but all aggregates of loss should be kept within a minimum limit, or the business should be concentrated and expenses made to conform to the amount handled.

It is now, more than ever necessary to hedge in the position of our banks by the creation of large *rests*. New manufacturing enterprises are being launched, involving the building of mills, and factories. Railway, municipal and many other bonds are being floated, and to a very large amount. Foreign imports are increasing, and vast public works are being inaugurated and carried on. These absorb large amounts of money, and will naturally make it harder to obtain. For six months we have seen money exceptionally cheap, but it is certain that a change cannot be far off. Good profits are pretty well assured to ably managed banks in the near future, but all positions, with the exceptions of a few of our leading institutions ought to see to it, that they are well fortified with *reserves*, otherwise they will work at more or less disadvantage, and lose the opportunity of making profits which may be afforded them by the revival of all interests.

Alluding once more to the discharge of duty by directors : It is a subject which will bear a great deal of comment, so long as that comment is temperate in tone. The author can offer no better excuse for this further trespass upon the patience of his readers than to beg them to consider the experience of the past decade, and the troubles which might have been avoided, had some of the members of our bank boards recognised more earnestly the necessity of a closer analysis of the reports presented to them. While it has been the custom in other lands as well as here, to select names for directors which wield influence, it has not been an uncommon thing to find these men, who are not always the most practical, serving upon the boards of two, three, four or more distinct incorporations. Taking all this into consideration, can it be expected that without change in our apparent theory of appointment, we are still left in security? The tone of the reports submitted by some directors in the past has, apparently. been well considered, and even deliberate in pointing conclusions, yet in the light of after events, how has the situation of our suspended institutions borne out the utterances so evenly spoken but a very short period prior to the event which brought suffering to many, and helped to undermine that confidence which is so essential in all business situations ?

There are other men much in demand as directors. These men represent ability and genuine talent as business managers, but there is not enough of them, and they, too, allow themselves to be pressed into the service of several corporations at the same time. There is a limit to human capacity, an overdue strain may be withstood for a time and excellent service rendered, but it cannot last, and in time, even these men, in many cases, find that they are not so well informed as to the condition of their respective trusts as they ought to be, if they continue to allow the use of their names upon these Boards. To point the force of this argument it is in order to state that merchants highly esteemed for their probity, energy and ability, have been known to appear as Directors in no less than five to seven different corporations. In other cases, prominent men have each held the Presidencies of three or four companies, simultaneously, while others sit as Directors on three or four Boards of Management. It is certainly a safe rule to follow, that no man should assume a trust which he cannot fully discharge. The temptation is great, and pride is strong, yet the strongest man is he who can so far command his inclinations as to refuse to overstep the limit which may lay within his powers. It should be remembered by those who weakly remain where they are, conscious that they cannot do justice to the interest so long graced by their names, that reputation often survives ableness, as an able writer has said, " If a really good business man cannot give a Presidency or a Directorship due attention, he becomes a mere figure ; and whenever a *name* is paid for, we may be sure the article is not worth the money. A figure-head may be competent or incompetent, the question is, *what are the functions it discharges ?* The Presidency of companies is probably destined to become obsolete. A working manager is generally better, though there *are* Presidents who devote themselves as fully and as conscientiously to their duties as any one could, but these are not mere figure-heads ; and they rather form the exception than the rule. We return to the fundamental point, men should not undertake trusts which from any cause they are incapable of administering." Let *elegibility* be founded upon other considerations than the mere possession of a great amount of stock. It is said that a Director upon the Board of the Bank of England is not allowed by law to hold over £4,000 of the bank's stock, and that the Governor is limited to half that amount, presumably with the intent to check speculation in the shares and the using of information derived as Director or Governor to this end. The difference in the theory between that bank and ours is, that Directors with large interests are supposed here to watch their personal stake with solicitude, and this helps them to make their trust a success, but as has been said before, unless the men are business like, able and energetic, or if their time is taken up by other Directorships, no particular check can be established upon transactions, whose individual amounts are moderate but whose *character* and *aggregates* need to be closely scanned.

By the provisions of our Banking Act, Directors are enabled to exercise great power over the administration details of routine. In fact, they are in every way *assisted* in the discharge of their duties. In sect. 33 of the Act, it can be learned that Directors, or a majority of them, have power to frame by-laws and regulations so long as these do not impinge upon the prerogative and ordinances of Parliament, as may to them appear needful and proper touching the management of the stock, property and effects of the bank, and touching the duties of the officers and clerks. And they also have the power to appoint as many officers, clerks, &c., and to pay such salaries as they may deem proper and meet. In sect. 37, they have access to all the books, correspondence and fund accounts of the bank, are allowed full powers to demand that these shall be exposed to them, and to inspect the account of any particular case or cases. Directors then, most assuredly possess the facilities necessary to a thorough fulfillment of their duties, and it may well be asked why these duties have been glossed over, when failure comes.

In December 1881, a circular was issued by the Government calling upon all loaning banks to make an unusual exhibit of:

1st. A statement of loans, discounts and advances for which stock, bonds or debentures of municipal or other corporations, or Dominion, Provincial, British or Foreign public securities, other than Canadian, are held as collateral securities, being the same as column 11 in the monthly return rendered to the Canada *Gazette*, except that the details are required in full.

2nd. Other current loans, discounts and advances to the public, with full particulars as regards the currency of the loans, the endorsers, if any, and the securities held, being the same as column No. 16 in the monthly returns rendered to the Canada *Gazette*, except that the details are required in full.

3rd. Notes and bills discounted, overdue, and other overdue debts secured by mortgage or other deed upon real estate, or by deposit of, or lien on stock, or by other securities, being the same as column 19 in the monthly return rendered to the Canada *Gazette*, except that the details are required in full.

4th. Other assets not included under the foregoing heads, being the same as column No. 21 in the monthly return rendered to the Canada *Gazette*, except that the details are required in full.

5th. A list of the names of each staff at head offices to include head office clerks, transfer clerks and clerks in all branches.

6th. A list of the bank shares, if any, held in the names of the staff, whether in trust, or individual names, upon which advances have been made by the bank, or which are held as collateral security by the bank.

The course of the Treasury Board in asking for these details, was most unusual. It was, however, conceded that the Government had received some information which, under the provisions of the Act, led it to make this request. No definite declaration of the real cause for the demand for these details was made, though the majority of opinions held that it was formulated for the purpose of checking speculation in the shares. Whatever information came to the cognizance of the Finance Minister, its character was unknown; but if it definitely bore—as was generally conceded, upon the subject hinted at, its object was good. The banks generally objected to the form and much of the detail required by the circular. Had it desired information simply upon the point of loans made upon stocks, as to any possible evasion of the law in this particular, there would have been little objection upon the part of our banking institutions to make prompt returns in compliance with the terms of such document, but the feature in it of asking for discount details as required by clause No. 2, created a general feeling of reluctance in accepting the conditions of the circular.

The banks were asked to make a full return at the date of the 16th of December. So far, it was likely to cover its apparent object, as it was impossible for banks to have been prepared for the issue of this request, and coming as it did between their monthly return dates, without the least preliminary notification it was well calculated to bring out a pretty clear exposition of the condition of the heads enumerated, and in a way which would not admit of evasion.

Upon the 27th of December, however, the following letter was sent to the banks from the Treasury Board at Ottawa, which modified the terms of clause No. 2, and significantly shewed the true purposes comprehended by the original circular.

" I have the honor to inform you that for the purposes required by the circular of the 16th inst., it has been decided to strike out the second question and to submit therefor the following : "other current loans, discounts and advances *to stockholders and others, for which bank stocks are held either directly or indirectly as security.*"

(Signed,)   J. M. COURTNEY.

In addition to this change, the circular was generally modified, and its original significance was lost.

Had the terms of the original circular been adhered to, it would still seem to have been within the power of the banks to satisfy Government without going into onerous and uncalled for detail work, for a bank's affirmation generally, as to whether it had any overdrawn or other accounts in any way secured by the lodgement of stock might have been accepted, and the necessity for preparing a mass of irrelevant detail avoided. There is little doubt that our banks generally have lived up to the laws requirements, as regards lending upon stocks, but the Banking Act provides that the Minister of Finance shall, in addition to the regular returns as specified in the Act, also have power to call for special returns from any bank, whenever, in his judgment, the same are necessary in order to a full and complete knowledge of its condition. This, together with the amendment in 43 Vic. chap. 22, accords the Government pretty broad privileges.

Our banks were each originally constituted under Special Acts of Parliament, these being their charters. The separate charters of all our banks have for some ten years back been continued by one general uniform Act, though originally there were diversities.

This general Act continued the charters to July 1, 1881, and from that time to July 1, 1891, as per Act 34 Vic., Chap. 5, entitled "An Act relating to Banks and Banking," and 43 Vic., Chap. 22. "The said charters or Acts of Incorporation of the several banks mentioned in the schedule " B " to this Act,—to all of which this Act applies, are hereby continued and shall remain in force, subject to the provisions of this Act, until the first day of July, in the year of Our Lord one thousand eight hundred and ninety-one, except in so far as they or any of them may be or become forfeited or void under the terms thereof, or of this Act or any other Act passed or to be passed in that behalf, by non-performance of the conditions of such charters respectively, insolvency or otherwise."

An eminent authority among our own bankers says that Canadian Banking, in its origin and main characteristics is partly British and partly American. The frame work of our charters and the Acts of Parliament continuing them, are after American models. The rights, duties and responsibilities of stockholders, and the officers elected by them to manage their affairs, are nearly the same in both countries. From the United States, we have derived the system of limiting the liability of stockholders to double the subscribed capital. Our system of returns to the Government is far more detailed than anything known in the United Kingdom, and in this, we resemble the United States construction of returns, rather than those of the country with which we have a political connection. In the important matter of advances upon warehouse receipts and kindred documents, and the rights and powers of banks with respect thereto, we have adopted American ideas as being most suitable to our circumstances. We have long ago discarded any other form of money than the American. In spite of the obstinate adherence of a few persons here and there to the obsolete system of pounds, shillings and pence, not sterling, it may be said that the *dollar* is our standard. The dollar, however, is gold, and always has been. Here, however, the resemblance between Banking in Canada and Banking in the United States, comes to an end, with the exception of those fundamental matters essential to the very idea of the business, which are common to banking in all countries.

The underlying idea of Canadian Banking will be found in its inception to be of Scottish origin. The greater part of commercial interests were from the first, swayed by Scotchmen in Canada, it was therefore natural that in establishing Banking institutions in our new country, Scotland's model should be largely adopted ; specially as the system had, in spite of occasional disasters, proved its working and application result to be the finest known in the world. In pursuance of the plan then, a few banks of large capital were established first in Quebec, and afterwards in Montreal, Halifax, St. John, Toronto and other centres of business, but though the frame work of these banks was Scottish, the details of the Acts have been largely American. As population increased and good openings for the extension of banking interests were afforded, the head banks established agencies or branches exactly as the great banks of Edinburgh and Glasgow had done before them, but unlike the policy practised in the United States. Thus every large bank in the Dominion is represented by these branches. The advantages or disadvantages of the Canadian system have often been discussed. In its favor, it may be urged that the system gives to depositors in all parts of the country, and in small places, the advantages of the security afforded by the large institution at the head, which possesses a large capital and has a double liability upon shareholders behind it. There can be little doubt also, that the diffusion of sound business ideas over all parts of the country is aided by these representations, or branches, wielded as they are by trained men, while at their head institutions a vast amount of knowledge as to the conditions and changes of business situations is naturally accumulated. The large capital and resources of the central banks are available for the carrying on of enterprises which, if the banks centred in smaller towns, would require a far larger amount of accommodation than any local institution could in all probability give them. But the system, no doubt, has its drawbacks. The very fact that large masses of capital are available in small places, encourages what proves to be often an unhealthy development of business. It must be confessed, too, that the task of keeping the loans and discounts of twenty or thirty offices, in widely diversified districts, in a sound and healthy condition, is one that has at times overtaxed the ability of even our ablest bankers. With whatever drawbacks it may be attended, however, there is no doubt that it has the effect of training great numbers of men among us to habits of wide and accurate observation, of large generalization, and of careful judgment upon the great movements of commerce and speculation over their area of the country. It necessitates a watchfulness over deposits, circulation, discounts, and reserves, which is of great value.

The banks of Canada differ from those of the United States, and are like those of Scotland in having a free circulation, limited only by the amount of their paid-up capital. Though on two occasions attempts have been made by the Government to assimilate the circulation of the Canadian banks to that of the national banks of the United States, and compel the depositing of Government Bonds as security for issues, these attempts were met with strenuous resistance, and Government has courteously listened to the expression of public feeling as manifested through the efforts of members of Parliament, and the banks have been left with their free circulation, the provisos being such as could readily be met.

The banks of Canada have not been subjected to such an oppressive load of taxation as that by which the financial institutions of the United States are burdened. Our Government has always appreciated the fact that in 'taxing banks they would only be burdening trade, hampering manufacturers, and finally injuring their own revenue. This tax is felt by Canadian banks in an onerous degree only in such instances as where they are represented at New York and Chicago.

While the Canadian system of banking may not, in many respects, be superior to that of other countries, it excels the Scottish system so far as shareholders are concerned, for while a Scottish bank may, in many cases, exact almost unlimited liability from the shareholder, and in occasional instances ruin him beyond hope or drive him to suicide, a holder of Canadian bank stock has a chance left him in life when bank troubles come, and may retrieve his loss.

Our system is not, however, weak in respect to the security given to the public. As for the shareholders, or those contemplating the investment of their funds in banking securities, they must select such banks as have men of probity, common sense, and generally recognized ability at their heads. All banks, like other business enterprises, are subject to reverses even under good management, but the risk of serious loss may be reduced to a minimum if good and careful, judgment dictates the investment. It is believed by many that the branch or agency system practised by our banks, extends their ramifications to too great an extent, and lays them open, through the eagerness of their branch managers, to losses and shrinkages which might be avoided by more concentration, and produce quite as good results in so far as dividends go. It would certainly appear reasonable that many annual statements would throw light into the ordinary shareholders mind, and leave him generally better informed as to the condition of his stake, were the interest to be compressed into more closely narrowed boundaries, as it might also tend to make the central management easier and sounder. Would it not be feasible as well, to make more Presidents of *General Managers* ? Our leading bank sets an illustrious example, may it not be followed with the best results ? It is doubtless well—to a certain extent, to select *influence* to represent our bank interest, but rather let it find a place upon the *Boards or Committees* of our banks, if it be accompanied by the great desideratums, *i.e.*, *honesty and ability*, then, with a Manager-President, shareholders might be just as certainly assured that their interests would be cared for, while depositors and customers would feel that whatever a bank lacked, it would be at least shielded from rottenness and consequent deceptive statements. Allusion to the fact that we are too heavily loaded with bank interests has been made in the earlier pages of this work, men of title and circumstance have, in more than one case, launched upon the commercial world banks for which there was no room, and in other cases have, through the influence of their names, amalgamated the wrecks of institutions which ought to have been allowed to die out of existence. Let us now look at the practical side of all this, and place men in the presidential chair, who have deserved the honor and won their right to it by long years of service, and from a purely business-like standpoint, decide whether we shall subscribe to stock which it may never be safe to float. Finally, our most sagacious and experienced bankers can easily convene, and by a safe form of deliberation, adopt and recommend, if they find it practicable, some restrictions upon the extension of branch interests. Capital ought to be the regulator of this, and if we were to hit upon the plan of establishing only two, or at the most, three branches for every million dollars of capital represented at the centre, and locate these with the best possible care as to their surroundings, would not results prove to be more certain and satisfactory ?

There can be no doubt that sound organization in banking systems renders supervision and inspection comparatively easy of accomplishment. Good machinery got well together, and methodically operated, will exercise great control over the multifarious transactions of any bank. Daily, weekly and supplemental reports from branches covering discounts by name, extent, terms, &c., advices of deposits and withdrawals, increases, or otherwise of circulation, local causes for the variations experienced, the submission of all important requests for credits to the head office and directors, before granting the same, &c., all tend to keep a bank's affairs in a sound condition, and in many cases must be of more value than even the periodical visits of inspectors, who must at best trust largely to the judgment of the local manager, and cannot possibly enter into the merits of the situation in most cases, beyond going through mere routine examination.

A Government audit of the affairs of each bank is deemed impracticable, and wisely so. Were it to be enforced, an immense number of officials would be required to cover the ground, in any thorough manner, for the work should be done at all points where a bank is represented, at a given time, besides this, it has been suggested that Government machinery is very liable to degenerate, and that it might require another staff of men to " inspect the inspectors." It needs something more in the way of supervision and inspection, than the mere checking of accounts and counting of monies and securities on hand, it is true that an inspector might be required to work certain sections of the country, where interests differ widely in character from those at other points, and with assistance cover each section at a given time, the head bank following him and his work closely, and checking each other section's business until the officer gets to them, but after all, we come back perforce to the central truth, that upon *thorough organization, and the close attention of the directors and officers*, depends the safety of banks generally.

In the opinion of the writer, too much has been said through the columns of some of our journals, by writers who would, if they could, be considered able critics upon this and other banking matters. During the depression, and since, these gentlemen have favored the commercial world with windy prescriptions for the cure of what they chose to consider a disease in the banking system of our country. Their vaporings have not been directed with judgment, and have failed, in most cases, to produce the slightest effect upon men conversant with the difficulties attending the subject of inspection. Their weakness has also been aggravated by the tone in which they appeared. Censorious, sensational attack always misses its object. Occasionally an article has appeared which, temperately and deliberately framed, has attracted attention from those astute men who have, it is to be assumed, made the subject almost a life-time study, but unfortunately no avenue to a sterling remedy of what the writers were pleased to call weakness, has been opened in a practicable way. Opinions must be fortified by something more than theory, but if a way can be traced by which our bankers can step to perfection in this matter, they would undoubtedly consent to allow the mantle of reputation to fall upon the shoulders of him who brought the idea to the light of the present day, and would gladly adopt a measure which would bring relief and absolute safety to their doors. In the words of one of our leading bankers—writing in 1879—" a system of audit, either by a Government official, or by an officer or officers *other than the executive of a bank,* who is supposed specially to represent the shareholders, has been recommended as a panacea for all our troubles, but how could any one of our largest banks be effectively audited by such an official? How can it be possible to accomplish an effective *audit* of the affairs and transactions of an institution of such magnitude? For an auditor to give a full account of the actual state of a bank, he must value every security, and be in a condition to follow every transaction; in fact, he must acquire a knowledge of all the affairs of the bank, as intimate as that possessed by the directors or the manager himself. Most of our Canadian banks have many branches. The auditor would require to visit these, one after the other in person. Yet, were his examination ever so exhaustive, he could at no time have within his purview, any more of the business of the bank at large than that carried on at the point at which he might then be pursuing his investigations, while the most disastrous transactions might be transpiring elsewhere. Suppose the auditor were to form an opinion that the shareholders' property was in jeopardy at any time, what then? If his estimate of the position were correct, *the mischief would have been done,* and the chances of retrieving it would be but slight. Nor would the auditor's opinion be conclusive proof of what he might assert. A particular bill of exchange may be the very best or worst asset of a bank, and it depends upon the judgment of the person examining the asset whether he pronounces it good or bad. An asset of great importance might be pronounced good by the manager and bad or doubtful by the auditor, and *vice versa.* It might be difficult to persuade either party of the accuracy of the views of the other, and there might be a diversity of opinion amongst the directors themselves."

As before remarked, it is not all that is required, to count the asset securities and check the accounts of head and branches, but to *value these* securities. Doing the first is mere child's play to the man who has passed a fair banking education, but to do the second, a man or men would have to be ubiquitous, and to possess a knowledge of the character and phases of each district, as well as the constitution and personnel of each large individual account of the bank, and after all this, be prepared at a moments notice to give the General Manager and Board correct advice as to the acceptance of any proposed transaction, whether he be on the ground where the business is offering at the time, or deep in the affairs of a branch five hundred miles away. No! The handling of great banking interests are safer and divested of much complication, in the hands of able, trained officers and a business like Board. Results and close analysation of returns each month, is a criterion by which a bank management must be judged, only let the Board be selected more for its sterling component qualities than for its integral influence among men. This latter power is often required by adventitious aids, accessories which make a position, but do not in many cases, fit its occupant for sound deliberation upon the stern realities and emergent situations, in which the modern bank director must exercise the highest qualities of business acumen.

Alluding again, but briefly as possible, to circulation, there has been afforded during the depression, some examples of enforced, unnatural and illegal expansion under this head. It has been pretty clearly shewn in the case of one institution now, happily for the community, defunct, that a commission was paid by it to secure such success. Our Banking Act, in its provisions as to the restrictions upon circulation, is brief but explicit. In sect. 8, it declares that "The amount of notes intended for circulation, issued by the bank and outstanding at any time, shall never exceed the amount of its unimpaired paid-up capital." That the limit has been exceeded, and that punishment might have been inflicted with perfect propriety, had there been any adequate provision for it, has been quite patent to the careful onlooker of the last decade. What term can be too severe by the use of which the practice may be condemned? The only food for wonder is that Government has not found in this matter strong grounds for causing its proposed measures to be adopted, despite the greater objections which bankers have to such substitution. Fortunately, any general tendency to illegally expand note circulation can be easily discovered in any bank of size, and is easily checked by the discovery, and when money is plentiful, there is no profit in forcing the automatic duty of circulation. The " Free Banking Act " of some twenty-eight years ago, afforded an opportunity for our bankers to accept a situation, where a Government guarantee of circulation secured by security deposits lodged with Government was the conditions, but with the exception of the Bank of Montreal, no other institution entered into the scheme. The Government measures of 1868 re-introduced the same plan, but there was almost general disinclination manifested in regard to placing issues upon that basis. It is plain that the acceptance of the conditions attached to the Government guarantee are inimical to the banking interests, and had these been in force in 1875—the year of crucial test among banks in Canada—it would most certainly have entailed upon us a legacy of disaster, for together with circulation lessening and redemption necessities growing, discounts increasing and Government deposits being simultaneously withdrawn, there was enough load placed upon our home institutions, without their having to lock up money in the purchase of Government notes, or the purchase of securities which must be lodged with the Government. At certain times the situation, were Government guaranteed ciculation to be put into effect, would be open to severe and unnecessary stringency, as reserves by the Act, must be maintained.

Reliable bank returns when followed closely, indicate with great certainty the conditions of trade. A careful comparison of these valuable exponents of the state of trade, for a given time, and with those which have preceded them for a few years in the past, can hardly fail to create a basis upon which the intelligent business man can frame his policy and plan of operations for the immediate future.

They inform him of the tendency toward accumulation of loanable capital at the banks, or the reverse, the consequent ease or per contra of the money market and the probabilities of its continuance, the contraction or expansion of circulation as the different periods of the years affect it, the amounts of public and Government deposits, the interchanges between banks, the amounts due from one to another, the loans out, the discount ranges, &c., etc., and if he be an earnest observer, he may to a great extent be enabled to analyze the character of the items they present to his attention.

Our banks make regular returns to the Government, and as soon as published, are open to the criticism of the commercial public, the organs of finance and competing banks. No bank can unreasonably expand its discounts or diminish its reserves without being almost instantly checked, yet how much depends upon the honesty and ability of the cashier and the directors in preparing the statement which issues from their hands. During the depression the construction of bank statements has necessarily been attended with great difficulty—in so far as the correct valuation of sundry assets have been concerned, even when the management has been all that could be desired, the culmination of foregathering events could not by any human foresight be located within many months of the date of their actual occurrence, nor could the effect of the stoppage of interlacing interests be determined except at hazardous estimates. These conditions of the banking situation—notably during 1875-7 and '9, increased the natural tendency—inherent in most men despite all the conservatism to which they may lay claim or be reputed to possess—of many bank direc- tors to impart a gloss to the character of their different headings which was worn off long before the next meetings were convened, and the superficiality of their conclusions was left fully exposed. As an eminent banker wrote in 1879, regarding the annual reports of some banks at that time. " Take these reports, lay them side by side and compare the phraseology, readers will become penetrated with admiration for the fer- tility of a language which admits of so many different modes of saying the same thing. With hardly an exception, the tone of these reports is a blending of condolence, apology and that quality of hopefulness which grave physicians express at the bedside of moribund patients. A species of arithmetical sleight-of-hand has been employed in manipulating the profit and loss accounts which is most bewildering to laymen not endowed with the faculty of analyzing figures. How many persons outside the half- dozen officials *who know*, are there who could so analyze these statements *as to determine with even approximate* accuracy what the losses have been? The figures given are, in the hands of experts, susceptible of analysis, but so skilfully arranged are they that many a mathematician who found no difficulty in achieving the *pons asinorum* would utterly fail in any attempt to dissect them. It has become the fashion for directors to segregate the " losses which have developed out of the business of former years " and to treat these with a frankness and candour which are quite refreshing. Enormous sums have been written off with perfect complacency under this caption, as if the directors had had nothing at all to do with the transactions out of which these losses have grown. Yet in four cases out of every five, the directors of the day are chargeable with the responsibility of these very transactions. Indeed this class of losses has been made to serve as a foil, the comparative magnitude of the figures making the " losses on the business of the past year" seem but trifling. The heading " notes overdue and unsecured " is capable of conveying the most fallacious and misleading impressions of the real state of things, and readers who imagine that they know much of the real position of these after conning over the returns, should banish the delusion, it is not under the head of "notes overdue and unsecured " however, that losses are alone to be apprehended. In the category of " notes and bills current " there is a far wider field for investigation. We venture to say that at this moment bad debts to a very serious amount are being carried by some banks under this apparently innocent heading. How many debts secured are fully secured? how many of them are really secured *at all?* In hundreds of cases the use of the term is mere prevarication. A second or third mortgage may be held on property not worth the first mortgage, yet that is called " security." Bank directors cannot be said to deliberately utter statements and reports which they know to be incorrect, indeed to a certain extent it may be a question of opinion when to write off a debt as irrecoverably bad, and directors in reviewing the accounts of a bank must perforce trust largely to the opinions of the executive officer."

There is no doubt but that the entering of notes overdue, secured or unsecured, current discounts &c. &c., as well as other matters of mere bookkeeping detail, are correctly entered, but these entries or figures do not necessarily convey correct impressions as to a bank's real asset strength. Nor does a small return of overdue notes give assurance that the current discounts are all good. It is an easy matter to renew poor paper, in fact it is easier than to face the music and write it off, so long as it can be truthfully said to possess even the merest lingering remnant of life or hope. As before remarked, the sound representation of a bank's position is only to be hoped for when at its head is to be found an honest, able and sound banker in the cashier, and an uncompromising directorate, who are willing to face losses *when they culminate*, and start with renewed strength upon the course of another year, certain that the evil they know of is eradicated, and that for it remains no further dressing in strained or superficial colors.

The Banking Act 34 Vic., chap. 5, 36, provides, " At every annual meeting of the shareholders for the election of directors, the outgoing directors shall submit a clear and full statement of the affairs of the bank, containing on the one part the amount of the capital stock paid in, the amount of notes of the bank in circulation and net profits made, the balances due to other banks and institutions, and the cash deposited in the bank, distinguishing deposits bearing interest from those not bearing interest, and on the other part the amount of the current coin, the gold and silver bullion, and the amount of Dominion notes in the vaults of the bank. The balances due to the bank from other banks and institutions, the value of the real and other property of the bank, and the amount of debts owing to the bank, including and particularizing the amounts so owing upon bills of exchange, discounted notes, mortgages and other securities, thus exhibiting on the one hand the liabilities of, or the debts due by the bank, and on the other hand the assets and resources thereof; and the said statement shall also exhibit the rate and amount of the last dividend declared by the directors, the amount of reserved profits at the time of declaring the said dividend, and the amount of debts due to the bank, overdue and not paid, with an estimate of the loss which will probably accrue thereon."

Provision 36, As *to penalties:* " The making of any wilfully false or deceptive statement in any account, statement, return, report or other document respecting the affairs of the bank, shall, unless it amounts to a higher offense, be a misdemeanor, and any and every president, vice-president, director, principal partner *en commandite*, auditor, manager, cashier, or other officer of the bank preparing, signing, approving or concurring in such statement, return, report or document, or using the same with intent to deceive or mislead any party, shall be held to have wilfully made such false statement, and shall further be responsible for all damages sustained by such party in consequence thereof."

Provision 57, As *to insolvency, &c.* : " Any suspension by a bank of payment of any of its liabilites as they accrue, in specie or Dominion notes, shall, if it continues for ninety days, constitute the bank insolvent and operate a forfeiture of its charter, so far as regards the issue or reissue of notes and other banking operations. And the charter shall remain in force only for the purpose of enabling the directors, or the assignee or assignees, or other legal authority—if any be appointed in such manner as may by law be provided—to make the calls mentioned in the next following section of this Act, and to wind up its business. And any such assignee or assignees or other legal authority shall, for such purposes, have all the powers of the directors."

Provision 58, As *to liability of shareholders, &c.* : " In the event of the property and assets of the bank becoming insufficient to pay its debts and liabilities, the shareholders of the bank shall be liable for the deficiency so far as that each shareholder shall be so liable to an amount—over and above any amount not paid up on their respective shares—equal to the amount of their shares respectively. And if any suspension of payment in full in specie or Dominion notes, of all or any of the notes or other liabilites of the bank shall continue for six months, the directors may and shall make calls upon such shareholders, to the amount they may deem necessary to pay all the debts and liabilities of the bank, without waiting for the collection of any debts due to it or the sale of any of its assets or property. Such calls shall be made at intervals of thirty days and upon notice to be given thirty days at least prior to the day on which such call shall be payable. And any such call shall not exceed twenty per cent. on each share, and payment thereof may be enforced in like manner as for calls upon unpaid stock, and the first of such calls shall be made within ten days after the expiration of the said six months. And any failure upon the part of any shareholder liable to such call, to pay the same when due, shall operate a forfeiture by such shareholder of all claim in, or to any part of, the assets of the bank, such call and any further call thereafter being nevertheless recoverable from him as if no such forfeiture had been incurred, Provided always, that nothing in this section contained shall be construed to alter or diminish the additional liabilities of the directors hereinbefore mentioned and declared. Provided, also, that the bank be *en commandite* and the principal partners are personally liable. Then, in case of any such suspension, such liability shall at once accrue and may be enforced against such principal partners, without waiting for any sale or discussion of the property or assets of the bank, or other preliminary proceedings whatever, and the provision respecting calls shall not apply to such bank."

Provision 59, *As to liability of shareholders who have transferred their stock:* " Persons who having been shareholders in a bank, have only transferred their shares or any of them to others or registered the transfer thereof within one month before the commencement of the suspension of payment by the bank, shall be liable to calls upon such shares under the preceding section, as if they had not transferred them, saving their recourse against those to whom they were transferred. And any assignee or other officer or person appointed to wind up the affairs of the bank, in case of its insolvency, shall have the powers of the directors with respect to such calls, provided that if the bank be *en commandite*, the liability of the principal partners and of the *commanditaires* shall continue for such time after their ceasing to be such, as may be provided in the charter of the bank, and the foregoing provisions with respect to the transfer of shares or calls shall not apply to such bank."

Such are the points of our Banking Act which hedge about and detail the duties and liabilities of bank officers, directors and shareholders, the construction of statements, &c., &c. The Act would appear to be explicit, easily complied with, and is undoubtedly followed as closely as any Act could be, barring the occasional instances where too much is left to one man who may be honest enough, but whose classification of all items under the specified heads for such classification may be, to a certain extent, faulty.

In completing this sketch, some general remarks may properly be made in reference to the influences and natural tendencies developed by the class of middlemen, known as brokers, their mainsprings of action, temptations, &c.

Speculation has been likened to a tree, which grows in the richest and poorest soil alike, and bears no fruit but leaves. The roots and trunk represent capital, the larger boughs are great financiers and the money articles. The smaller ones, the jobbers, brokers, &c. The twigs are the few experienced speculators, with but small capital.

The leaves are the lambs. These fall off and wither but return the next season. The trunk stands firm upon the " Root of Evil." The storms of rumors and panics often shake off the leaves before their time, and even sadly bruise the smaller branches and twigs, but the trunk grows larger every year, and the roots more widely spread.

It is, unfortunately, a fact that the excitement of speculation is the life breath of many a man, an absorbing game whose pursuit seems to furnish a sort of exhilaration similar to that found in other games of chance, but far more intense, and because allowable, more generally sought. Even the small operator who has lost his all, comes back sooner or later, in many cases, to dabble in the intoxication and stern excitement, opportunities for which are afforded without limit in our leading centres.

It is a vast error—though commonly concurred in—to suppose that it is the lust of gain only by which stock gamblers are impelled along their courses, it is not the desire of greed, nor the longings of avarice so much as the intense craving for excitement. The money won : they toss it back and risk its loss without a moment's hesitation. Greed is but little part of the delirium which allures many with so exhaustless a fascination. The spell that binds them is the *hazard.* Give an operator thousands, he will care only for the intoxication of chance which the money purchases. There is a glorious intensity of *sensation* in the swing between a fortune and beggary, which lends to life a sense never known before, indeed, once tasted, it is rarely abandoned.

It has been pointedly said by a keen fellow, whose life was passed amid the whirls and eddies of the London Stock Market, that the personal vanity and that spice of conceit which is inherent in us all, and which can only be lessened by education or suffering, makes men still keep betting, although they know that it requires *talent* to win, and though they see their friends being ruined all around. This same conceit and vanity makes speculators still play on the losing game, although they daily see other speculators lose all they have, and know the odds to be great.

Those who do not speculate, and they are yearly becoming fewer, profess to wonder at this trait in human character, and often plume themselves on being free from such insanity. They are insane perhaps on other points as bad, or worse. Each small, or outside large operator thinks all are fools but himself, and when a speculating friend is ruined, instead of experiencing fear and learning wisdom from the event, he feels a slight contempt and says to himself, " why was he not like me ? " and then with some elation, he will add " yes, I shall be one, perhaps the only one, to show men how to play the interesting game successfully." How sweet a thought to human vanity.

This class of gentry find it very sweet for one with a hundred dollars to deal as though he had a thousand. For one who has a thousand, to speculate with men who have from five to twenty thousand at command, to mix and talk with bigger men, enunciate views to other aspirants to these transient honors, to fancy they are wise, and that ere long they will be rich. All this is sweet, very human, very vain.

" De'il take the hindmost " is the cry now in the race for gold. Each wants to show his neighbor that he is getting on, this breeds a general dislike to do the steady work of life. We hear of those who *have* got on, but no word of the hundreds who, in every city, have succumbed silently in their illegitimate pursuit of wealth. No one can startle others with a dazzling, swift success unless one runs some fearful risks.

Those outside the "Money Street," or beyond the pale of the Broker's Board, are handicapped from the start. A new crop of these innocents arise each season, they will not understand that it is upon them that many brokers live. They go on paying out their commissions both ways, interest surprises them with its aggregates when the broker's statements of current accounts are laid before them, they lose as a *matter of course*, and are from the moment of the first " drop " bound more closely to the course which, in the great majority of cases, is paced until the last dollar is paid away, and they awake from the fascination which has so long controlled them. What folly for these outside people to argue that they can reach success by going into the " street," if money could be made there so easily, why does it not occur to them that the brokers would make it for themselves, and avoid the bother and trouble of acting for them, and replying to all their senseless questionings? Can they learn knowledge in the Stock Markets which brokers have failed to acquire through daily experience during a long life passed in the manipulation of stocks?

Marginal operators, particularly, have the least chance to speculate successfully. Capital must always win whatever it elects to do. The pieces on the chess board are all moved according to a pre-determined plan, of which the brokers may possible get some hints, but of which outside operators on margin can know nothing. It must be remembered that the true broker does not advise his client, he cannot do so, besides this, he has customers upon both the " bull " and the " bear " sides of a stock. You cannot expect from him advice of definite character even if he is able to give it. There are brokers who cannot, so long as man is human, but feel and act in the interest of their more influential client, whose brokerages are mainstays. The business of the small marginal operator is but of small moment to these, and only in a general way can they give the attention, which is all important to the small outsider, whose interests often hang upon a half per cent., whose orders often serve, perhaps unintentionally, as a peg upon which to hang the transactions of larger size. Other men still, who usurp the name of broker, will make the orders received by them from the outside lamb, serve as a peg upon which to hang their *own* operations. These men will manipulate a "limit" as advantageously for themselves as though it were a " put and call " option, and unless the market runs away from the limit, there may be much gain to the broker who practices this style of business and is fortunate enough to secure several lambs upon which to operate.

The man who is most successful—being an outsider—is the one who refusing to be guided by newspaper conclusions, carefully selects a stock possessing intrinsic merit, buys and pays down for it, feeling confident that it is sound, and that if it goes off a peg, it will right itself in time, he sits quietly down, takes his dividends which pay him a reasonable interest, and does not fidget over and around his investment if a street combination forces its quotations temporarily down.

In *London Charivari*, some time ago, could be found the following lines :—

> " When panics come, who seems to wear
> A calm, serene, superior air,
> As though it wasn't his affair ?"
>
> My broker !

It is difficult for some victims to the " street," to avoid believing that as a class, brokers are unreliable, unfeeling, *sharp*. This belief is encouraged by the moves of the class itself. The adroitly written articles upon stocks, which appear periodically in the money columns of our leading papers are, in some cases, known to be inspired by certain members of the fraternity whose largest clients have a point to make, the reporter may or may not act in good faith to the public in becoming the exponent of the temporary situation in this way, but certain it is that during our depression, and the rapid transitions of stock-quoted values, the members of the Fourth Estate must be clearly held responsible for placing before the investing public some of the baldest, most ridiculous theories in support, or per contra, of certain stocks, which ever graced (?) the columns of the representative papers of any country. The mystery of a *close Board* of brokers, as at Montreal, during so many years whose days and months have witnessed enormous transactions in ever varying securities, has helped to throw over the street and its general complexion, a cloak of suspicion and colour which ought to have been long ago removed, reporters for telegraphic purposes, are now admitted within the pale of its operations, but the "Street" should make further innovations upon a practice belonging to the dark ages, remove to a commodious, well-lighted building, and rail off a respectable amount of room for the public to occupy, and all, within sight and hearing of each call and the responses to it. The idea of an open Board is, however, working into favor, a considerable number of brokers being favorable to the plan, and in time, some definite policy to this end will probably be adopted, but a new building must first be provided, any enlargement of the present one being an impossibility.

The interruptions to business upon the Stock Exchanges of our country has also led to a feeling of great dissatisfaction in the minds of many investors, both large and small. Let the following comparisons between the legal holidays, against which many business interests are opposed in the Province of Quebec, and the legal suspensions of business in London and Paris be considered. These days being legalized in the Province of Quebec, it remains for all to simply accept the inevitable owing to the peculiar constitution of our religious *personnel*. But when these are augmented by the adjournments of our Board for the purpose of allowing some of its members to attend races, horse sales, &c., the investor, whose interests and calculations are too serious to admit of this child's play, naturally feels irritated to find the basis of his computations upset or disarranged by the sudden and unlooked for, to him, adjournments of the Broker's Board.

The Province of Quebec, by law, observes the following holidays : Sundays, New Year's Day, Good Friday, Christmas Day, the birthday of the reigning sovereign, the first of July, the day of general thanksgiving, the days next following New Year's and Christmas Days—when these days fall upon Sunday, as in 1881–82, the Epiphany, the Annunciation, the Ascension, Corpus Christi, St. Peter and St. Paul's Day, All Saints Day, and Conception Day. In September 1881, the Board was adjourned for three consecutive afternoons at Montreal to allow its members to attend the races and the exhibition. On the 13th of October, only a morning session was held, as the hunt club meeting was called for the afternoon ; at another date the Board adjourned to attend Dawes' sale of horses. In addition to these breaks in the current of most important business, there can be witnessed a hegira of many brokers, and some the very ones whom a client expects to meet, to regattas, torpedo explosions, &c., &c.

The English non-juridical days are Sundays, Good Friday, Easter Monday, Whit Monday, first Monday in August, Christmas Day, Boxing

Day, or day after Christmas, New Year's Day, first of May and first of November, the two latter days because the Bank of England's transfer books are then closed. No precedent for the closing of the Exchange for the purpose of attending a horse sale, or race is there established—though many members may be found on Epsom Downs on Derby Day, and also at Putney boat races.

The legal holidays upon the Paris Bourse are Sundays, New Year's and Christmas Days, Ascension Day, the National Fete Day on 14th July, the 15th of August, All Saints Day, and *only* these in a Catholic country. A special law would be required to close the Bourse upon any other day, and there is no knowledge of a general exodus for the purpose of attending horse races or other superfluous occasions. For in Paris, they admit that such indulgence would bring about a perturbation in affairs generally. It may be said, that we copy from England as well as other countries in many things that we do, but even England, with her well-known love for field pleasures, does not go to the lengths witnessed in Canada. Again, it may be contended that even here, the Exchange is not really closed upon all the days named, but upon any one of them if the investor goes down into the "Street," he is never sure of finding the broker he wishes to meet, nor is he sure but that the few who remain at their posts will succeed in checking his proposed advantage and throw him out for the time being.

There are brokers *and* brokers. No sweeping condemnation of this or other recognized integers of our financial *ensemble* can ever be administered and fail to do injustice. Brokers have been known, are known to-day, who feel their clients losses keenly, who act for them as they would for themselves had they funds at stake, where the opportunity for a fractional per cent. advantage occurs. Brokers there are among us, who have shewn evident signs of depression at a client's losses, whose hearts are in the right place, who are as human as men can be, who would, if allowed by the Board, to which they daily do honor, sacrifice their own commissions in favor of a client, and these brokers in some cases are not rich men at that, neither do they wear this evidence of sympathy as a cloak or bid for future business. To these then, this tribute is due. Others there are whose life-time dealing with stern facts, has tended to make them mechanical, but has also impressed them with the need of promptness and care for the interests entrusted to them, who deservedly pride themselves upon the reputation they have acquired, whose judgment is good, and whose course is always a business-like one. If these do not recognize feeling as a necessary attribute in the conduct of their weighty interests, can they be blamed? Finally, there are brokers in the wide field of speculation from which the world will never free itself, who by cleverly managed juggles, bubble schemes, &c., amass, in a few cases, great wealth, but who cannot as a rule thus thrive in this Canada of ours. Let the class then be congratulated upon its record as a whole, and refuse to follow the brilliant but illusory and remorseful careers of men in larger centres. The development of the resources of our country, or of other sound interests, can be encouraged to the advantage of our people, production can be fostered, unsound schemes or ridiculous inflation can be discouraged, and evasions of our laws become unknown offences. Mutual satisfaction will then be the result of all transactions, and no blot can mar the pages of our " Street " history.

LUMBER INTEREST.

This industry may be considered a leading one, and second to none in the greater part of our country. Over-production, and a curtailed demand from the United States during the depression, caused it to languish for some five years or more, requirements from England, South America, &c., also falling off, the result was a paralyzation of the interest and a large increase of debt to banks, culminating in heavy failures and general distress in all localities where the stake in the manufacture of lumber was paramount.

In 1879, fresh demands from the United States, followed by a better tone in the old country and elsewhere, gave new life to the business; prices rallied rapidly, advancing greatly, and once more this great element of strength to our country began to return our manufacturers a better proportion of business and profit. Capital long unemployed, and liabilities which had borne interest compounded for years, felt the good effects, the one found instant use, the other was reduced, claims held by banks acquired a surer value, because the assets they represented took on a new lease of life, and becoming active, began to fulfil the mission for which they were originally created.

During 1881, however, there was a check given to the interest to a certain extent by the lowness of the river waters, over one and a half million feet being stuck upon the Kippewa and other streams, or "hung up" in lumbering parlance. The fire fiend also visited some limits, and the unfortunate owner had to suffer a considerable loss, as it is useless to try to stay its ravages in the woods, the buildings upon the limits being the only assets whose security is attempted. In consequence of these drawbacks business for a time was almost at a standstill, what timber arrived at shipping points had to be sent away in half loads, as the barges could not go down to the St. Lawrence if they were deep in the water, and the sawing capacity at Ottawa was for a considerable time unworked to its full limit. While this locking up of material was then a present loss to mill owners, it was evident that there would be a good supply with which to commence the next season, and as the cut of timber was a large one, this detention by natural causes could not be a permanent evil. During the season, however, the mills lost time in the early part of it, for the scarcity of logs prevented them for starting until a month after the usual time, or in some cases, until June. The season's cut is estimated as below, and is from reliable sources :—

E. B. Eddy, Hull	40,000,000	feet.
E. B. Eddy, Deschenes	20,000,000	"
Bronsons & Weston	35,000,000	"
Perley & Pattee	30,000,000	"
J. R. Booth	35,000,000	"
Gilmour & Co., Hull	25,000,000	"
Gilmour & Co., Chelsea	35,000,000	"
Sherman, Lord & Hurdman	18,000,000	"
John Rochester	8,000,000	"
McLaren & Co., New Edinburgh	15,000,000	"
McClymont & Co	10,000,000	"
Capt. Young	10,000,000	"
Total	281,000,000	"

In isolated cases, a stock of logs was on hand early in the season ; Mr. J. R. Booth, notably, getting a prompt start and sawing along within a good margin ; Messrs. Bronsons & Weston also cut up a considerable amount as the season got well under way.

The amount of logs " hung up " on the rivers above was, as the late fall advices came in, found to be about 1,000,000 pieces. Of this large aggregate about 725,000 logs were stuck around the. " Chats," and 275,000 between the " Chats " and Ottawa. The amount below Ottawa being very small. Thus there was, when the ice took in December 1881, all this vast quantity of timber cut but not sawn on the Ottawa and its tributaries.

The returns for the Chaudiere slides for the current year, 1881, are as follows :—

	Cribs.	Pieces.
Square Timber	6,213	162,843
Round Piles	254	5,213
Flatted Timber	82	2,356
Dimension Timber	31	
Spars	4	80
Total	6,584	170,492
Last Year, 1880	3,441	82,814

To the year's figures may be added the eight rafts of square timber stuck on the upper river—say 500 cribs, and 10,500 pieces by rail, equal to 500 cribs; this would give a grand total of 7,584 cribs, or considerably more than double the cut of the preceding year.

The rivers were never known to be as low as during 1881, at least within the experience of the oldest lumber manufacturer now in business; there is, however, a report that they were in a similar condition some thirty years ago, but this was at a time when the lumber business was in its infancy.

The shipments of deals from the Port of Montreal to the United Kingdom during the season of 1881, consisted of 38 cargoes, containing 21,838,287 feet, against 19,781,885 feet in 1880; showing an increase of over 2,000,000 feet. The total shipments from the Port of Montreal to United Kingdom and to South America of deals and lumber for 1881 season, amounted to 34,704,228 feet, against 28,250,919 feet for the season of 1880; or an increase of over 6,000,000 feet for 1881. The following is a detailed statement of deals sent from Montreal to the United Kingdom and the continent for 1881, as compiled by Messrs. Anderson, McKenzie & Co. :—

Name of Vessel.	No. of Feet.
Thule	626,764
Carla	426,391
Haab	739,924
Lord Palmerston	514,085
Mallard	518,952

Name of Vessel.	*No. of Feet.*
Alida	282,012
Lindola	314,967
St. Kilda	870,732
Lake Simcoe	211,860
Statsminster	270,930
Falde	381,892
Adele	573,595
Arnim	240,432
Aeger	378,730
Memlo	336,715
Lake Nepigon	65,000
Port Royal	227,727
Prince Llewellyn	242,027
Elizabeth Mary	235,042
Hilda	663,600
Amal	394,671
Beaconsfield	595,580
Xenia	572,220
Texas	277,100
Mississippi	198,741
Texas	140,561
Fido	155,127
Dronning Louise	427,130
Montreal	39,600
Virgo	426,360
Glendonwyn	140,580
Wayfarer	601,920
Roycroft	518,760
Ocean King	196,020
Laura Emily	607,860
Garden Island	762,300
Nebo	536,580
Dampier	326,700

FROM PIERREVILLE.

General Burch	745,415
Indiana	476,255
Framines	638,495
Cap	520,167
Mary A. Wilson	318,230

From the interesting annual circular compiled by Messrs. J. Bell Forsyth & Co., of Quebec, I glean that the exports from Quebec, for the past five years, were as follows :—For 1877, 30,639,851 feet ; for 1878, 18,565,499 feet ; for 1879, 15,765,057 feet ; for 1880, 26,252,094 feet ; and for 1881, 20,309,155 feet. For these five years, the export of Oak averaged 2,238,152 feet per year ; Elm, 791,192 feet ; Ash, 252,320 feet ; Birch, 347,856 feet ; Square and Waney White Pine, 9,800,360 feet ; Red Pine, 1,276,040 feet ; Pine Deals, 4,587,199 feet, and Spruce do. 3,003,574 feet.

The prices current at Quebec on 15th December 1881, were, for White Pine in the raft, inferior and ordinary average, 20 to 24 cents ; for fair average do., 24 to 28 cents ; for good and good fair average, 28 to 32 cents ; for superior do., 32 to 37 cents ; in shipping order, 24 to 40 cents ; for Waney Board, 18 to 19 inch, 37 to 39 cents ; and for Waney Board, 19 to 21 inch, 39 to 42 cents.

Red Pine in the raft, measured off, according to average, was quoted at 13 to 22 cents ; and in shipping order, 35 to 45 feet do., 20 to 24 cents.

Oak, Canada, by the dram, according to average and quality, 43 to 45 cents ; do. Michigan and Ohio, 48 to 50 cents ; Elm by the dram, 40 to 50 feet, 25 to 28 cents ; Elm, 30 to 35 feet, 23 to 26 cents ; Ash, 14 inches and up, 28 to 32 cents ; Birch, 16 inch average, 18 to 19 cents ; Tamarac, square, 12 to 14 cents ; Deals, bright, according to mill specification, $108 to $112 for first, $70 to $72 for seconds, and $37 to $39 for third quality ; Deals, bright Michigan, $120 for first, and $75 for second quality ; Deals, dry floated, $102 to $104 for first, two-thirds for second, and one-third for third quality ; Deals, floated, $92 to $96 for first, two-thirds for seconds, and one-third for third qualities ; Deals, bright— Spruce, $40 to $44 for first, $26 to $28 for second, and $20 to $23 for third qualities. It is to be borne in mind among foreign purchasers, that timber sold in the raft subjects the buyer to great expense in dressing, butting, and at times heavy loss for culls, if sold in shipping order, the expense of shipping only to be added.

The arrivals from sea of sailing vessels at the Port of Quebec during the year were not up to the expectations of trade members, but a steady increase was perceptible in the extent of deal shipments by ocean steamers, from the Port as well as from the Port of Montreal.

The comparative statement of sailing vessels clearing, lumber laden, at the Port of Quebec, for sea, for the past eight years is as follows :—

	Vessels.	Tons.
1874	854	636,672
1875	642	478,441
1876	786	624,110
1877	796	670,627
1878	476	399,833
1879	433	364,628
1880	634	555,451
1881	459	380,186

The market for White Pine, at the beginning of the year 1881, did not open with the brisk demand which had been looked for, and a few rafts in market and to arrive were purchased at moderate figures. As the spring shipments were being completed, however, it became evident that the stock on hand was unusually small, and new timber was eagerly bought up, in some cases before the rafts had left the Ottawa district. A lull occurred in August, and for a time little business was transacted, but this idleness was of short duration, and subsequently prices were paid for rafts of choice qualities, such as had never before been given. In some instances, 39 to 40 cents for Waney board, and 35 to 37 cents for Square in the raft were paid, the purchasers having to bear all loss from culls and defective wood as well as the expenses of putting the timber in shipping order. The greatest care and attention was paid last winter in the selection of timber, in some instances miles of limits were traversed to hunt up good and choice trees ; yet, after all, a great falling off in the percentage of first-class goods was noticeable, generally in rafts, though some exceptionally fine ones were placed on the market. The supply this year has been under the average of former years, though in excess of 1880, and it is estimated that if the present winter is favorable for manufacture, an increased production may be looked for should all reach market next season ; this is certainly to be desired, seeing that the present stock is so light, and scarce sufficient for spring requirements at Quebec.

In Red Pine the year's production was considerably over that of last year, the increase, however, being entirely in small and inferior wood, a good deal of which was unfit for shipment and had to be utilized for local requirements. Large and choice wood is becoming scarce on some limits and was in good request all the season ; of this description the quantity in stock at the end of last year was very limited.

Oak.—Notwithstanding that the quantity measured to date is over the manufacture of 1879 and 1880 put together, this wood has maintained its price for choice parcels, though inferior and common were difficult to sell. The scarcity of good wood, and the enhanced cost of production, forces manufacturers to hold their timber, unless something like our highest quotations are realized. The estimated production of good Oak is light and the weather was unfavorable for the manufacturers.

Elm.—The supply was slightly over that of the preceding year, the shipment fair, and the stock wintering below the average. It is difficult to procure good Rock Elm, the trees being scattered, and the prices asked for standing timber so high, that unless full rates can be obtained, the production for this market must be greatly curtailed.

Ash.—Of this wood a good deal of small inferior came to the Quebec market. Manufacturers should get out nothing but good White Ash, large and good wood is in request at the quotations named.

Birch and Maple.—The production was light, the export about an average one, and the stock reduced. These woods are more easily obtained than others dealt with in these reports, and the supply for some years to come must depend to a certain extent upon the rates offered.

Pine Deals, compared with 1880, the supply was a million standard short, the exports also show a diminution of nearly two millions standard. This latter situation arose from the limited tonnage obtainable after September. The demand for Deals up to July was not active, but after that date a better feeling prevailed. The increasing consumption in the United States will absorb a large quantity of sawn lumber and thus diminish the future supply of Deals.

Spruce Deals were in short supply owing to the lowness of the water late into the season ; this naturally prevented the logs from reaching the mills. The export is some 200,000 standard less than it was in 1880, and the stock wintering is about an average of the last five years. Deals commanded fair prices throughout the season.

Freights opened at about 24 shillings for timber and 60 shillings for deals to Liverpool, for 1881. To London the rates being 25 shillings for timber and 60 shillings for deals. To the Clyde, 22 shillings timber and 60 shillings for deals, the season closing at 24s. 6d., for timber and 67 shillings for deals to Liverpool, 71 shillings for deals to London, and 24 shillings for timber to the Clyde.

St. John, N. B. exported during 1881, to the United Kingdom and Australia, as follows :—143,243,941 sq. feet, as against 159,249,307 sq. feet in 1880. This immense amount was shipped mainly by nine firms, the July shipments amounted to over 29,000,000 sq. feet of deals carried in 48 vessels, the shipments of August summing up 26,875,000 feet in 45 vessels. The chief destination of these vast quantities being Liverpool, Bristol, Channel, Glasgow, Dublin, London and the Continent. The only ports to which square timber were sent were Liverpool, Carnarvon, Dundalk, Waterford and Wexford.

The following official returns of the total Ottawa exports for the season, give 158,243,000 feet, besides shooks, laths, sleepers &c., the value being $2,069,000, as against a value for 1880 of $981,000. The number of feet for 1881 was less than for 1880, but the value was greater because of the increase of prices over the latter year.

During 1880, the aspect of the wood trade in England was as follows : The year opened buoyantly, and the very favorable expectations then entertained were realized during a considerable portion of the year. Late in the fall, however, the unexpectedly large imports affected the healthy state of the market, and the result toward the end of the year was disappointing. Prices receded somewhat, and meantime the consumption, which had begun to show some activity toward the close of 1879 and beginning of 1880, assumed its previous quiet character, and although it had continued fairly steady through the year, it can hardly be said to have improved to the extent anticipated. Freights remained comparatively steady, though in October, Quebec freights experienced a sharp fall, followed by an equally quick rebound in November. The average variations were not, however, considerable. In the spring of 1881, the feeling in England was heavy, stocks of most kinds of woods being too large, created a pressure upon rates. In May, there was a very fair consumption, but prices continued to experience a downward tendency on account of the forcing of sales consequent upon the presence of considerable stocks. Later on in the year, the demand for Quebec square pine steadily increased, and fair prices were obtained. During the summer the import of American pitch pine was very heavy, consisting of 551,000 feet in one month, as against 281,000 for the corresponding period in the previous year. For the first five months of the year the receipts were 4,027 tons of woods from Quebec, 25,259 from St. John, N. B., 42,199 from the United States, and 24,817 tons from the Baltic.

The rapid consumption of the timber of the world's forests has, at the hands of a good many writers, been widely commented upon. Sweden and Norway, which still are able to do a large export trade in deals, are now compelled to buy their oak in Poland. In Russia, the forests along the shores of the Baltic, in Finland, and in the Southern Provinces, are so rapidly thinning that the forest acreage of the Empire is now only one in ten. There are about 34,000,000 acres of forest in Germany, of which 20,000,000 are in Prusso-Germany, estimated to be worth £500,000,000, and bringing in an income of £10,000,000 per annum. The State forests are taken great care of in all parts of Germany, in Prussia alone £100,000 being spent every year in replanting. The imports of timber exceed the exports by over 2,000,000 tons. The oak and the beech are the kind of trees which do best in Denmark, but the timber trade of that country is very small. Austria and Hungary have upward of 43,000,000 acres of forest ; but in Austria proper, the State does not possess more than seven per cent. of the wooden area, as, owing to the wasteful policy of the Minister of Finance from 1855 to 1872, more than five million acres were sold for sums so far below their value that there was a popular saying in Vienna : " If you want to become rich buy State forests." The speculation came to an end in 1873, but Austria is now obliged to buy most of her timber in Bosnia and Montenegro. Servia and Roumania have some very fine forests, but Italy, though her forest area extends over nearly

14,000,000 acres, does not do much in the way of a timber trade, as the roads leading to the forests are so bad that it is almost impossible to move the timber when cut. Much the same is the case with Spain, which has 8,500,000 acres of forest; while Portugal, which has only a million acres, finds a good market for her timber. Sweden and Norway export about £32,000,000 worth of timber, in deals largely, each year; at this rate their fine forests will soon be exhausted; while Russia, where the annual consumption of timber is put at £36,000,000, exports only £4,800,000 worth. In Germany, as mentioned above, the imports exceed the exports, but in Austria-Hungary the exports are £4,800,000 more than the imports. In France the annual imports are estimated at £8,000,000, and the exports £1,200,000. England buys about $10,800,000 worth and Holland about £2,000,000 worth per annum. Finally, the imports into Western Europe may be put at £36,000,000, taking one year with another.

In our own country, considerable waste of pine timber is reported in Ontario as a result of the mode practised in cutting, squaring &c. It is certain that our government would preserve most valuable assets, if, for the future, they would withhold from the market such portions of our timber territory as still remain unsold, until at least, it became evident beyond a doubt, that this course narrowed the business into so few hands that a monopoly of the interest would result, which *might* take shape, if other countries could not meet us in the world's markets with a considerable supply. In the United States, the subject is exciting great attention. At the meeting of the Chicago Lumbermen's Exchange, a few months since, the startling statement was officially made that owing to the enormous growth of the lumber business, it will take only twenty years to exhaust the forests of the country. That at the present rate of depletion, in the course of five years all of the black walnut timber large enough for logs will be used up, also at the rate the oak timber is being used for railroad ties, cooperage and other purposes, that in the course of a short forty years the oak forests will be consumed. Other varieties of timber are said by this authority, to be fast disappearing. This kind of statement is, however, no new thing to the ears of all lumbermen, and most of them discount these theories largely, still it is pretty certain that time—

whether it be forty years or a hundred—will bring about some approach to the points raised by the Chicago prophets, and we cannot on this continent any more than upon the shores of the Baltic, and other parts of the old world, hope to escape the force of natural laws. It is, then, a subject to which thought may be invited, and where practicable, the advisability of tree planting may be considered. In this connection, the tree known as the Western Catalpa is highly spoken of as the coming wood. It can be grown to advantage in temperate belts, such as the bottom lands of the Mississippi, Missouri, Ohio, in Illinois, Iowa, Wisconsin &c., or on the high prairies of the west ; though a broader idea can be got of regions favorable to its growth by following the presence of the Soft Maple, as the Catalpa will grow under similar conditions. The time of growth is forty years, at that age it has attained a diameter of three feet under favorable natural auspices, its growth is generally more rapid than that of the Soft Maple, and its wood has been known to last from fifty to one hundred years, set in the ground as posts &c. It is likely that it can be introduced into considerable areas in Canada, particularly in the vicinity of the great lakes, as our seasons for the past decade have not varied much as regards weather severity from that experienced in the Western States. Other woods, however, can be grown with the exercise of care as to fires, and precautions generally being taken against the inroads of squatters, as well as due attention given to thinning &c. It is, then, really a question if we ought not in this generation to contribute as far as possible to a legacy in favor of our successors and the world at large, by individual effort in forwarding tree planting and tree cultivation.

Dry Goods, Clothing, Millinery and Fancy Goods Interests.

The dry goods business is *the* one which, the world over, has always felt the dire effects of a general depression most keenly. In Canada then, we did not escape the realization of this seemingly universal law, for the record of casualities, both in number of failures and loss of capital, presents an exhibit of disaster whose proportions are far greater than those experienced in any other line of trade, lumber not excepted.

During the depression and commencing with its first year, the distress in this line resulted in the stoppages of some sixty houses, all of whom were wholesalers. The greater part of these had to relinquish business after paying, as a rule, but poor dividends to creditors, there being actually no room for them in the trade.

The profits of 1871-2 and 3 were largely unsound, as they were represented by figures derived from supply accounts, long-winded customers, and inflated ideas as to the outlook ; which naturally led up to an unsound estimation of the value of stocks and outstandings. These apparent gains were quickly wiped out by the very first following years of depreciation and loss, and it is believed that with the exception of a very few houses doing a business of much extent, annual balances up to 1878 could not show a real gain upon the exhibits of 1870. The good prices of 1870-1, 2 and 3 were caused by the general advance in Europe, which advance was created by the effects of the American, and also the Franco-Prussian wars. These difficulties stimulated over-production and over-buying and helped to intensify the subsequent depression. At the time Paris was invested by the Prussians the silk markets were demoralized, and English houses as well as through them, Canadian houses became alarmed lest supplies of these fabrics should for the time fail, this led to overbuying, and leading markets became overloaded at high prices.

As has been stated, the loss resulting from these causes quickly made itself felt, and observant traders in this line became aware before the first half of the decade had passed, that they had before them a condition of things for which there was no precedent in their experiences. We felt here the effects of over competition and "support account" trading as early as 1873, while in 1874–75 these effects became greatly aggravated, then at this time the great value shrinkage in Europe added to the distress here, and precipitated disaster from which there was no escape for many houses who were caught unduly extended. This depreciation in values may be said to have been the last feather weight on the camel's back, for it involved large losses in the higher priced goods, such as silks, dress goods and finer fabrics generally.

It was, from 1874, a long and weary course for our wholesalers to tread. Happily the climax was reached in 1879, then it was that the "support account" system was found to be among the things of the past, those weaker houses who had believed it to be their only safety in the absence of sufficient active capital, had been forced to succumb, and with them died all possibility of its hold upon life. It is true that there may, in a few small cases, still exist a trace of the evil, but in such shape only as it would naturally be left in at the close of a trouble so extended as was this to the dry goods trade, and this remnant of the result of an absurd business policy will soon disappear, though the same desperate plan of realization may, and probably will, be brought once more into life under similar circumstances. It would be well for all creditors in the future, however, to make this point as much a matter of inquiry in seeking information when times darken again, as to ask for light upon the other leading heads of a debtor's condition, for it may usually be argued that to find a merchant favoring the "support account" system in his own transactions is to find behind it all an insufficiency of capital and a dangerous expansion of interests.

The severest pressure was brought to bear upon the trade in the years 1877–8 and 9. Goods were sacrificed extensively, principally by the weaker houses, who had all along, and in the most wonderful manner managed to obtain immensely disproportionate credits in England in the face of evident signs of weakness, and despite warnings from good authorities upon this side the water. Bank facilities were curtailed in the latter year, for it was the most hopeless in its forecast for the future, of any which had preceded it, and we were nearer a disastrous panic than at any other time in the history of the decade. The culmination, however, did survivors good as it eliminated the useless houses from our midst and restored natural conditions. The total imports of dry and fancy goods, &c., got down in 1879 to $20,680,000, a decrease from 1875 of $15,500,000.

The following figures show the variations of dry goods, clothing, millinery and fancy goods importations during the most interesting years of the trade histories :—

1868	$21,155,741
1869	19,940,797
1870	21,111,017
1871	28,357,395
1872	34,426,469
1873	33,960,557
1874	35,310,475
1875	35,599,698
1876	23,833,219
1877	24,933,041
1878	23,494,000
1879	20,680,000
1880	25,450,000

Until 1876, the Province of Quebec, mainly at Montreal, imported a yearly average of nearly $4,000,000 more goods than did the Province of Ontario. In 1876, however, the former Province lost house after house through the cleansing processes of the times, and its business changed materially in extent, Ontario then began to gain, as it had lost but few houses, and its distributing power remained comparatively undisturbed. The averages for the Provinces of Nova Scotia and New Brunswick have not materially differed for the past twelve years, the figures by Provinces, for 1881, are not as yet obtainable.

The general trade outlook in the late fall of 1881 was excellent. The horizon had been cleared thoroughly, payments were never better, and business turnovers had increased—in some cases fifty per cent. over those of 1879. The winter, however, proved to be a mild and open one late into January 1882, and its effect was to curtail the sales of seasonable or heavy goods, and undoubtedly it affected spring sales as well. Confidence in the condition of the country, however, remained unimpaired, for so long as good prices were being realized by the farming community for their produce, mills running full time, wages good, and old scores from country traders reduced to a minimum or wiped out altogether, all the important factors of trouble were removed.

The trade generally note with relief that there is getting to be an increased demand for better goods, the trash bought so eagerly during the long depression being now seldom asked for.

Cotton, Silk and Woollen Manufacturing Interests.

The manufacturing of brown cottons is, comparatively speaking, not an old industry in Canada, its inauguration dating back only some eleven or twelve years, and though for some time after its birth a few of the older concerns made but little headway, through exceptional causes, mainly the lack of practical ability requisite in closely calculating the cost and bringing prices down to a par with the terms offered by the United States and the old country, as also the want, plainly manifest, of sufficient protection, it combined with the production of white goods, and sprang into new and vigorous life immediately after the new tariff went into effect, in 1879, and since that period has acquired an importance attained by no other industry within the same length of time. Its extension may be pointedly illustrated by a consideration of the fact that in 1877 we imported from other countries in the shape of brown and white cotton cloth, jeans, denims, drillings, tickings, ducks, &c., to no less a value than $4,173,996, while during 1881 the amount so imported had been brought down to $1,970,982. It is now approximately estimated that with the output of the mills at present in working condition, together with those now being constructed and proposed, the present importations of 30 to 40 per cent. will be reduced to some 15 or 20 per cent., and that if the present disposition, and belief in the industry is maintained, the importation of all classes of plainer makes of cotton goods will eventually be reduced to a minimum. It is to be understood, however, that the importation of finer fabrics and printed goods will probably be maintained at about its present proportions, unless our capitalists become in time willing to embark larger sums naturally required to finish these goods in their varied processes of manufacture. It is, of course, within the range of possibility that the manufacturers of the United States may, in the event of depression in their own country, again seek an outlet in the Dominion for the surplus product of their mills, at the closest rates, but at the present date they have a home demand equal to the output of their mills, with no surplus stock now on hand to unload.

Among the pioneers in the manufacture of plain cotton cloth in the Dominion may be named the Young, Law & Co. Factory, at Dundas, this being subsequently merged into a joint-stock business, under the style of the Dundas Cotton Company. Early in the last decade the Lybster Cotton Company, at Merriton, Ont., the V. Hudon Company, the Canada Cotton Company, the Stormont Cotton Manufacturing Company, &c. These older interests were supplemented the last half of the decade by the Coaticook Cotton Company, the Montreal Cotton Company, at Valleyfield; the Craven Cotton Mill, at Brantford; and after 1879, the encouragement afforded by the new tariff was such as to lead to the investment of some $400,000 in the Merchants' Manufacturing Company, as well as to the increase of facilities in the V. Hudon Cotton Company, the latter concern now working 80,000 spindles. Then followed the promotion and probable start of the following concerns :—The Halifax Cotton Company, which is to run 15,000 spindles; the Windsor, N.S., Cotton Company, with 10,000 spindles; a smaller enterprise proposed at Yarmouth, N.S.; a very large one at St. Stephen, N.B,; the St. Croix Cotton Company, with 30,000 spindles; the St. John, N.B., Cotton Company, with 10,000 spindles as proposed; one at Moncton, N.B., now organizing, with some 20,000 spindles; a new mill at Chambly to run on white cottons principally, running, say, 5,000 spindles; the Kingston Cotton Company, with 10,000 spindles; and a new mill at Hamilton, with a proposed outfit of 10,000 spindles. It will therefore be readily seen that, considering the present ratio of increase in the facilities for manufacturing, there is ample ground for the belief above expressed, that the home consumption of plain cotton goods will very shortly be wholly supplied by the products of our own mills.

Comparative statement of cottons entered for consumption in the Dominion for the following years :—

	Yards.	Value.
1877	50,957.105	$4,173,996
1878	49,622,556	4,035,467
1879	46,685,559	3,483,971
1880	13,604,229	1,400,919
1881	19,126,120	1,970,982

These importations cover the heavy staples most in use, such as bleached and unbleached cloth, sheetings, drills, ducks, denims, tickings, jeans, checked and striped shirtings, cottonades, ginghams and plaids.

The attainment of our Woollen manufacturing interests to their present prominent proportions, as a leading Canadian industry, is the result of the growth of the last twenty years or so. The Lower Canadian *habitant* has, from time immemorial, made his own " etoffe du pays," and in isolated circumstances, there were factories, where such goods as Halifax tweeds, coarse flannels, &c., were made prior to the period above stated ; but it is only since then, that the manufacture of woollen goods has been so largely developed. Among the early manufacturers who are still largely engaged in this interest are Messrs. Lomas & Son, of Sherbrooke, and Messrs. Barber, of Streetsville, with some few others, but later years have largely added to the list of extensive manufacturers, and have also witnessed the addition of other descriptions of goods made by these factories. The list of fabrics of to-day will be found most comprehensive, considering the few years during which ideas have met the encouragement of capital. There is now being made within our own borders, the following goods :— Fine tweeds and coatings, blankets, the finest flannels, knitted underwear and hosiery of all descriptions, Cardigan jackets, woven caps, nubias and shawls, yarns, &c. This is the result of the renewed life taken in by our manufacturers soon after the close of the American war, and notably between 1865 and 1869. During this period a number of mills, with superior facilities and capable of manufacturing the better grades of goods, were built, and our people then began to realize their independence of older countries, in the results as above shown of their own enterprise. The products of some of our leading mills have not only passed the test of local criticism successfully, but have earned the commendation of some of the world's best judges, for it is upon record that at the Great Exposition at Paris, and at the Centennial at Philadelphia, the goods made by our people have received some of the highest honors attainable, and as a result a demand has been realized from different sections of the globe, orders having reached us from as far distant points as Australia, Victoria, &c., where the goods have been received with the greatest favor. It may be said just here that the wools from which some of these goods are made, are imported, to a considerable extent, from Australia as well as from Cape of Good Hope. In this we can also take the lesson home, which has been strongly put forward in preceding pages of this work, *i.e.*, that our farmers, in wool growing as well as in cheese and butter making, can and ought to raise the best of stock, and our manufacturers aim to produce the finest makes, and this done, we ought to stand abreast of other countries in so far as the production of really fine goods is concerned.

Our manufacturers of tweeds, etoffes, flannels, blankets, knitted goods, &c., now number about 150 (not including custom mills), of which nearly three-quarters are in Ontario. Further extensions of the interest are spoken of, and our people may confidently look forward to a time in the near future, when the influence and power which attaches to a country dependent upon no other land to supply itself with, and export woollen fabrics, is acquired.

The figures below give the returns of raw wool imports for the last fiscal year, by Provinces :—

	Quantity.	Value.
Ontario	4,295,975 lbs.	$ 883,662
Quebec	3,718,993 "	712,037
Nova Scotia	7,398 "	1,423
New Brunswick		
Manitoba		
British Columbia	16,221 "	1,225
Prince Edward Island	1,700 "	500
Totals	8,040,287 lbs.	$1,598,847

The amount of wool shorn in the Dominion is closely estimated at about 5,000,000 lbs., and the amount pulled from the pelt about 2,500,000 lbs. We exported for the fiscal year ending June, 1881, 1,482,927 lbs.

The annual product of the total number of factories and mills producing the various lines of goods quoted above, but not including custom mills is, for 1881, estimated at nearly $8,000,000, of which amount the mills located in the Province of Ontario may be credited with a two-third proportion. Among the mills having the largest capacity are the Paton Manufacturing Company of Sherbrooke, the Rosamond Woollen Company of Almonte, the Cornwall Manufacturing Company, the Campbellford Mill (now being inaugurated), the Auburn Woollen Mills of Peterborough, Barber Bros. of Streetsville, Jno. Routh & Co. of Cobourg, B. Caldwell & Co. of Lanark, Jno. Penman of Paris, St. Willett of Chambly, the Coaticook Knitting Company, Albert French of New Edinburgh, Moorehouse, Dodds & Co. of Glentay, R. Forbes & Co. of Hespeler, Robinson, Howell & Co. of Preston, &c.

The silk industry in Canada is yet in its infancy. The year 1876 saw the establishment of the first enterprise. This house devoted its energies to the manufacture of silk twist and sewing silk ; the same concern has, since the framing of the new tariff, added the manufacture of ribbons to its original business. The success attending this effort, together with the renewed confidence experienced in business circles, led to the organization, a little more than a year ago, of a second concern— the Canada Silk Company—a joint stock interest who are engaged in the manufacture of the same class of goods as those produced by the house first mentioned. The Canada Silk Company intend to, eventually, engage in the manufacture of broad silks as well. The Corriveau Silk Mills are the only manufacturers of broad or dress silks at date. They contemplate increasing their facilities at once, in fact a reconstruction of the Company has been effected, and the capital enlarged to $200,000, a new mill is being built, into which the organization will move during the coming season. It is claimed for their goods that they are entirely free from the artificial stiffening used by some foreign manufacturers. A leading house in the dry goods trade here are forwarding the extension of this concern's business, which is proof enough in itself, that the quality of the product of this mill is such as to guarantee its success, and make the grades favorite ones.

There is certainly every reason to believe that our silk manufacturing interest is capable of as good proportionate returns as those of our cotton, and other interests, the business has been got well in hand, and is being carefully managed, while our demand for home-made goods is increasing.

Grocery and Sugar Refinery Interest.

Among our leading lines of business, that of the grocery interest is as important and prominent as any. Being closely competed, it was also among the very first to feel the advent of the depression. In fact, it was in this line that the first failures of size occurred, the forerunners of disaster appearing as early as 1872.

The first stoppages were of houses who had crept up to, and in some cases greatly exceeded, the limits of turnover to which their capitals should have confined them, and dealing with the weaker classes of accounts, were the first to feel the discriminating action of banks. Had our general trade situation been surrounded by less expansion, and our power of recuperation been less vitiated and weakened, it is probable that the annihilation of this class of wholesalers would have placed the general trade upon a safe footing, and enabled them to get sounder results from their collections, as well as to maintain a better range of margins, but we could not in a day, or a year, overcome the effects of the intense inflation of all interests, and until 1880 this line of trade was laid open to the inroads upon capital and credit induced by the inaction all around it, as well as by the fact that it stood second to but one interest— that of dry goods—in so far as the disability of over competition in its ranks was concerned. It has been constantly subjected to most rapid declines, as well as sudden rises in the current values given to its staples, through many outside causes, and it may be said to have been more at the mercy of natural as well as speculative effects in this way than any other line of trade in this country.

In no staple has wider variations of cause and effect been witnessed than in teas. During the earliest years of the decade, production had not become so excessive, as it was in the last years of this term, and many large houses in the Dominion, accumulated excellent gains. During 1875, however, speculation ran rife, those who had made large profits continued the enlargement of their interests in many cases, and the severest drop experienced in years resulted. The years 1876 and 1877 were also noted for a most unsatisfactory course of trade in this staple, but 1878 was probably the worst in the history of the line, as it not only was impossible to make any decent average of profit, but losses by bad debts and forced realization, made the whole turnover a losing one. In the early part of 1879, prices had touched a very low point, but in the autumn of that year an unwarranted advance set in, and ran the rates up some 25 or 30 per cent. This was due largely to the "short crop" cry, how well founded this "bull" plea was, may be seen when the facts were afterward found to be that the crop in that season was never larger, the importations from China and Japan having run up to over 40,000,000 lbs., as against an importation of some 20,000,000 in 1875–76. Prices were maintained for several months, all houses, more or less, had to face the situation with from good to very heavy stocks, and from that time down to the present, prices have steadily receded, until the fall of 1881 saw an almost unprecedented low range of values, in so far as all the lower grades are concerned. The higher grades are also low, but the retrogression is not so marked or likely to gain, as in these the supply is more limited, and purchasing power being yearly on in the increase, higher grades are more in demand. The outlook for the lower ranges is decidedly uncertain, but generally is discouraging, for there seems to be no limit to the production, and stocks are heavy on all sides.

Other ports have also imported far beyond their legitimate wants. It is impossible for us to escape in this line at least, the controlling influence which is brought to bear upon this market from other cities, these virtually *make* the prices which are in due rotation established here. New York cannot be shut out, and influences our home market more than it would seem possible for it to do under the present tariff. Exigencies, however, know no law or sound governing principle, relief must be had, and some one lose in wielding this immense production. It may be *apropos* here to briefly say that it is a question of grave doubt as to the policy of encouraging direct importations so widely, there is little use in questioning the fact that the outcome of the practice is a large stock shouldered upon the trader as a rule, his facilities must be good to turn with success, and while a number of our houses possess these, they are too often imitated by well-meaning traders who do not, however, lay claim to the same calibre, and who are more easily injured.

The year 1879 was, undoubtedly, the best year experienced by the general grocery trade since the early years of the decade, but from that time down the safety in tea handling has lain in the ability of our houses to effect rapid "turnovers," but a cause for good is at work, which in effect is now steadily being felt and gratefully, and if profits are still close enough, and competition be growing more keen each year, we have in it —*i.e.*, the limited loss by bad debts and the prompt payments and unprecedented minimum demand for renewals, a source of great encouragement. Old and strong houses may continue to advance with their greater facilities, their power to command and cull accounts, and their ability to get cash discounts, but merchants of moderate means must depend upon the promptness with which their outstandings are realized, and with these in the condition they are to-day, the smaller jobber, aided by economic management may gain, despite the untoward circumstance of smaller marginal returns. We are upon the second year of general improvement in all trade conditions, with harvests for two seasons got in well, our country traders have been repaid old scores by their farmer clients, and are now well upon their feet.

Referring briefly to Sugars, it is gratifying that we have the energy and ability to produce and build up such self-contained enterprises as those promoted by our refiners. For three years from the spring of 1876, they languished for want of adequate protection, but in 1879 were fostered as they deserved to be by a wise policy, and are to-day among the most important factors of our commercial fabric. From them the trade get better quality, and in more suitable packages, than importations gave them generally speaking, and there is just sufficient competition between the refineries at Montreal, Halifax and Moncton, to keep prices at reasonable rates.

Nothing is now imported excepting raw, or an occasional small line of low grade Scotch Sugars. It is true that at times when the market is in a rapidly advancing state, some purchases can be made in the States, but these occurrences are now rare. Raw Sugar, from refining to good grocery, is imported from places of growth, and chiefly *via* the St. Lawrence, as imports *via* the States are subject to additional expense.

Our market is, however, influenced in this interest as in other staples by the condition of that in the States, and is consequently a point for speculation to be felt at. Granulated Sugar has, during the past five months, fluctuated one and three-quarters cents per pound, and at date is down to within one-quarter cent. of the lowest point. Raw and Yellow Refined have not varied so greatly, but as in most other lines of trade, speculation has become more common whether here or in the States, and some feel that what was once known as *legitimate business*, is yearly becoming more difficult to practice. Each season a few lines of goods are " talked up " through rumours of short crops, &c., &c., and though these attempts at " bulling " the market are getting to be discounted to a great degree, there are many who find their regular margins small, and will load up to a certain extent, with a view to catch the benefit of a rapid turn. This has been particularly noticeable in the handling of sugar during the past season. In speaking of the general grocery interest as having suffered a steady decline, in so far as values go, during the past year, it is only a matter of history to state that there are exceptions, and that during the latter part of the fall of 1881, more or less rally has been experienced in several lines, and that with the exception perhaps of raisins, the prices of several staples are more reasonable.

Comparative statement of Teas imported and entered for consumption in the Provinces of Ontario and Quebec, during the last four fiscal years :—

YEAR ENDING JUNE 30, 1878.

	Lbs.	Value.	Duty.
Ontario	3,827,184	$1,012,646	$223,094
Quebec	3,707,868	794,568	213,634

YEAR ENDING JUNE 30, 1879.

	Lbs.	Value	Duty.
Ontario	5,031,828	$1,216,168	293,537
Quebec	5,022,187	1,043,546	283,461

YEAR ENDING JUNE 30, 1880.

	Lbs.	Value.	Duty.
Ontario	4,144,864	$997,290	241,497
Quebec	4,432,408	991,603	244,105

YEAR ENDING JUNE 30, 1881.

	Lbs.	Value.	Duty.
Ontario	5,871,933	$1,363,961	352,466
Quebec	6,432,753	1,305,785	341,321

During the last fiscal year, the amount of teas imported from the United States into the Province of Ontario for consumption was only 2,385,144 lbs., against imports from other countries of 3,486,789 lbs. The amount imported from the States into the Province of Quebec during the same period was, 1,490,855 lbs., as against imports from other countries of 4,941,898. This shews the changed course of trade under the new tariff plainly, for prior to its inauguration nearly four-fifths of the total amount brought into the Dominion came from the United States.

The general condition of this interest is, however, not satisfactory to large or smaller operators, it is getting to be believed that middlemen must go to the wall in time, and that the only way in which a decent regular, or average profit can be made by large handlers, will be in the establishing of representatives at the depots of production, who will pack for their houses. The large amounts which are steadily coming out upon consignment render necessary the intervention of *some* agency which will tend to unravel and equalize the intricacies which surround the modern tea dealer upon this continent.

Hardware and Metal Interest.

Merchants engaged in these departments of business, experienced during the depression many severe shocks, long periods of stagnation and great losses. It may safely be said that no one interest felt more keenly the adverse effects of sudden transitions and unlooked for culminations than did this trade, nor did any other line present at certain periods a more hopeless outlook. Merchants, in both light and heavy goods, suffered intensely through over competition, large stocks, the cutting of rates, and losses by bad debts and by speculation.

Early in the decade margins were good, and losses few, these satisfactory conditions of trade were in turn strengthened by a steady market at first, and by a rise in values which gave rapid gains to the majority of houses, but unfortunately did not satisfy many, particularly the younger and more ambitious members of the trade. These houses had at best but moderate means, and might well have foreseen that at the first symptoms of impending commercial distress, their bank limits and general credit facilities would be criticized and curtailed to such an extent, as to render it an impossibility for them to finance except at a serious disadvantage. During 1870, 1871 and 1872, however, their rose-coloured surroundings encouraged the belief in their minds that brilliant possibilities awaited extension of interests, and houses were found doing an annual turnover of business running into hundreds of thousands of dollars, upon actual capitals of less than $25,000—in some cases considerable less—and at a time and in a line of business sensitively open to declining values, inasmuch as considerable advances had been experienced.

The first failures occurred, properly speaking, in the grocery line and from the same causes, but the storm which broke upon the junior hardware houses was not long in following. The first evidences of certain disaster were recognized as present in 1873, and from that time for a long, weary eight years uncertainty and distress haunted this interest, with a malignity unparallelled in its record, and seldom approached in any country or in any line of trade. Next to that of dry goods, this hardware interest was notable for its tendency to encourage the realization of stocks by the "support account" system, while in the wrecks of the class of house chiefly alluded to, the presence of accommodation paper was often detected, though its character had been for long most cleverly concealed.

The record of this interest is different from that of any other throughout the depression. It was singularly delusive in its outlook from year to year, its terrible value drops were succeeded quickly by delightful contrasts in the shape of advances, alternate fear and hope being constantly opposed to each other. The average hardware merchant led a most exciting life, until at last he grew blunted to the effect of these alternations, and resigned himself to the inevitable. It was here that sound original strength aided by conservative action had its triumph, those houses lacking in these attributes, one by one disappeared, the record of casualities, including even some of the very oldest in the trade, and bringing to the light indisputable evidences of books unbalanced for years, accommodation paper and large unsafe credits.

The members of no other line of trade witnessed as much recrimination as unfortunately passed between rival houses of medium calibre in the hardware interest. Legitimate traders, while they did not share in creating a cause for these interchanges of abuse, acknowledged their inability to prevent its continuance, and simply went on in their strength, hoping each year for a change of the conditions which trammelled the general situation. During the eight years of vicissitudes which were inherited by the trade, numberless attempts were made by its members to establish a uniform policy in so far as prices, &c., were concerned. In most of these cases there is no doubt but that the prime movers were actuated by sound motives, and really meant to carry out individually, the course indicated by themselves, but they reckoned without due consideration of the causes which were operating against the success of their wellmeant endeavours, and agreements fell through because of the continued stress placed upon the trade in the shape of weak houses, overdone business situations, and necessities which could only be met by the forced realization and consequent sacrifice of goods. All this was very natural under the circumstances, and the position could not be altered until more failures had taken place, more houses forced to retire, old country market conditions changed, the consequent hand-to-mouth system of buying done away with, and the state of our own Canadian commerce reformed.

The fall of 1881 saw all these essentials attained. The representative houses met and with unanimity settled some points where harmony was the paramount object to be desired, such as establishing certain advance percentages, regulating of the discount upon sales, the commission to brokers, &c. The trade at this date was in a general good condition, and is since maintaining the advantages which it ought to share after the crucial experience it has had. There are no apparent reasons for any of its members departing from mutual understandings, and until our internal interests are again overloaded, it is believed that the dignity of this important branch of business will remain intact.

In 1872, when values tended skyward, the press and every one else, nearly, spoke of this period as being the "iron age." Poets might rave about golden and silver eras, but this was the era of *iron* which turned everything *into* gold. Speculation in iron of all kinds was rampant, it was the metal brokers' harvest time, many having been known to sell the same ton of iron many times over. Money was generally made through this and the two years following, but was more than wiped out by the years of depression immediately supervening. Pig iron in 1872 reached $48.50, this rise being mainly accomplished within eight months. The subsequent decline to normal rates was more gradual than it might have been, and is to-day a matter of surprise, and can only be explained by referring to the craze that seemed to affect every one's ideas in regard to their own pet asset at this time. Side by side with these figures and by way of pointing a comparison, may be set those at which pig iron, taking the fluctuations of many years into account, usually averages, which is from $21 to $23.

It is often impossible to forecast or even satisfactorily account for the sometime surprises in fluctuations in the metal markets. Even the shrewdest men in the trade acknowledge their inability to do this at *all* times, speculation cannot be checked, and is indulged in under the *warrant* style and other modes of operation. 1880 witnessed the most demoralizing stages of rates, and these were all the more intense in their effect because of the long-drawn out character of the stagnation which prevailed, no life being evidenced for over six months, and the disgust was increased because this lethargy was experienced when other interests were taking on brighter aspects. Summerlee iron in February of 1880 was worth $33, but in the following July could be bought for just half this. In May, 1881, it could again be bought for about $17, but advanced later on some 40 per cent. Late advices report 650,000 tons of pig iron in yard at Glasgow and unsold, and production is going on at a pretty round rate.

Coke tin, an article of large consumption, could be bought in 1881 at $4.50 per box, as low a price as it ever reached. It is emphatically stated that 40,000 to 50,000 boxes of Canada plates were sold last season without a cent of profit; these low prices, in the face of the increased demand arising from the great extension of the canning business, are accounted for by the fact that the production in Britain is altogether disproportionate and in excess of even the increased demand. Many extensive factories, started during the inflation of nearly ten years ago, are being continued by the creditors or trustees, who hope to eventually realize their claims, but it would have been better for them to have faced the first loss.

At Montreal, centred the heaviest losses and the worst general effects of the depression. The recuperation of the interest at that point, was also delayed in turn by the fact that much of its business had become scattered during the paralyzation of the latter half of the decade, and the demoralization of its country connection, caused by the failure of five of its larger houses, notably between 1875 and 1878. The Western houses then saw their advantage and improved it by making every effort to extend their trade connections. It has been computed that one-third of the trade volume was diverted from Montreal to the West. At the end of 1881, however, we find the remaining and representative Montreal houses doing more sound business than they could readily cope with, in fact the belief is expressed that there is, as trade conditions now stand, room for at least one more good, legitimate house at that point.

Great Britain produced in 1880 7,721,833 tons of pig iron, an increase of 1,712,369 tons on the production of the previous year. These figures represent the largest production of pig iron that has ever occurred in the United Kingdom. The largest total previously was, in the year 1872, when it reached 6,741,729 tons. The Bessemer steel production has also increased, reaching a total in 1880 of 1,044,382 tons, or about 25 per cent. above 1879. The coal raised from the mines amounted in 1880 to 147,320,000 tons against 133,000,000 for 1879; of the amount mined in 1880, 33,599,000 tons was used in iron making.

During July, 1881, it became evident in Britain that the powers of production had enormously developed, and that large stocks were accumulating. Some hope existed that a fresh demand would spring up from some quarter of the world and absorb the greater part of the surplus, but the expectation was not fulfilled, and during the early shipping season stocks showed no signs of decreasing, and quotations continued to tend downward. Prices obtained through June and July would not more than cover the bare cost of production at the furnaces, and in many cases the works could not be used without loss. Some improvement was noticed early in August, but it extended only to finished iron, pig iron still being dull and showing excessive stocks. At some of the works reduction of the makes was determined upon, but no concerted action could be arranged and no relief was felt. The consumptive demand at this time may be said to have been fairly outpaced by the enormous production and gradual accumulation of stocks. In September, however, it was found that a number of furnaces had been " blown out," and the production to a certain extent was diminished. To the fact, however, that the world was shaking off the cloud of depression which had clogged its commerce was due, in the main, the active rally which now took place in values, and from this time the interest resumed its normal condition.

In a review of the metal trade for 1879, 1880 and 1881, eminent authorities in the old country coincide in the conclusion that the rise in values in 1879 was caused by what might fittingly be called the

" American boom ;" while in the latter part of 1881, the improvement
had birth in *many* quarters, home and foreign, and while the United
States demand was heavy for rails, blooms, &c., their requirements for
finished iron were of very moderate extent, in fact they might be called
" overflow " orders and unimportant in their bearing upon values. The
great pressure of the revival in 1881 was, first, for sheet iron—the most
sensitive department of the trade. This can easily be understood when
it is considered that, independently of the ordinary consumption and
export requirements, the galvanizing corrugating works use up fully
200,000 tons per year at home. Any increased foreign demand then, at
once alters the balance and puts prices in motion. Bar iron followed
next in active request, the requirement near the close of the year being
exceptionally large, and the entire output of several of the ordinary
priced well-known shipping brands were taken up readily. Hoop iron all
along continued the most neglected portion of the trade, but late in the
year manifested more life in so far as a few specialties were concerned.
Puddled bars were scarce, and the " Shelton " and " Dallam " grades
could not be found in market during the late year. Taken altogether,
the improvement in the last half of the year hardly balanced the deficiency
of the first half, the rise in prices did not materially benefit producers or
shippers, raw material keeping corresponding pace with the upward
movement, and the producers and shippers had to work off engagements
taken at lower figures. Years ago it was not difficult to buy a few thousand
tons at current prices for forward delivery ; but in 1881 ,manufacturers,
with the lesson still fresh in mind of the over speculation which was so
strong a factor in the last collapse, acted with unusual caution, and
in many cases would only name quotations against actual specifications.
This, no doubt, acted to the general advantage of the trade, and proved
a contrast to the reckless manner in which iron was sold to outsiders in
1879 and 1880, these buyers on the first appearance of weakness, throwing it on the local markets, and intensifying if they did not precipitate the
universal demoralization. December, 1881, closed with British works in
possession of better lined order books than at any time within ten years
previously, the feeling that the corner was finally turned on the last seven
or eight years of depression being generally experienced.

The British exports of iron and steel for the four years preceding 1882, were as follows :—

1878... 2,296,860 tons.
1879... 2,883,484 "
1880........ .... 3,787,000 "
1881... 3,750,000 "

Exports to Canada decreased about 20,000 tons in pig iron as compared with 1880, but increased 25,000 tons as regards rails, bars, hoops, sheets, plates, &c. 1882 commences under favourable auspices as far as the outlook is concerned, a strong disinclination is manifest against unnecessary change in rates, and as an eminent authority upon the interest puts it "hope is strong that we may see a few years of steady trade instead of the brief excitement and the wild 'saturnalia' which has characterized some periods in the history of the interest in late years. A local English sheet has described it as a cruel piece of satire to have wished anybody in the iron trade 'a Happy New Year' since 1875; but it is believed that it may now be done safely, and that it is but reasonable to expect a tolerably prosperous year in 1882."

SADDLERY HARDWARE INTEREST.

That branch of the business known as the Saddlery Hardware Interest is now conducted upon a distinct basis. It is comparatively new to find it apart from the regular hardware line, its separation from that only covering some fifteen years.

During the depression it was affected considerably, and all the more because from its nature, it must take up with small and weak country and city accounts, which very often prove hard of collection, and where closed by note these present an array of paper such as is not very easily handled, and must be taken at bank mainly upon the score of the seller's reputation.

The stock-in-trade of a saddlery hardware merchant consists very largely of goods which up to this time have to be imported, harness goods being brought into our country to the extent of some seventy per cent. These goods must be had, and a change of tariff affects the matter but slightly. The staples in the line are mainly tinned and japanned malleable iron, and nickel-plated trimmings, the tinned and japanned goods have been affected by the widest fluctuations as regards values, the variation during the depression sometimes amounting to fifty per cent. Owing to a break up of the previously existing combination among the manufacturers of the United States, values at the end of the decade for staples were materially lowered, and goods in 1881 were laid down in Canada much more cheaply than during the former years.

Considerable change has taken place in the relative commercial positions of the harness makers during the past few years. Formerly this class of men confined their energies to work at the bench, and turned out harnesses of nearly a uniform pattern; now, the majority of these men have become merchants as well as manufacturers, though in a small way often, and keep varying stocks of trunks, sleigh bells, horse blankets, &c., and as a rule meet their bills quite fairly.

The development of the North-West has opened up a large market for the saddlery hardware merchant, driving by road being as yet the principal means of locomotion and transport, and trade is prosperous in this line on this account. Generally speaking the outlook is quite good ; during the hard times people made their harnesses go as far as possible by patching up, &c., but these are now being replaced by new ones and of later style and better finish, while the small makers can hardly get enough men to fill their orders.

Another branch of the business is the Carriage makers and their trade materials. The principal change under this head, or department, is that which has taken place in the terms of credit given by the wholesaler to the carriage maker. Formerly these terms were very long ones, and credits too large, as a consequence the business was overdone and goods sacrificed, many failures resulting. A revolution has set in, the long terms were reduced to strictly a four months basis, and have been for some time now kept at that. The staples in this department are hubs, spokes, wheels, springs, axles, carriage bolts and trimming leathers, as well as iron. The imports under the new tariff being about 25 per cent. The fluctuations in quoted values have been insignificant.

The general saddlery hardware trade in Canada exhibits a tendency to follow in the course pursued in the United States somewhat. It is likely that we shall find the interest centred in larger concerns, joint-stock or otherwise, who will supply the small dealers their goods *ready-made*, and this will leave to the village carriage maker only the work of repairs.

The number of small and large carriage makers, &c., in the Dominion is now estimated at over 5,000. Allowing an average of five men to each shop, there must be fully 25,000 men engaged in the industry. This estimate is believed to be a moderate one when it is considered that each regular shop must have at least one blacksmith, a painter, a wood-worker and a trimmer. It is a point worth noting that all these mechanics are full-grown men who are generally heads of families, so that the total number of beings supported by the occupation must be considerable.

DRUG AND CHEMICAL INTEREST.

This particular branch of trade was not exempt from the stress and trying vicissitudes to which the commercial world at large was subjected during the past decade, and more particularly during that period of intensified depression extending from 1875 to 1879. Of course, allusion is made here more especially to the wholesale trade ; the members of the Retail Drug trade did not feel the effects of the all-prevailing lethargy to the same degree that dealers in most other lines of goods experienced, as commercial panics have no healing effect upon the ills that human flesh is heir to, and the sales of drugs and medicines are maintained at pretty much a normal standard.

It is, therefore, not to be wondered at that there should have been comparatively fewer failures among retail druggists than in some other branches of business. The wholesale druggist, however, does not depend solely upon the business done with retail druggists, a very large proportion of his trade lays with country general storekeepers. In a comparatively young country such as ours, especially in the more rural and recently settled districts, the ordinary country storekeeper has to keep such a varied assortment of goods as would astonish a city-bred shopman, and large numbers of this class of customers are to be found upon the books of the wholesale druggist, as buyers of crude and coarse drugs, such as castor oil, salts, senna, &c., of dye stuffs, patent medicines, and many other articles which are in daily demand at the counter of the country general merchant. This being the class of traders from whose ranks was recruited the largest contingent that went to form the vast army of insolvents enrolled during the years above alluded to, the wholesale drug trade suffered almost as severely as did the wholesale grocery, dry goods or hardware trades. Had the business been carried on under its usual conditions and in its old grooves, the effects of the depression upon the trade at large would not have been so severe in their character, but, unfortunately, the years leading up to 1870 had ushered in an epoch marked by an amount of unhealthy competition which served to empha-size the effects of the wide-spread depression as felt a few years later. Fortunately, the system of supply accounts has never obtained any degree of foothold in this trade, and although some few houses had pretty large interests which they had to nurse for a time, still the bulk of the trade had their risks well spread, and though for several years balances showed no increase, the trade may be congratulated upon the fact that none of the old familiar names have been wiped out by failure, but still exist to-day with unshorn laurels and undiminished vigour.

It is proper here to note that values did not shrink in sympathy with the depreciation that ruled in many lines of goods appertaining to other branches of trade. Prices as a rule were fairly maintained, and except in the case of a few important staples such as iodine, and the class of drugs into which iodine largely enters as a component part, there was compara-tively little fluctuation. The somewhat marked fluctuations in the case of the article named, however, were not so much due to the stringency of the times as to the effects of a combination among the manufactures of the article, which combination eventually fell through.

As already indicated the returns in the wholesale drug trade are not so large as they were ten or fifteen years ago. Within the period named, a number of new houses have embarked in the business, and the opinion is freely expressed that the number of wholesale houses is rather dispro-portioned to the amount of trade to be done. The more extended system of selling through travellers now in vogue, has added materially to the expense of doing business, and profits have been gradually getting smaller and smaller, owing to the efforts made by younger houses to secure trade by offering extraordinary inducements in the way of discounts much beyond the limits usual to the trade. To such propor-tions had this evil attained that a strong effort was made last fall to provide a remedy. A meeting of the trade was held in Montreal, at which a set of conditions and terms was agreed to, and a deputation sent to call on the western trade with reference to the matter met with a favourable reception, but the scheme fell through owing to one or two small patent medicine concerns, whom it was not originally contemplated to include in the combination, refusing to sign, and the evil still remains. To the uninitiated, the number of retailers, especially in the larger cities, would also seem to be much larger than occasion required, but such does not seem to be the case, and it is stated that the great bulk of the retail trade are in prosperous shape. It is curious to note in this connection that Montreal, with a population two-thirds larger than Toronto, has only forty-eight drug stores, while the latter city has some sixty, but this is accounted for by the fact that a number of the Toronto dealers have a large country trade and connection.

The tariff as recently amended has had little effect upon this branch of trade in the way of diverting the current of of trade from its usual channels. The great bulk of goods is still imported from Britain; the only kind of goods that can be imported profitably from the United States being those which are free by their tariff, principally drugs in their crude state, and some few articles that can be bought in bond. Dye stuffs are mostly imported from the United States, and the tariff has not affected the importation of these, as they are free here. In the general experience of the trade, the tariff has affected the business in patent medicines more than any other article. Formerly, all patent medicines came into Canada at a duty of 25 per cent., but by the new tariff the duty on liquid patent medicines was increased to 50 per cent., which to a certain extent is prohibitory on such goods. The result has been that many of the more popular of these articles are now manufactured here for the Canadian market, among the preparations thus made being Perry Davis' Pain-Killer, Radway's Remedies, St. Jacob's Oil, Vegetine, Dr. Ayer's Preparations, Green's August Flower, Kendal's Spavin Cure and many others. The Government, however, still derive some revenue from these, as duty-paid spirits have to be used in their preparation, upon which the Government receives the excise duty.

In conclusion, it may be stated that the volume of business has, for the past fifteen or eighteen months, been gradually increasing ; the amount of business done during the last six months of 1881 has been greater than that of any corresponding period in the experience of the trade, and if the unhealthy cutting in prices and terms now prevalent were only modified, there would be little to be desired.

Paints, &c.

In taking a backward glance, extending over the past ten years or so, it is worthy of remark that the record of commercial disaster, in connection with this particular branch of trade, is singularly slight, and is marked by no appalling run of failures such as some other lines were subject to during the trying years of depression, from which we have recently emerged. Of course, this interest is not of so prominent a character, nor does it assume the dimensions of some others, but even comparatively speaking, the proportion of failures in it has been small. Some smaller concerns of recent date, and of weak make-up as regards capital and the business qualities that go to form the elements necessary to success, have been obliged to go to the wall, but all the older houses— with the exception of one that retired from business—still remain. There is no doubt that the depression found some of these laden with heavier stocks than was altogether advisable, entailing a certain proportion of sacrifice and loss, but the bulk of the trade saw the days of tribulation coming, and trimmed their sails accordingly, successfully weathering the storms of commercial depression which have been so fraught with ruin and disaster to the business world at large. It must not be thought, however, that because failures among the trade have been few, that money has been generally made during the past decade ; such is not the case. Prior to 1875 fair profits were realized, but during the succeeding five years it is not to be supposed that balances showed any material gain. The spring of 1880 opened with favorable prospects, based largely upon the revival then becoming generally manifest, but, unfortunately, the trade at large, and more particularly manufacturers, have not realized the anticipations then formed, to any appreciable or marked degree. This is owing to an unhealthy competition and rivalry as regards prices, which are now being cut down dangerously fine, and this fact is causing serious apprehension to many in the trade, which it is to be hoped may lead to such a thought-ful discussion of the situation as may result in the effectual checking of the evil.

The manufacture of paints and colours in Canada has been consider-ably increased of late years, and it is a question with some if the industry does not now stand a chance of being overdone. The increase of duties upon foreign goods following the adoption of the new tariff, led to the establishment of some large manufacturing interests as well as to the extension of others already existing, and it is now considered by compe-tent authority that the home production of goods of this class has more than doubled within the last ten years. It may be queried however, with a fair show of reason, whether this particular interest is in a better position as regards outside competition than it was under the old tariff, or is benefitted to the same extent by the changed duties as some other branches of manufacture, as several of the ingredients entering into the composition of paints, &c., are themselves subjected to heavier duties, which fact goes to counterbalance the apparent better protection upon the manufactured article. Taking for instance one article, linseed oil, which is an essential component part in the preparation of white lead, paints, &c., we find that it is subject to a twenty-five per cent. duty, being the same as is charged upon foreign-made paints, which come into competi-tion with the product of our own paint factories. This is a matter, however, which the members of the trade have brought before Govern-ment, and hope to have remedied. Nearly all the prepared leads and paints used here are now made within the Dominion, as well as a fair proportion of dry colours ; mostly all the mineral ochres, lampblack, &c., are still imported. A duty has been placed upon Paris green in anticipa-tion of its being manufactured here, but the demand for this very dangerous article is uncertain, some houses have sold from forty to fifty tons of it in a season, but should the present all ubiquitous potatoe-bug disappear the sale would decline to a mere bagatelle. The principal centre for the manufacture of leads, paints, varnishes, &c., is at Montreal, where there are located about a dozen factories, out of the nineteen or twenty that the Dominion possesses. A factory for the manufacture of window glass, which is an important item entering into the make up of this trade, has recently been established at Napanee, in which neighbour-hood, it is stated, there are deposits of suitable sand, but all the other ingredients and chemicals have to be imported, and it will need close and careful management to enable the concern to make money in face of the advantages possessed by Belgium, whence we at present derive our prin-cipal supplies of this article. In Belgium, manufacturers have coal, sand and chemicals all at their doors, and even England, with all her advantages, cannot compete with Belgian makers of those grades of glass which enter most largely into common use.

FUR AND HAT INTEREST.

This line of trade being to a considerable extent made up of articles costly in their character, and that may almost be considered as luxuries, naturally felt the years of depression from which the country at large has recently emerged, to a greater extent than most others. Furs are unlike boots and shoes, the ordinary run of dry goods, or any other class of goods for which there is any normal demand. In times of depression, when tightness of money makes economy the rule, their term of usefulness is extended beyond the limits which would otherwise be allotted to them, and as the changes of mode and fashion do not very largely affect this class of wearing apparel, the furs which have already fulfilled their just mead of faithful service are compelled to perform a prolonged term of duty. However, with the clearing away of the dark shadows of commercial disaster, and the return of better times, this trade has, as a natural sequence, experienced the effects of the general revival to a correspondingly marked degree. Prior to the setting in of the bad times, fair profits were realized as a rule, but from 1874 or 1875 to 1880, it may be pretty fairly stated that there was very little money made in the wholesale fur trade. The latter date was the turning point, and in 1881 the demand for furs was unprecedented in the history of the country, and notwithstanding the largely increased competition—several new houses having recently engaged in the trade—the business of the year just closed has been singularly large and profitable. Such has been the demand for furs of all kinds, that several of our larger houses did not send their travellers out upon the usual sorting-up trip in the fall, as they found it almost impossible, even working their hands overtime, to keep up with the orders in hand.

The large and growing trade with the new Territories of Manitoba and the North-West is a marked and noticeable feature of late, and there is every expectation and prospect that the trade with this section will continue to increase, and become an important item in the business of future years, more particularly as the climate there is such as makes furs, more or less, an essential for winter wear.

The foregoing remarks apply more particularly to the manufacturing and wholesale trade, but retailers generally have felt the benefits attendant upon a free circulation of money as well, and report increased turnovers all around, although the unusually open fall seasons of the last two years have, no doubt, prevented sales attaining to the extent they would have, had winter set in when usually expected. Owing to this cause, some over-sanguine dealers who re-ordered largely upon the strength of active sales early in the season, may have to carry over more stock than they calculated on, to their own inconvenience, still, the position of the trade generally is vastly improved to what it was a few years ago, and there is much ground for hearty congratulation.

The recent tariff changes have not materially affected the fur trade. Raw or undressed furs continue to be admitted free of duty, while dressed furs, not made up, pay fifteen *per cent*. Of manufactured furs, which are subject to a twenty-five *per cent*. duty, none at all are imported from the United States, and only a very small quantity from Europe. Such as are imported are of a cheap variety of material, and inferior to domestic goods in quality as well as in general style and finish. The only exception to this general rule is in the case of fur-lined circulars, which, properly speaking, can hardly be classed with furs. The other goods imported are mainly the deep tippets and shoulder-capes with muffs to match, which have been so much worn of late, and which are made in London of some cheap fur, such as common hare (dyed black), these, with a few Astrakhan lamb jackets, may be said to comprise all the goods imported. Singularly enough it has not been the furriers who have imported these goods, but several leading retail dry goods men last year bought quite freely of them in England. It is understood the experiment, for so it may be called, has hardly proved a success, and there is very little prospect of future importations attaining any degree of importance, a state of affairs with which our furriers are not likely to be displeased. Our own tradesmen in this line have a knowledge of the requirements created by our peculiar climate, which no foreign manufacturer can be expected to have, and in point of taste and general excellence of manufacture, they are not surpassed by any country. Americans in want of furs prefer as a rule to buy from dealers here, and a very considerable number of Canadian-made fur coats, sacques, &c., have found their way across the lines, notwithstanding the very high duty to which this class of goods are subject under the American tariff.

Aside from the foregoing remarks, which indicate the varying conditions of the trade for the past few years, it may be interesting to a good many to know something with regard to the sources from which we draw our main supplies of furs, and some of the more important facts in connection therewith. Taking the prominent item of buffalo robes, we learn that comparatively few have found their way East of late years, and in 1881 the Hudson Bay Company did not sell any upon the Montreal market. The few that were sold came through American sources, and for a pair of untrimmed robes as high as twenty-five dollars was asked, a price so high as to put them beyond the reach of most people wanting them. This dearth of buffalo robes here is accounted for, partly by the growing scarcity of the buffalos themselves, but more largely by the increasing demand for them in our new Territories of the North-West, that is to say in the land of the buffalo itself, where, the ever-increasing emigration absorbs the supply of robes, the severe winter climate rendering them a necessity, more particularly in travelling. To meet this scarcity something else had to be found that would supply the place of the traditional buffalo robe, and that could be sold at a comparatively low price. Wolf skins, from which a good many robes used to be made, are virtually out of the market, as the poisoning of this animal has been actively prosecuted in the West of late years, and the Hudson's Bay Co.'s list of November 1881 shows that only 1,458 wolf skins were to be offered at their January '82 sale; bear skins are too expensive to be generally used for this purpose, so the choice fell on Japanese goat skins, which are now largely made up into sleigh robes and rugs, no less than 150,000 of these goat skins having been imported last year. Seal and Persian lamb continue to be the furs most in demand for personal wear, though prices have continued to advance of late years. The bulk of the Persian,

Bokhara and Astrakhan lambskins formerly imported into Canada, used to be bought from the great fur houses of Leipsig, Germany, but of more recent years our buyers have penetrated into the producing districts themselves, and large quantities are now brought direct from Nijni-Novgorod, and the more Eastern Provinces of Russia, whence are also obtained large quantities of squirrel skins for linings, &c. Seal and sea otter, most largely furnished by Alaska, are bought by our merchants principally in London, but the latter fur is now so costly as to be beyond the common reach, skins sold at the spring sales of 1881 in London, realizing an average of twenty pounds apiece. A large number of otter skins are sent to China, where they are used to make the *button*, or insignia of rank of the Mandarin, which may account in some degree for their costliness. Strange as it may seem, nearly all our native furs are sent away for foreign consumption, while we import foreign furs for our own use. All our mink, fox and beaver skins go to Europe, though a good many of the latter find their way to us, after being dressed, dyed and with long white hairs sewn in them, as plucked otter. The generally prevalent idea that the beaver is about exterminated, does not seem to hold, as upon reference to the Hudson Bay Co.'s circular of November last, we find that they then had 107,000 to offer, while Sir Curtis Lampson and other extensive dealers had large quantities also. About the only fur of which we import any quantity from the United States is raccoon, which is used for making coats, our own native raccoon, which is much finer than the American, being used principally for trimmings.

The remarks made at the opening of this sketch with regard to the fluctuating conditions of the fur trade for the last ten years or so, and the recent notable improvement, apply with almost equal force to the hat trade, a line of business usually linked very closely with the fur interest. The tariff, as amended, has also done something to increase the production of domestic made goods ; we are not now so largely dependent upon outside sources for our supplies in this line, and our importations, particularly from the States, are not so extensive as they were. The finer grades of felt hats, such as fine hards, half stiffs, and fine soft felts, continue to be largely imported, the first mentioned from England, and the latter two from the States. A number, however, of our leading retailers have lately been making a fine quality of fur-felt hats, much in demand, and known as the "pullover," themselves, importing the felt in an unfinished state, and shaping and finishing the hat here. Of silk hats, which have lately gone much out of wear, a fair quantity is also made here, but as a good many who still affect this particular style of head gear, will wear nothing but a "Christie" or a "Lincoln & Bennett," some silk hats of English make continue to be imported. Of fine fur-felt hat factories, we have at present only one in operation, being the Canada Felt Hat Company of Hamilton. Messrs. James Coristine & Company, of Montreal, have a factory for this class of goods fitted up and ready for operation, but owing to temporary labour complications it is laying idle. Of the medium and cheaper grades of felt hats, into the composition of which wool enters principally, large quantities are made in Canada, the production having been much increased the last few years. The factories engaged in this business are located as follows :—Three in Montreal, one in Hamilton, one in Newmarket, one in Marieville, Que., and one in Truro, N. S.

To summarize and conclude ; while the past of the fur and hat trade, say from 1875 to 1880, has been generally lacking in profit to those engaged in it, the present is prosperous, and the future, as far as it can be at present gauged, promising. The late setting in of winter last year may cause some retailers to carry over more stock than they would like to, and thus lessen the sales, of wholesalers next season, but with a continuance of good times, the demand will continue active, and prices remain good.

Paper Interest.

Contrary to the generally received belief, the manufacture of paper in Canada is not an industry of even comparatively recent origin and growth, but its first inception dates as far back as the opening decade of the present century, a period at which our native industries were naturally few in number, and limited in their scope and general character. It is nevertheless a matter of record that Messrs. Mears, Wall & Jackson, a firm of Americans, commenced the building of a paper mill at the village of St. Andrew's, in the then Province of Lower Canada, in 1804, and paper was made therein in 1805. The mill was subsequently bought in 1807, by a Mr. Brown, who ran it for twenty-five years, only shutting down upon the expiry of the lease of the water privilege. The second mill was, as nearly as can be ascertained, built in the County of Portneuf, on the Jacques Cartier River, in 1810 or thereabout. The first mill to run in the West, was built by the Hon. James Crooks at Flamboro, near Hamilton, while Nova Scotia boasts of having had one at Bedford, near Halifax, some seventy years ago.

Though so early established, the development of this industry was by no means rapid, but, on the contrary, was of a very gradual character until comparatively recent years. The very early mills alluded to made, as a rule, only coarse wrapping papers, but as years advanced and the country grew, the manufacture of news, print and book papers was gone into somewhat extensively, until at the time of writing this industry has attained such an importance, that there is a fair prospect of the local demand for all qualities of paper, except writing papers of the finest and most expensive grades, being filled nearly altogether by Canadian mills.

It may here be stated as a fact of interest, that up to a year after the Confederation of the British North American Provinces, all the paper used by publishers in the Provinces of Nova Scotia, New Brunswick and Prince Edward Island, was imported from Belgium. This was of a very inferior quality, heavily loaded with clay, and the total yearly importation did not much exceed $30,000. Upon the consummation of Confederation, the paper-makers of the Upper Provinces went into the field, and aided by the heavier duties imposed under the new Dominion tariff, secured the trade, supplying a better article at fair prices, and have ever since retained the business of the district.

The years which witnessed the closing scenes of the American war were exceedingly profitable ones to Canadian paper-makers, and the recollection of those palmy days of active business and handsome returns still lingers gratefully in the memory of those who were then, and are still, engaged in the trade. A number of the American mills had been destroyed during the war, while others had failed or were closed down, so that the demand was larger than the mills running could well supply, and common news print was worth *twenty cents* a pound and over. Of course, allowance must be made for the then greatly depreciated currency, and the heavy duties on goods going into the States, still there was money in it for Canadian makers, and considerable quantities of paper were sent into the American market at prices netting large profits. Some idea may be formed of the extent of the trade then done in this direction, when it is stated that a first sample order from a large Boston firm to one of our prominent mills amounted to some $24,000.

This, together with the generally prevalent prosperity in our own country, naturally led to the extension of the interest, and during the years from 1865 to 1873, a number of new mills were projected and built, at Newburg, Napanee, Joliette, Kingsey Falls and other points, until at the last-named date there were in all thirty paper mills in active operation throughout Canada. Despite the consequent largely increased production, the supply did not seem in excess of the demand, prices during the period designated were very fairly maintained, and yearly balances evidenced substantial gains ; indeed, such was the belief in the money-making possibilities of the trade, that in one case parties were found willing to be charged interest at the pretty round rate of from twenty to twenty-five per cent. upon money borrowed to invest in the erection of a paper mill, and this at so late a date as the year 1873. It is needless, however, to state, that even a paper mill cannot sustain such a load of interest and survive, and in this particular instance, after a brief proprietorship of about two years, the original projectors of the mill had to give up the struggle and the works passed into other hands.

Confining ourselves more particularly to the past decade, we find that the years 1871, 1872 and 1873 were those yielding the best returns to the trade at large, fair profits being the rule in all grades of paper and general stationery goods. The years dating from 1876 to 1880 were those most unfavourable to the interests of the trade ; the all-pervading depression seriously affected the demand, and prices dropped till margins became excessively narrow ; losses by bad debts were alarmingly frequent, the smaller country printers being a notoriously weak, long-winded class of risks, and the situation, thus bad enough in itself, was still further aggravated by the fact that American makers sought an outlet for their surplus in the Dominion at such prices as tended to completely demoralize the already much weakened market. This combination of adverse effects resulted in a tension and strain which most effectually tested the strength and resources of all engaged in the trade, and revealed all the weaknesses of the feebler concerns, not a few in this latter category being driven to the wall. The following figures will clearly illustrate the vastly altered condition of the trade in 1878 and 1879, as compared to what it was in the prosperous days closing with 1873 and 1874. At the last-mentioned date, as already stated, there were in operation, in various localities of the Dominion, thirty paper mills, representing an investment in buildings, plant and machinery of $1,960,000, with a stock to the value of something over $1,000,000, bringing the total capital involved, up to rather more than $3,000,000. In 1878 and 1879, of these thirty mills, *ten* had actually failed, with a resulting loss of $550,000 ; *seven*, representing a locked-up capital of $280,000, were idle, while *thirteen*, with an estimated capital of $1,910,000, were in operation. It is thus considered that there had been a total shrinkage of between twenty-five and thirty per cent. in value of assets between these two dates, or in other words, that from $800,000 to $900,000 had been sunk and dissipated by various firms in the interim five years.

At the period when the effects of intensified competition among manufacturers was most keenly felt, an effort was made to effect a combination to regulate the price of news print—the line most subject to cutting—to newspaper men and publishers. The arrangement, however, was only partial in its character, several mills declining to come in, and the articles of association, &c., were so lax in their provisions, that manufacturers of elastic conscience, while observing the letter of the agreement could in various ways evade its spirit and still not render themselves amenable to the penalties provided for non-observance. The combination was, therefore, one in name only, and it died a natural death in the course of a few months.

The year 1880 witnessed the turn of the tide, and the dawn of returning activity. The wave of general trade revival which had spread all over the United States, before its influences had been appreciably felt by us, had created there a largely increased consumption of paper, more particularly news print, and makers were unable to meet the demand from the simple fact, that so suddenly had the rush of orders set in, that the necessary paper stock was not to be had. Prices of ordinary news print advanced from 6½ cents per lb. to 10 cents and over, and all quarters were ransacked for paper stock at fancy prices. Canadian makers took advantage of the situation, and, notwithstanding the heavy duties, were able to send considerable quantities of paper into the States, and realize reasonable returns. This little " boom," however, was not of long duration, the dearth of paper stock in the States was soon remedied, supplies pouring in from all quarters ; prices there resumed their normal condition, and our manufacturers were again restricted to the supplying of the Dominion's wants. The ball, however, had been set rolling, and trade conditions have continued to improve. Mills that were formerly idle have resumed work, some new ones have already been built, while several others are projected and even in course of erection. At the present moment there are actually in operation throughout Canada thirty-two mills, representing an estimated capital of $2,880,000, while three more are building, or about being built, involving an outlay of $320,000, the most important of these being an extensive mill now in course of erection at Cornwall, where it is contemplated making fine papers. It is well to understand that what are called " pulp mills " are included above. While these, properly speaking, can hardly be called paper mills, still their product is essential to the regular paper maker, most of whom have heretofore made their own wood pulp, but latterly there is an apparent disposition to separate the two processes into distinct industries. These pulp mills, of which several have lately been built, convert several kinds of soft wood, such as basswood, spruce, poplar, &c., by grinding or by boiling with chemicals under pressure, into "pulp," which, mixed with varying proportions of rag stock at the paper mill to give texture, &c., is turned out in all the different grades of news and book papers. Quite an amount of this wood pulp is already shipped to the States, and it is proposed by some of the newer mills to try and open up a market for their product in Europe. Similar mills in Norway are sending pulp to Britain, and with the large quantities of suitable wood, readily accessible, which Canada possesses, it is argued that there is no reason why we should not secure a share of the trade.

The present outlook indicates fair prospects for a steady trade with moderate profits. The existing capacity for manufacturing is fully equal to the present consumption, but an increased demand is anticipated for coarse papers to meet the growing requirements of sugar factories, cotton mills, and other manufacturing industries which are springing into active existence. It is also expected that after this year, when new mills are built, and improvements in existing ones are completed, that there will be a material falling off in the importation of the cheaper grades of writing papers, which can then be profitably bought at home.

The position of this branch of trade with regard to tariff charges is not materially altered from what it was before the last change of Government. A duty of twenty per cent. is still levied upon printing papers, calendered and writing papers have an additional protection of two and one-half per cent. The only important tariff change in which the trade is interested, is the altered classification of patent medicine almanacs and pamphlets, which at one time were classified as "*literature*," and admitted free, an evident injustice to our paper men and printers, when it is considered with what immense quantities of this class of *literature* the country is flooded. This item to the uninitiated may seem insignificant, but there is no exaggeration in saying that many tons of paper are used annually in the production of these advertising pamphlets. The existing arrangement provides for a duty upon these, which remedies the disadvantages of which our paper manufacturers and printers heretofore complained.

Leather and Boot and Shoe Manufacturing Interests.

It is estimated that the Leather Trade has doubled its size and importance in the Dominion since 1870. The growth of production has been aided most materially by power manufacturing, and the consumption seems to have pretty well kept pace with the former, except at periods during the past decade when the boot and shoe interest was upon an overstrained basis, and when superfluous houses created stocks out of proportion to the needs of the country.

Many tanneries have been erected since 1870, their output being largely in what is known as black or upper leather. Some new sole leather tanneries have also been built, and others enlarged and improved. During the depressed periods referred to, the supply of leather was largely in excess of healthful demand, and the pressure of stock upon the markets of our country led to the liberal giving of credit to, and the encouragement of weak boot and shoe houses. It also led to the practice of consigning large parcels to the European markets, the realization of these being often attended with loss and disappointment. The goods so consigned and experiencing such loss, being principally common black leathers ; sole leather made from foreign hides has sold more profitably, being handled by fewer and stronger houses who controlled large resources.

The years witnessing the best profits in the leather manufacturing business were those of 1871, 1872, 1873 and 1874, the worst years for the interest being those including 1875 and extending to the end of 1879.

During the depressed years in this line of trade, it was, as a rule, treated with liberality by the banks which carried the respective accounts. In 1875, and particularly in the spring of 1878 and through 1879, when about a million dollars of dead loss must have been made by our tanners and leather merchants, many accounts were supported which must otherwise have failed to retrieve their exceptional losses, but by bank advice and advances, prominent handlers of material pulled through, and have since rapidly reduced their liabilities and are making money.

At the end of 1879, the general effect created by the troublous times through which the interest had passed, resulted in a contraction for some time, of the leather consumption of the country. A shortening of credits to weaker houses also followed. During 1881, it is estimated that over fifty per cent. of the leather buyers paid cash, or thirty days, for material, and the trade was in a normal condition, save that in common black leathers the supply was still largely in excess of the demand, and these goods were consequently sold without profit.

Among the staples in this line are Spanish sole leather, so named because the hides used, come chiefly from the Spanish-American districts, slaughter sole, which is made from domestic or slaughter-house hides, black leather, upper or cow hide, buff, pebble, patent, enamel, &c., &c. In 1875, sole leather ruled low in price, and is usually one of the most speculative of the staples. In 1876 it was high, as also in 1879. Black leather was at the lowest point in 1877–78, domestic hides being low also. Early in 1880 Spanish sole leather was high but fell gradually from 29 to about 25 cents, where it remained in the fall of 1881. This is about the nominal price. Other leathers followed this article and steadily fell off with it, about 15 per cent. ; remaining fairly steady, the tendency being however, downward, owing solely to over-production. At the opening of 1882 the outlook was very fair for the interest, very few failures having occurred in the shoe business, and a fair year is looked forward to. Values are expected to hold, and should the result of the boot and shoe manufacturing business be up to the mark, a good output of leather will be realized.

During 1875, the manufacturing of boots and shoes received a severe check by frequent failure and because of a grossly overdone state of business. Again, in subsequent years, the interest was plunged into a fearful condition of doubt and uncertainty because of the same surroundings. The industry rallied from time to time in the most surprising manner, only to be set back again and again by natural forces, and it was not until the spring of 1880 that it could be said to have before it a future which promised sound conditions. Heavy losses were sustained by the leather trade through this over-extension of business among the shoe manufacturers, these losses culminating at three periods, notably, 1875, 1878 and 1879, though intermediate drops occurred. In 1881 the number of manufacturers swept out of existence in previous years were found to be pretty well made up by the addition of new factories, but these were encouraged because of the good turn which had come to the general commerce of the Dominion. There is, however, grave doubt if the interest be not again in an abnormal state, owing to the large number of small manufacturers which have sprung up in the suburbs of Montreal and Quebec, and which number, particularly about Quebec, is being constantly added to.

There is, on the whole, a better feeling at the opening of the present year, 1882, for though margins in some trade connections are narrow, and competition in certain lines great, the country stocks are low as a rule, payments are good, almost too good, and there is a greater outlet than for many years before.

The production of the two cities, Montreal and Quebec, is now at the rate of about $6,000,000 per annum, in a wholesale way. It is divided about as follows :—Montreal produces about $4,000,000, and Quebec about $2,000,000. The low wages paid at the latter point and the adaptability of the French-Canadian employés of both sexes to the work, is perhaps destined to work up for Quebec, a proportion of the business in certain makes which may in time overshadow Montreal, and it is at the ancient capital that the greater number of small manufacturers have been started.

CORDAGE, SAIL AND BAG MANUFACTURING INTERESTS.

The staples in the cordage line of trade are chiefly Manilla, Sisal, Russia and Jute cordage. The imports of manufactured goods from the United States have never been very large, though the raw material imports have been. Such goods as were imported, after being manufactured, were of the Manilla cordage class.

Previous to 1876, the profits realized in this line were very fair, but from that time to 1881, margins were close and business was curtailed, competition also affected the returns, and for several years the trade was not in a hopeful condition. Even during 1881, profits were not in satisfactory proportions, as competing houses continued producing more goods than were readily absorbed by the country.

There are at present, four manufacturers of cordage in the Dominion, and it is estimated that the two leading concerns could easily supply the whole country, and if run to their full capacity, they might even create a surplus of stock.

The outlook is, however, more favourable at the opening of 1882, the demand has increased during 1881, and the amount turned out and actually worked off, represents larger figures than was attained to, even prior to 1876. The demand for Manilla hemp, notably, has increased, and is likely to continue enlarging, as the requirements for one line alone —twine for self-binding harvesters—is consuming an immense amount of raw material. In this regard one concern bought during the late fall for future delivery, some sixty tons, valued at about $18,000.

During the summer months of 1881, there was a sharp rise in the value of hemp. Prices jumping from £40 to £41 in the old country to

£44 on the spot, and advanced some £3 more within thirty days. The explanation being, that many American and other farmers prefer it to the wire which has been used in binding corn, and began to buy it direct from the place of production. Stimulated by continued strong advices then, from Manilla and from America, the markets advanced as stated during the early summer months, and lots of 3,000, 6,000 and 7,000 bales were disposed of at from £47 5s. to £48 5s. for later delivery. Sisal also shared in the general improvement, sales of 6,000 bales being made at £29 10s. in London and Liverpool. Mauritius strengthening to £38.

The sail and bag industries are more or less affected by the condition of our shipping interests and our carrying trade. Many of our steamer lines now use their own bags, and do not have to buy at our ports, while our shipping interest from several causes already described, has shewn a falling off during the past year, 1881. It is believed that another season will see this shrinkage made up, and interests largely dependent upon it will then improve.

Jewellery Interest.

During 1871, 1872, 1873, 1874 and 1875, this line of trade experienced satisfactory returns, but inasmuch as it dealt in articles of luxury, it subsequently felt the weight of the depression to an extreme degree. It continued dull and open to large losses through 1876, 1877, 1878 and 1879, but in 1880 commenced to rally, until in 1881 the interest got back into the old, sound and profitable grooves.

Of all the years of the depression, the year 1878 witnessed the greatest general disturbance in this line, its losses by bad debts was the chief cause of distress, and this was supplemented by the diminished turnovers resulting from inability upon the part of individuals to gratify their tastes, or to indulge in expense not strictly necessary to their comfort.

Though the times did thus affect this interest, values continued pretty firm in the main among the staples, such as gold chains, watches, clocks, diamonds and sterling service ware; diamonds notably holding their own, and really gaining in value, while they were the only article for which the demand was comparatively steady, and though this may seem paradoxical, they found purchasers nearly as quickly through the darkest years of our late troubles, as they did in 1872. Since the early part of the past decade, the diamond turnover of the country has increased nearly 30 per cent., though the sale of other unset precious stones has been materially reduced through the imposition of a 20 per cent. duty on unset stones, which prevents home manufacturers from finishing and setting in competition with foreign countries. The principle reason for the maintenance of the diamond trade in all years, whether depressed or otherwise, would seem to lay in the fact that the investment not only pleases the taste, but is a sound one in a realizable sense, values instead of diminishing, rather tend upward, and the same people who bought them in former years, have all along—though comparatively few in number—been able to buy as though there were no depression.

During the dull years named, this trade was singularly open to losses through the failures and easy settlements of their country customers under the Act of 1875. Feeling competition more keenly than most lines, it was harrassed continually by compositions granted to unworthy traders, or by the favorable purchases of insolvent stocks for the insolvent who could not get a discharge, and who immediately began to realize upon the margin he ought never to have had conceded to him. With the natural turnover lessened greatly all over the country, these traders rendered it impossible for the solvent jeweller to get a profit, or in many cases to keep whole, and the injury done to the general trade in this connection was severe.

Nearly one-fifth of the total turnover in this line of business is made up of gold chains—chains, which are a leading staple, are now being largely made in the Dominion, and meet with a good demand. Since the new tariff, the manufacture of plated ware has been inaugurated at Hamilton and Montreal with success, the establishments at both points being identical in interest, and likely to develop well.

It is gratifying to be able to state, however, that the demand for sterling ware is increasing. These goods are more generally appreciated, and there is being experienced a considerable importation from the States of such lines as the Gorham make, while the patterns and general make-up of English manufacture are not now in as great favor as formerly.

The best ordinary goods in the clock line are mostly brought from the States, while the higher-priced makes come from France and Germany, the work in both the latter countries being of superior quality. The American makes of watches in medium-priced grades, together with the Swiss products, meet with the largest sale, the English common watch being a poor affair. The best English goods are highly prized, but are almost out of the market owing to the cost.

It is estimated that watches of American manufacture now make up half the total sales. The cheaper Swiss watches the balance, and also find their way to the States largely.   More English goods would be sold in Canada were the English manufacturers to aim at getting out a good watch at medium rates.

The competition in the general jewellery line is now getting keener each year.   It is believed that 1882 will see the trade grossly overdone, but as long as bad debts are avoided, our best known houses will continue to keep the lead, and with increased turnovers will gain.   The legitimate wholesaler usually makes a good living as long as his accounts are well culled.   The retailer, if he possesses a practical knowledge of how his wares are put together, and has a repairing or manufacturing department in his store will always make a living in the worst of times, it being granted that he is temperate and attentive.

Sewing Machine Manufacturing Interest.

The invention of the sewing machine has created an important industry in the world. It has led up to the development of much native genius, and to the education of skilled workmanship.

The changes in this industry have, however, been proportionately as great as in other lines of business; successive new ideas and the abolition of old principles, have had their effect in promoting changes and new administrations in the sewing machine world. With manufacturers of these useful goods it has certainly been a race to keep in the van of onward progress, and the central truth that only the fittest should and generally do survive, has found its exemplification among them.

Out of some fifteen manufacturers only some seven or eight now exist. Concerns with lack of enterprise, watered capitals, lack of brain fertility, and poor detail management, have been forced to concentrate, retire or amalgamate. The immense turnout of 1872, 1873 and 1874 has seen its outcome in the paralyzation of the class alluded to, until at the present date we have only some five makes of sewing machines which can be called deserving of every recommendation, and are at the same time popular with the people.

The "Wanzer," "Williams'," "Raymond," "Lawlor," and the "Osborn," seem to lead the march of improvement in all their features, and where others are attempted, they have not sufficiently developed their prospects to admit of a close prophecy as to the future in store for them, and their progress has been interfered with to a certain extent by changes which have kept them out of the first rank.

The palmy days of the sewing machine manufacturing interest seem to have occurred during the first five years of the past decade. The succeeding years, 1876, 1877, 1878 and 1879, were close as to gains, and more generally unsatisfactory ; the depression marking its record here as well as in other enterprises.

The conditions under which machines are being sold, through the force of heavy competition, has cut the business of some of the junior concerns considerably, and imposes a great deal of detail care upon the larger ones. The instalment plan of payments is responsible for this, and as the pressure of stocks grow greater, the necessity for realization has forced down the deposits upon purchases, until the hazard in some sections of the country is altogether larger than a sound policy would seem to warrant. The business is consequently requiring the most skilful and attentive management, and any flaw in this is felt more seriously than it would have been years ago. Better terms of payment should be arranged upon by combined action if possible, or the general position of this interest will be one of more or less disadvantage.

One of the leading manufacturing houses, the "Williams'," has extended its facilities greatly within a short time, its works at the Tanneries, in Montreal suburbs, are most complete, and it is said that the Company contemplate the further extension of works at Plattsburgh, N.Y., where they propose to invest something over $100,000 to that end. A large amount of means is employed by the different concerns in this line at Montreal and in the West, and as our population increases, wider avenues for the home output of machines will present themselves. It is to be remembered, however, that a very large proportion of Canadian-made machines find a ready sale in foreign markets, where they compete successfully with the best American makes, and the names of our largest manufacturers are well and favourably known in Europe, South America, and even still more distant Australia and Cape of Good Hope.

Liquor and Brewing Interests.

It is difficult, if not impossible, to review this line of business in detail during the depression, and, at the same time, comment fairly and justly upon its phases for the period. This consciousness then, particularly at this time, requires that the sketch should be brief and general in its deductions.

The best years the liquor interest experienced during the past decade, were those of 1870, 1871 and 1872, the Franco-Prussian war aiding the gains. Directly after this, losses were made in heavy proportions, the consumption of some brands fell off, and forced sales narrowed results, until the business paid some of the largest sellers but very limited gains after travelling and advertising expenses were defrayed. Heavy stocks had also accumulated through the force of the inflation of trade in the first years of this period, this being fostered by the trade policy—if not necessity, of granting long and large credits.

The widest fluctuations probably occurred in 1875 and 1876 for wines, and in 1877 and 1878 for French wines and spirits. These were largely caused by varying opinions as to probable production, but prices hardened eventually, some considerable advance being secured owing to a succession of poor vintages, and values still continue firm in some specialties because of this.

The opinion as expressed by some authorities in the trade, is to the effect that the new tariff is inimical to the general interest. It is called irksome, and likely to diminish, in dull periods, the sale of many foreign wines and spirits, though these parties admit that it must encourage the consumption of domestic manufactures, such as native wines, &c. This might be well, perhaps, but there appears to be good ground for the fear that high duties upon wines and spirits, as in cases of other luxuries, may result in the creation of imitations, and, in the end, flood the markets with goods made out of high wines and flavored with essences. There is no doubt, however, but that the consumption of ale, porter and lager beer will increase, because of the cheaper cost, such increase being at the cost of the spirit trade. Apparently, then, there is but one condition which confidently promises satisfactory results to the general liquor trade, i. e., continued prosperity and good gains in general trade interests. This condition being present will, so long as it is felt, still carry with it a pretty certain demand for higher priced wines and spirits.

Our malt liquor interest is in excellent position. We are well represented in this line by old and favorite makers, their output is large and returns good, and there is every promise of an increase in the dimensions of the trade.

The following is a return for the past four fiscal years, by lbs., covering the amount of malt consumed in manufacturing processes, &c. :

	Manufactured during the Year.	*Taken for Consumption.*
1878	48,229,293 lbs	26,534,587 lbs.
1879	46,291,230 "	27,795,037 "
1880	58,940,565 "	28,902,354 "
1881	45,290,500 "	

Total revenue accrued, including license fees, $1,616,220. It may be interesting to add that the revenue derived from this head is not so large for these four years as that obtained from tobacco in its various forms in *one* year, the figures for the latter, in 1881, being $1,717,630.

TOBACCO.

The record of the tobacco trade of Canada for the past ten years has been, on the whole, of an uneventful character, and unmarked by any very special or striking features. The production of manufactured goods in this line has, of course, increased, but only so far as to keep pace with the augmented demand as developed with the growth of the country, no fresh markets having been opened to our manufacturers. Taking the average for the last three years as furnished by the Custom House statistics, the amount of raw leaf imported (included in which is cigar leaf) is about 8,700,000 lbs. per annum, an amount not greatly in excess of the importations of previous years. The number of factories has not been added to of late, but several of the larger ones have greatly extended their facilities, the increase of manufacturing capacity thus afforded being sufficiently ample to meet any legitimate demand that can at present be put upon it, and, indeed, among manufacturers themselves the complaint is common that there are too many in the business. All told, and even including several very small concerns, the tobacco factories of Canada number eighteen, located as follows : seven in Montreal, two in Halifax, three in Quebec, and one each in Charlottetown, Pictou, N.S., Toronto, Hamilton, Paris and Windsor. The great bulk of the goods made is in the form of plug tobacco in all its various grades, from black chewing to bright smoking, but cut smoking tobaccos, snuff and fine cut chewing tobaccos are also produced in fair quantities. Most of our manufacturers have certain lines for which they have a special reputation, and on which they run largely, this is noticeably the case with Mr. W. C. McDonald of Montreal, whose black tobaccos have met most widely the popular taste, though the Adams Tobacco Company, and one or two others have their own peculiar processes, and turn out a class of goods in this line which meet with a large amount of favour, and a very considerable sale. In bright smoking tobaccos, the " Myrtle Navy " brand, made by Messrs. Tuckett & Billings, of Hamilton, is generally considered to take the lead in this class of goods, and probably has a more extended sale than any other brand of similar quality, though frequent efforts have been made by other manufacturers to produce a smoking tobacco that would equally please the popular palate. These efforts, though meeting with varying success, have not been unavailing, as it is generally conceded that a much better class of smoking tobaccos are now turned out than were made a few years ago.

In fine cut chewing tobacco the Globe tobacco Company of Windsor and Detroit, figure prominently, as well as in cut smoking tobaccos, of which latter D. Ritchie of Montreal, J. Lemesurier & Sons of Quebec, and a few others are considerable manufacturers. In this last department, however, there has been some diminution of production this last year or two, as the law compelling the putting up of cut tobaccos in small packages has been complained of as irksome by several manufacturers, who have given up making this class of goods. Very many of the present generation look upon snuff-taking as an almost ancient habit gone out of vogue, but very large quantities of snuff are still manufactured, altogether in Montreal and Quebec, and it will probably be surprising to many people to learn that the annual production of snuff in these two cities is close on to *one hundred and ten tons.* The figures as given in the blue book for September, 1880 (no later ones being available), show that for the year ending at above date, no less than 218,000 lbs. of snuff went into consumption. The manufacture of this article calls for the most scrupulous care in all its processes of grinding, sweating, &c., and the flavouring or scenting has to be very accurately performed to suit the varied tastes of the consumer. The most expensive perfumes enter into its compositions, the costly attar of roses, worth more than its weight in gold, is imported specially from the far East to scent the finer grades, which require from four to six months in their preparation.

In the way of foreign competition our manufacturers have little to contend with. The specific duty of twenty-five cents per lb., with an *ad valorem* duty of 12½ cents added thereto, almost effectually shuts out foreign made goods. There are some few fancy brands of American tobaccos, such as Paces plug and Durham smoking mixtures, which find their way into Canada, but the demand for these goods is very limited, and it is estimated that the total yearly importation would not reach 25,000 lbs., an amount too small to be in any way felt. It will thus be seen that outside competition can have no effect on prices and profits, but the internal competition, that is the competition among our own manufacturers, is so keen, that for a good many years past prices have been cut exceedingly fine, and except on standard brands, which have a name and reputation, there is at present a comparatively small margin of profit. From 1870 to 1874 competition was not carried to such extremes as in more recent years. In the latter year (1874) prices went up some twenty cents a pound in bond, owing to a scarcity of leaf in the United States, and as Canadian manufacturers had all laid in their stocks before the rise, the year's operations resulted in handsome profits to all engaged in the trade. This is the one exceptional year of the decade as regards good profits; since then fine cutting of prices has been the rule, till, at the moment of writing, it is considered that the limit in this direction has been reached.

There is one phase of the tobacco trade, particularly affecting the Province of Quebec, which has been yearly growing in importance, and which is at present exciting the earnest attention of manufacturers, and that is the increasing growth of native Canadian tobacco, and the terms (most unfavourable to manufacturers) upon which the Government allow farmers to grow, cure and sell the home grown article. The growing of Canadian tobacco in the Province of Quebec has developed amazingly for the last few years, at one time each *habitant* was content to raise in a little corner of his garden sufficient for his own wants, but now very large areas are planted, fields of ten or more acres are not uncommon, and some growers are known to have harvested some 50,000 pounds, while holders of from 25,000 to 30,000 pounds are quite numerous. The Government allows the farmer to take out a free licence, that is a licence for which he pays nothing, to cure and manufacture this tobacco into rolls, and to sell it upon affixing stamps, which he buys the same as postage stamps, at the rate of four cents a pound. The manufacturer, if he wishes to buy this tobacco and work it up in his factory, has to pay *twenty cents* a pound excise, the same as upon American leaf; or if he chooses to go to the expense of fitting up a separate and distinct

factory, in which to work up this Canadian leaf, he can take out a
separate licence, which is not *free* to him, and he can manufacture it in
these separate premises by paying *sixteen cents* a pound excise. This,
the manufacturers claim, and with some reason, is most unfair to them,
especially now that the production of this native tobacco has reached such
dimensions, it being estimated by parties who have been examining into
the matter, that there is now annually grown close on to three millions of
pounds, and though the greater portion is imperfectly cured, and coarse
and rank in flavour, yet, owing to its great cheapness—being sold at from
fifteen to twenty-five cents a pound—its consumption is largely increasing,
even among the better class, to the serious detriment of the regular manufacturer. It is further urged that there is no efficient check against fraud
upon the part of the producer, there being few excise officers in the country
parts; there is no method of cancelling the stamps when affixed to the
rolls, and it is positively asserted that the same stamps are used more
than once, the farmer buying them back from the storekeeper at half
rates. The matter has assumed such dimensions and importance, that
several manufacturers are moving in the premises, and endeavouring to
bring about some concerted action on the part of all interested in the
trade, and it is more than probable that a strongly supported petition
will shortly be presented to Government, urging the serious consideration
of the whole question relating to tobacco duties.

CROCKERY INTEREST.

The mutations to which this line of business has been subject, during the past ten years, have been not a few, and some of these changes are of quite an important character.   The current of trade in many lines of goods, has been diverted into altogether different channels from those in which it used formerly to flow, and the location of the source of supply has altered.   A very considerable number of leading articles which help materially to form the make up of this trade, and which have hitherto been imported from Great Britain, Germany and the United States, are now largely made within our own borders, and under the existing tariff, the prospects are that the proportion of goods of this class, made in Canada, will be increased.   The cheaper grades of crockery, such as Rockingham, Cane, " C C," and white granite wares, which were formerly imported altogether from Great Britain, are now largely made in St. Johns, Que., and Montreal.   There is at the present date (1881) six potteries engaged in the manufacture of these goods, which find a ready market.   Among other staple articles in this trade, are coal oil lamps, lamp chimneys, burners and wicks, fruit jars, goblets, and glass table ware, all of which are now made largely here.   Lamps are made at Montreal and at New Glasgow, N.S.   But as yet only the cheap lines have been attempted, the more expensive goods being still imported.   Of chimneys, a very small proportion is now imported from Germany or the United States, the glass factories at Montreal, Hamilton and New Glasgow now turning out large quantities of an excellent quality.   A fair proportion of burners is now made here, but as yet this industry is in its infancy, and the goods are not up to the average of American made goods, in finish or durability.   These defects will doubtless vanish with growing experience, the same remarks apply to wicks.   Fruit jars are largely made at the two Hamilton factories, but a certain proportion of American jars is still brought in, being by some considered superior to the home-made article. Up to this year, goblets, tumblers, and glass tableware generally, were not manufactured in Canada at all, being mainly bought from the large American glass houses at Pittsburgh, Wheeling and elsewhere, but the managers of the glass factory recently established at New Glasgow, N.S., are showing considerable activity and enterprise in this direction, and are now taking orders for this class of goods from the wholesale trade, and their samples are spoken of as being of good design and finish. The duty on this latter class of goods is only twenty per cent. as compared with thirty per cent. on most of the other glass goods mentioned, so that it is probable that additional protection will be sought, now that they are made within the Dominion.

It will therefore be seen, as stated at the opening of this chapter, that the conditions under which the trade is done have been largely altered within the last few years, and, for a good many lines we are not dependent to so great an extent, upon foreign markets as we formerly were. This is especially true of the cheaper grades of crockery and glassware. The Canadian made goods, as a rule, seem to give fair satisfaction as to quality, there are, of course, some exceptions, but it is hardly to be expected that infant industries, comparatively speaking, such as our potteries are, can jump at once to perfection. Their first establishment was attended with a considerable amount of misfortune, and consequent serious doubt as to their future, but the later prospects are more encouraging, and with time and experience, the qualities of the output will naturally improve. The import duty upon crockery generally, is thirty per cent., and at the prices which have been ruling, it has not been possible to import similar goods to what are made here, and sell them at a remunerative profit, even though they may be of somewhat better quality; but, as the leading pottery has recently made an advance in its prices of about ten per cent., an example which the others may follow, the tendency may be toward a larger importation from Great Britain, more especially as there is a growing demand which our home facilities may not be able to keep pace with.

All the finer qualities of crockery and glassware are still imported, principally from Europe, as also are all china goods, none of the latter ware being made in Canada, though something is done in the way of decorating plain china in Montreal and Toronto. In this connection it may be stated as a fact worthy of note, that the tastes of our people seem to be tending more and more to the expensive and artistic, in this class of goods. The importations of fancy and art chinaware have largely increased of late, and the year 1881, surpasses all others in the imports of this description of goods. Several of our leading crockery houses make a specialty of this line, and in looking over their establishments, one is well nigh bewildered with the variety of the articles there shown, and the eye charmed with the exquisite taste and finish displayed. It is to be presumed that the growing taste above indicated, is a natural outcome of the good times at present prevailing, and the only fear is that a possible reaction may find the shelves loaded with a heavy stock of these goods, upon which the loss would naturally be heavy.

It may be interesting to briefly notice a few particulars concerning the first inception of our pottery interest as well as its later growth. The St. Johns Stone Chinaware Company was the first concern organized to enter upon the manufacture of Crockery in Canada. It was started in 1873, with a capital of $50,000, which was subsequently increased to $100,000. Owing, no doubt, to a want of knowledge of the detail of the business, and also to expensive management, the Company did not prove a success, and in 1877, it passed into private hands, since which time the business has been prosecuted with vigour and more satisfactory results. The only white granite, or stone chinaware, made in Canada is turned out at this pottery, as also are large quantities of cheaper goods. In 1877, a second pottery was established in Montreal, and since then, four others, one of these of considerable magnitude, have been put into operation at St. Johns, several of these being started by former employés of the St. Johns Stone Chinaware Company. The establishment of these latter potteries is no doubt largely due to the extra protection afforded by the new tariff, the duty being raised from 17½ to 30 per cent. upon most of the grades.

Taking a retrospective glance over the last twelve or fifteen years' record of this department of trade, it can be seen that it has been subject to all the varying fluctuations experienced by all lines of business. From 1866 to 1873, both years inclusive, good prices were obtained, and money was generally made in the trade. Then followed the depression, and from 1875 to 1880, not only were prices cut fine, but losses by failure also helped to wipe out what profits might otherwise have been made.   The year 1881, has shown more activity, and a much larger demand for goods has set in, but the competition in prices is very keen, and the absence of loss by failures is the main feature upon which the members of the trade base their estimates of probable profit.

THE MERCANTILE AGENCY'S RECORD.

This valuable integer of modern business was established in June, 1841, by Lewis Tappan, a merchant of New York. His well-known character for sterling honour and truthfulness secured to him the confidence of business men generally, and an amount of patronage which, in an untried enterprise of new character was highly gratifying. He succeeded in elaborating with great care a system, uncompromising in its integrity and just in its administration; in August of the same year had got details well in hand, and from that time added fresh elements of strength to his great undertaking. In 1849, the business was succeeded to by Messrs. Tappan & Douglass; in 1854, by Messrs. B. Douglass & Co., and in, 1859, by Messrs. R. G. Dun & Co., the present proprietors.

During the first ten years, the growth of the business was not rapid, though from the beginning it steadily acquired the support, and strengthened its claims to the confidence of the leading commercial men in the principal cities of the United States. As the enterprise gradually enlarged its field of operations, however, and became a representative institution at all the chief business centres upon this continent, its facilities were multiplied and it drew ahead with wonderful strides; a retrospect of the past twenty-five years of its history, furnishing an exhibit of results attained to by no other strictly commercial enterprise within the writer's knowledge. The Mercantile Agency's position to-day is a fitting monument to the tireless zeal, honesty and ability of its promoters, as well as a splendid tribute to its present proprietors, all of whom have been identified with its management for many years.

In 1857, the Montreal office was opened, and in the year following the connection was extended to Toronto. Links were soon formed between these cities and those of Halifax and St. John, Hamilton and London being subsequently added to the circle (all these offices doing business under the firm style of Messrs. Dun, Wiman & Co.), and at the close of 1881 an opening at Winnipeg was decided upon and promptly inaugurated. The Mercantile Agency thus presents facilities afforded by no other reporting interest, and its merits are universally recognized,

The same year witnessing the extension of the business into Canada saw also the foundation laid for what is now a large business in the old country and upon the continent; the London (Eng.) office being inaugurated simultaneously with that at Montreal. Manchester was the next point of opening and dates from 1871. Then followed the immediate extensions at Glasgow (Scotland), Paris (France), and shortly afterwards at Berlin, Germany. These offices were established for the purpose of concentrating at the leading exporting centres in Britain and upon the continent, information concerning the merits of importers on this side the Atlantic, thus facilitating the movements of commerce between the old and new worlds, and bringing merchants together who would otherwise have remained unknown to each other for many a long year.

The Mercantile Agency has now a circle of eighty-six associate offices in direct connection and communication with each other, all managed by well-tried men, selected because of their especial fitness for the duties of their respective posts. These men from the first have realized that the business is a *profession*, and that its close study was imperative upon them if they were to succeed. They have also recognized the fact that in no other business would a single case of unfair bias, weakness or relaxation of well-known rules, be followed so quickly by sweeping censure and loss of prestige as in their own; and though they have been called upon to meet exigencies before which untrained, weak men would succumb, still there is not an established instance, throughout the circle of offices, of wrong-doing or of a committal of the Agency's fair name between reporter and reported. As a consequence but few changes occur, and managers become so closely familiar with the tendencies and general make-up of merchants in their districts as to make the use of their offices *very* advantageous to subscribers.

Common honesty, ability, method and application are the requisites of successful Agency management. No one of these can be lacking if success is to be attained and satisfaction given. In many other businesses close watchfulness over departments may be relaxed at certain seasons, and duties be deputed to juniors; in the Agency business never. Neither can one day's duties be suffered to overlap into another before being worked out; here indeed, vigilance is safety, for the system deals with figures and conclusions which involve the deepest interest, and which, if carelessly handled, might easily lead to grave misunderstandings and complications. Fully conscious then of the important trusts devolving upon them, the employés vie with each other in earnest endeavour and pardonable pride to checkmate all approach to any infringement of fundamental rules, while the reporters, condensing clerks and any others who may have the framing of reports to do, are selected men, promoted from the office staff, and thoroughly familiar with their especial duties.

The object sought by the Mercantile Agency is to place within the reach of wholesale merchants, manufacturers, bankers and others, such information as will help them to decide with whom it is desirable to do business. To enable these dispensers of credit readily to ascertain those whom it is safe to deal with, is of as great importance as to discover those whom it is wise to avoid, and for this double purpose the Mercantile Agency exists—namely, to promote trade as well as to protect it.

The system embraces the collection and distribution of information, under certain restrictions, and for defined, legitimate business purposes, the main object being to furnish the home standing of the merchant, obtained from intelligent and reliable sources upon the ground. If, in his own little circles at home, the trader is considered honest, attentive to business, of good business qualifications, doing well and with a sufficient capital, is not the statement of these facts a positive benefit to himself, and the community in which he resides, as well as to the city merchant from whom he buys his goods? If, on the other hand, the trader is notoriously dishonest, or otherwise so disqualified for business, as to have no credit at home, is it not right and proper that it should be known in places *away from home*, where he may seek to obtain a credit? Would not the interests of the community where he may reside as well as the interests of the wholesaler from whom he attempts to buy, be equally preserved by preventing him from obtaining goods? In both cases, the legitimate ends of healthful trade are alike met, and the Mercantile Agency has the proud satisfaction of knowing that it is promoting the real interests of society. The life of the credit system is confidence, yet confidence must rest upon knowledge, and the Mercantile Agency in bringing creditor and debtor together through the light of this knowledge, is steadily proving its value to the general trade interests of the country, as no other factor of the century does. In case after case, the reports furnished by the system affords the wholesaler a degree of confidence which is equivalent to a personal acquaintance with the buyer, this confidence is *the* indispensable basis of credit, its acquisition is of the first importance, and saves many a long and harrassing delay to the country trader between the purchase and receipt of goods, as well as a vast amount of time, labour and expense, to the city merchant; all of these drawbacks having been experienced by both before the birth of the Mercantile Agency system.

The records of this representative Agency, then, present for legitimate use, and *for legitimate use* only, the best knowledge obtainable from the most reliable and intelligent authorities throughout the country. These authorities have been carefully selected through a long course of years and experience, until the list, as it stands to-day, reflects credit upon the system which has created it. Advices from such sources in the true interests of commerce must, then, and do command the serious attention and respect of the subscriber and credit giver, and supplemented as they are by information from trained travellers who regularly patrol every section of the country, deservedly earn for the Mercantile Agency the faith and support which meets it upon every side.

During the darker years of the depression, the merits of this carefully planned Agency shone forth conspicuously. Always on the alert to foreshadow the probable effects of the times upon weak, undeserving trade combinations, it became in no sense a ruthless *breaker* of honest interests, to whom continuance of life meant relief and safety to these, and to their creditors. Its conclusions were natural ones, not forced upon the attention of an already over-excited community, but legitimately and quietly given to its clients with advice of a calm and reasonable character. It did a great work in allaying the prevailing uneasiness and in clearing up uncertainty; it invited, as it always does, a close study of the antecedent history and inherent tendencies of each case for which there was much inquiry, and it urged upon its subscribers a consideration of pros and cons which were fully thrown open to all clients who had anything at stake in the way of credit. These points were—through the exigencies of the times and the natural desire of the Agency to do its full part, worked up by its representatives to such stages that the fullest light shone upon them, and in many cases contributed to the shaping of a business policy, in the treatment of debtors, which helped to avert a panic. At three distinct periods during the depression, *i.e.*, in 1875, 1877 and 1879, disappointment, loss of confidence, and a dark outlook, nearly culminated in a general overthrow of extended business interests, and every day brought with it a new crop of rumours and attempted sensations. It was at these epochs in our commercial history that the Mercantile Agency worked out an important part of its mission, and by its systematic course in sifting these mischievous rumours to the bottom, and throwing into bold relief the chaff from which they were made, did much to re-unite the scattered fragments of confidence and hope, and in turn was the first instrument to announce—through its failure returns and other comprehensive channels of information, their union and restoration.

The Birth and Growth of Canada:

Its Advantages and Disadvantages.

"Not institutions alone, but geographical position, climate, and many other natural conditions unite in forming the influences which, acting through successive generations, shape the character of nations and individuals."

Three hundred and forty-eight years have elapsed since Jacques Cartier, the bold fisherman of St. Malo, planted the standard of France, with its *fleur de lis*, beside the Cross at Gaspé, and opened in history's record a page for our country.

All was as yet, a nameless barbarism. A cluster of wigwams held the site of Stadacona, which afterward, under the more modern name of Quebec, furnished so much eventful history. The aborigines upon the shore were under the sway of that royal savage Donnacona; the rugged promontory at this point, and the forest solitudes were mute but threatening in their aspects as the Breton navigator and his fearless band gazed upon them; yet nothing daunted, they, after a brief delay advanced up the St. Lawrence, and at the base of a majestic rock, one hundred and eighty miles above Stadacona, found a second and larger Indian settlement named Hochelaga, whose huts and corn-fields were destined eventually to give way to the massive structures and squares of Montreal.

Retracing their lonely course down the St. Lawrence, the little band made a halt at Stadacona, and prepared as well as they were able, to meet the severity of the coming winter. This period passed, a return to France

NOTE.—For much of the historical data contained in the first pages of this sketch, the author is indebted to the standard writings of Francis Parkman, whose powerful style and wording in this connection have, to some degree, been introduced. His "Old Regime in Canada" is the work chiefly consulted.

was determined upon, for disease had decimated the expedition, and the allurements of the country were only a rigorous climate, a savage people, and a soil barren of gold. Jacques Cartier was tempted to other fields, but returned in May, 1541, being succeeded by Roberval, who built the first regular houses, locating them at Cap Rouge. His reign, however, was short and unpromising, and as France had become involved in war, Canada, or New France, was left for more than half a century as it was found.

In 1578, French vessels were visiting the coast of Newfoundland for codfish, and subsequently located upon Anticosti for the purpose of carrying on a traffic in furs. Laroche, Champlain, De Monts, De Chastes and others followed, each contributing to the history of those early days, and succeeded in colonizing "Nouvelle France." Poutrincourt, Lescarbot, Biard and the Jesuit Fathers followed. The Jesuit Brotherhood had found its way into nearly every known and accessible region with its potent influence, to meet in its early experiences in New France greater hardship and trial than ever before, yet subsequently doing a great work in assisting the feeble settlers in their faith. These however, for the time, suffered reverse upon reverse, though still keeping a hold upon the new shores, until the long and memorable struggle between England and France, proper, a war of state and religion was inaugurated, and which for a century and a half shook the struggling, weak communities of North America, closing at last in the memorable triumph on the Plains of Abraham.

In 1608, Champlain with his axe-men, priests, soldiers and peasants fell to work vigorously, and built up with wooden habitations a part of the present Market place in Quebec Lower Town, surrounding all with a moat and other means of defence. For a time matters went smoothly, but the weak colony soon felt the ravages of the Algonquin and other savage tribes, who subsequently became allies. Champlain undertook expeditions up the river and southward from the site of ancient Hochelaga, even so far as into what is now New York State, his name being given to the great lake on its eastern border. During these tours he came into collision with the fierce Iroquois, and here was the beginning of a long course of murderous conflicts, which continuously embroiled the weaker settlers of New France.

In 1610, the first attempt in regular fur trading was made. Tadousac was the headquarters of the interest, and vessels from France loaded up rapidly with the spoils of the forest and rivers ; but divisions occurred between rival leaders, and their effect was augmented by the uncertainty of the Indian attitude, until this business became irregular and lapsed into a state of lethargy.

In 1616, the little colony at Stadacona, or Quebec, had but little gain to show since its first settlement, yet it was here that Champlain's qualities as a man and soldier shone forth conspicuously, and nursed the puny nucleus into stronger life. He had, however, the greatest odds to contend with, though struggling with all in a most manful way. In 1635, on Christmas Day, this remarkable character died. To use the words of the historian : "The Colony could ill spare him. For twenty-seven years he had laboured hard and ceaselessly for its welfare, sacrificing fortune, repose and domestic peace, to a cause embraced with enthusiasm and pursued with intrepid persistency. His character belonged partly to the past, partly to the present. The *preux chevalier*, the crusader, the romance loving explorer, the curious, knowledge-seeking traveller, the practical navigator, all claimed their share in him. His views, though far beyond those of the mean spirits around him, belonged to his age and creed. He was less statesman than soldier. He leaned to the most direct and the boldest policy, and one of his last acts was to petition Richelieu for men and munitions for repressing that standing menace to the colony, the Iroquois. His dauntless courage was matched by an unwearied patience, a patience proved by life-long vexations, and not wholly subdued even by the saintly follies of his wife. He is charged with credulity, from which few of his age were free, and which in all ages has been the foible of earnest and generous natures—too ardent to criticize, and to honourable to doubt the honour of others. Champlain was no religious formalist, nor was his an empty zeal. A soldier from his youth, in an age of unbridled license, his life had answered to his maxims ; with the death of this faithful soldier closes the opening period of New France."

Up to 1660, Canada had writhed for many years under the scourge of the Iroquois war. During the greatest part of that time, the entire French population had never exceeded three thousand. The settlements were grouped around three fortified posts—Quebec, Three Rivers and Montreal—which in time of danger gave refuge to the settlers. The sufferings of the country were increased by the discord—religious and otherwise, which invaded her interests. In 1662, Argenson arrived from France to assume the Government, but was recalled, and Intendant Talon became the agent of Royalty in its attempt to build up a colony. The Government of Canada now assumed the features of that under which the laws of a French Province were framed. The Intendant held the reins of Government, but more as a confidential agent of the French king, being his careful correspondent and commentator upon the course and actions of the Governor-General, though inferior to the latter in rank.

The spirit of monopoly had ruled from the beginning of the foundation of the several small trading centres in the country. The old Governor Lauson, who was for a while, seignior of a great part of the Colony, held that Montreal had no right to trade directly with France, but must draw her supplies from Quebec; and the preposterous claim was revived in the time of Mezy. The successive Joint Companies, in whose hands the business of the country began to centre, had a baneful effect upon individual enterprise. In 1674, the charter of the West India Company was revoked, and trade was declared open to all subjects of the king; yet commerce was still compelled to wear the ball and chain. New restrictions were imposed, meant for good but resulting in evil. Merchants who had begun to congregate in the little centres, were forbidden all trade, direct or indirect, with the Indians. They were also forbidden to sell any goods at retail except in August, September and October; to trade anywhere in Canada above Quebec, or to sell clothing or domestic articles ready-made. This last restriction was designed to develop Colonial industry. No person, resident or not, could trade with the English Colonies, or go thither without a special passport. Foreign trade was stifily prohibited; if engaged in, the goods so trafficked in were liable to seizure and the holders to a fine. In addition to all this, merchants in France were obliged to show their invoices to the Council, in order that a fixed price might be established which should pay the seller only a certain profit, and if seller or buyer agreed to a larger margin they were liable to heavy penalties. Resident merchants, however, were favoured as to their profit limits, and could sell at any price they saw fit, so long as the territorial limits alluded to were observed.

Probably the earliest attempt at manufacturing lumber was made before 1700 by one Hazeur, the spot being Mal Baie. He got a large stock of planks and timber on his hands, and through the assistance of the French king, sent two vessel loads to France. A second venture was inaugurated at St. Paul's Bay, and about this time, a whale and cod fishery was established, though in a weak way. The king, however, gave his assistance and helped a firm to start, one of the partners being the Sieur Chalons. The importance of the fishery interests to the Colony was now strongly advocated, and they began to be considered the *mines* of the Colony. There is no doubt but that the French Government now listened generally to the numerous petitions for help, and sent out artisans of many grades, and in the time of the Intendant Begon, 1714, coarse fabrics of wool and linen were made.

The finances of the Colony, however, were not prosperous. In the absence of coin, beaver skins long served as currency. Wheat was also declared by the Council a legal tender, and moose skins subsequently became the equivalent of money. In 1714, common playing cards were also used as a medium, but were converted into bills of exchange by the Government, as every one made card money *as they saw fit*, notwithstanding all precautions, however, the Colony floundered in drifts of worthless paper at its end, under the old rule.

In 1717, the first establishment of a *Bourse* or Exchange was permitted at Montreal and Quebec, by the Government, the latter having previously been so jealous of popular meetings of all kinds, that for a long time it forbade merchants meeting together to discuss their affairs. The French king resumed possession of the districts formerly held by the West India Fur and Trading Company, when, in 1674, the charter of that interest was extinguished. These districts, together with the Post at

Tadousac, were subsequently farmed out to one Oudiette and his associates, who paid the Crown 350,000 livres for their privileges.

The great future fur trade of Canada was now started with vigour, and for many years was the pre-eminent industry of the country. The Government tried without ceasing to control and regulate this traffic, but it never succeeded. It aimed, above all things, to bring the trade home to the Colonists, to prevent them from going to the Indians, and to induce the Indians to come to them. To this end a great annual fair was established, by order of the king, at Montreal. Thither every summer a host of savages came down from the lakes in their bark canoes, meeting the Colonists on a common between St. Paul street and the river. A similar fair was established at Three Rivers, for the Algonquin tribes north of that place, but these annual markets did not fully answer the desired object, as many of the Colonists would go *above* Montreal and quietly intercept the Indians on their way down, drench them with brandy, and get their furs from them at low rates previous to the dates upon which the fairs were to be held.

The chief characteristics of the fur trade of Canada, however, were yet to be brought out. Oudiette and his associates not only collected the revenue, but were also vested with an exclusive right of transporting all the beaver skins of the Colony to France. On their part they were compelled to receive all the beaver skins brought to their magazines ; and, after deducting a fourth interest belonging to the king, to pay for the rest at a fixed price. This price was graduated according to the different qualities of the fur ; but the average cost to the collectors was a little more than three francs to the pound. The *habitants* could barter their furs with the merchants, but the merchants must bring them all to the magazines of Oudiette, who paid in receipts convertible into bills of exchange. He soon found himself burdened with such a mass of beaver skins, that the market in France was completely gutted. The French hatters refused to take them all, and for the part which they consented to take, they paid chiefly in hats, which Oudiette was not allowed to sell in France, but only in the West Indies, where few people wanted them. An unlucky fashion of wearing *small* hats also came into vogue, diminished the consumption of fur, and increased his embarrassments, as did also a practice common among the hatters, of mixing rabbit fur with the beaver. In his extremity he bethought him of setting up a hat factory for himself under the name of a certain licensed hatter, thinking thereby to alarm old customers into buying his stock. The other hatters, however, petitioned the Minister against this, and the new factory was suppressed, and Oudiette soon became bankrupt. Another company of men under-took the farming of the contract in his stead, but this venture also proved unfortunate. The end of the matter was that the action of the law of supply and demand was completely arrested by the peremptory edict which, with a view to the prosperity of the Colony and the profit of the king, required the companies to take every beaver skin offered.

In the meantime, all Canada, thinking itself sure of a good price, rushed into the beaver skin trade, and the accumulation of unsalable furs became more and more suffocating. In 1700, a change was ordered, the monopoly of exporting beaver skins was placed in the hands of a company formed of the chief inhabitants of Canada; although some of the parties to this hesitated at first to take the risk, about one hundred and fifty merchants finally subscribed to the stock of the new company, and immediately petitioned the king for a ship and a loan of seven hundred thousand francs. One of the conditions to the formation under Government of this new company was that they were required to take off the hands of the former interest an accumulation of more than six hundred thousand pounds of beaver, for which, however, they were to pay only but half its usual price. This done, the French market refused to absorb it, and the directors of the new company saw no better way than to *burn three-fourths* of the troublesome and perishable skins. In order to rid themselves of what remained, the directors begged the king to issue a decree, requiring all hatters to put at least three ounces of genuine beaver fur into each hat, but all was in vain. The affairs of the company fell into confusion, which was aggravated by the bad faith of some of its chief members. In 1707, it was succeeded by another company, to whose magazines every *habitant* or merchant was ordered to bring every beaver skin in his possession within forty-eight hours; and the company, like its predecessor, was required to receive it, and pay for it in written promises.

Again the market was overloaded with a surfeit of beaver, again the bills of exchange went unpaid, and all was distress. In 1721, the monopoly of exporting beaver skins was given to the New West India Company ; but this time it was provided that the Government should direct from time to time, according to the capacities of the market, the quantities of furs which the company should be forced to receive.

Out of the beaver trade rose a huge evil, baneful to the growth and to the morals of Canada. All the more vigorous of the population took to the woods from the first. They defeated the plans of the king for the increase of families, and all led to want of discipline and order. Edicts were directed against them, and more than once the little Colony presented the extraordinary spectacle of the greater part of its young men turned into *couriers de bois*, or forest outlaws. A year or two of bush-ranging spoiled them for civilization, though their daredevil mode of life and carriage will always be joined with the picturesque in the memories of that grand world of woods which the nineteenth century is fast causing to disappear.

For another fifty years, the Colony went on with varying degrees of advancement. The English conquest was the grand turning point of Canadian history. Material growth, an increased mental activity, an education, a warm and genuine patriotism, all date from the peace of 1763. It is truly said that a happier calamity never befel a people than the conquest of Canada by the British arms.

From this date the shipping interests of Quebec and other ports steadily enlarged, new centres formed, the West was developed more rapidly, commerce rolled in upon its natural course, and the march of progress became accelerated. Our forests soon responded to the demand made upon their wealth, and this interest grew to be one of immense advantage to our country.

There were, however, checks given to this advancement at times, and for many years prior to 1820, it appeared difficult to roll up and maintain a great gain, either in business or population. After this period, commerce grew with astonishing rapidity as witness the history of the

Bank of Montreal in preceding pages. From time to time, there were pauses, it is true, but increased strength was felt and confidence was kept bright. The troubles of 1838 were passed, and for some years afterward our commercial interests may be said to have steadily, though slowly, assumed a wider importance. It is, however, to be regretted that our growth in population has since been so slow of accomplishment. The great want of our country is *people*, there is room enough in our broad areas for millions more than we have to-day, but a more comprehensive and attractive system of emigration facilities is called for and must be elaborated or our growth will continue to be slow.

There are many reasons which tend to make Canada a desirable objective point to the emigrant. More especially does it present natural and attractive phases to the old country settlers here. To them we offer room in such proportions as ought to dwarf all precedent upon old world soil, in so far as their particular experience has gone. All things being equal, it is to be argued that they must naturally choose to live under the old flag, which they find here, besides this, they find the same associations here, the same natural ties, customs—in great measure—modes of thought and the fullest liberty. Each member of the British Isles may in Canada find a wider liberality and acquire for himself a more important position as a man than he can ever hope to obtain at home, and to other people we offer a haven of rest, an asylum of peace and a recognition of human rights, which the German, with his military prescriptions, the Russian, with his Nihilistic terrorism and revolutions, the Frenchman, with his Communistic drawbacks, can never experience, at least for any great length of time. All nationalities can here pursue, undisturbed, their commercial ventures, having no fear of internal dissension or upheaval, nor aggression from our neighbours to interrupt their interests. There is, in fact, no country upon the face of the globe more free from dangers in these respects, at the same time offering as great a degree of civilization and equality to its people.

Canada for many years has struggled along between two fires, so to speak, bounded on the south by a great Republic, it has had to encounter the latter's ingenuity of device in competitive manufacturing, and in competing for emigration, while Great Britain's tried mechanical skill and wealth have, in many lines of fabrics, almost paralyzed our own feeble attempts at manufacturing, by throwing open a source of supply, and extending of liberal credits to such a degree that we have never been able to cope with its influence upon our own interests. Not only has its wealth and power overshadowed us, but it has failed to send us the *bone and sinew* that we want so badly, and which we have confidently looked for at its hands. Nothing is more astonishing than the apathy which has seemed to pervade the leading as well as the lower classes in the old country with respect to our pressing want of settlers. At London, count-less schemes have, from time immemorial, been floated in countless and unsound ventures. Attempts have been made by capitalists to colonize tracts of territory in other lands, but being inaugurated for individual gain, have seldom added to the strength of the district so selected. In fact, these selfish ventures have actually hindered by their effect the more humane endeavour of the few to create an interest in the subject of immigration. All this can and should be changed, and of late there seems to be more hope that Canada's claims will meet with more of the recognition to which they are entitled, among the middle and lower classes of the old country. The uselessness of their remaining upon a soil where every square foot must be made to contribute to a bare support, has long been seen by these, and systematic endeavour upon our part may yet result in imparting to them a broader knowledge of our advantages, and give a direction to their energies and labour.

There has been, and is, a great and surprising amount of ignorance among the possible immigrants of older countries as to our geographical position, our climate, and our progress in civilization. We have not in turn represented our country properly, but remaining quiescent in the matter, have allowed time to elapse which might have been utilized in advertising our claims in many quarters where light was needed. The elaborate and earnest method of our neighbours to the south of us, has not in the meantime failed to produce fruit. They *have* advertised their spare lands, their markets, their railways and their civilization, and, having brought within their borders every nationality, have acquired and worked out the ideas which came to them in crude form with their new citizens. Canada, with its vast mining resources, its timber, its water ways, its splendid grain districts, its untried—almost unknown, but virgin land strength, and its social attractions has, as a contrast, remained almost at a standstill, for the paltry gain shown by the late census is too insignificant to quote. We present to-day, a long strip of frontage development outlined by the St. Lawrence and Ottawa Rivers, and widened only by Eastern Township and Western Canada expansions; then we continue in straggling shape along the lakes until Manitoba is reached, leaving good arable and mining ground in a large part of the territory passed over, and making but partial attempt to familiarize the world's millions with our advantages. Not every settler cares to attack the forest in order to win a home. Many might come, and of better class, were they to be shown that in the older districts of our country they could find social amenities, education and a peaceful administration of law and order. These would bring money and brains with them, glad to escape from the limitations and closely drawn lines of the old country, they would give us the strength we need, but to get them we must unroll our maps, cite surroundings, nearness to markets, prices obtained for crops, &c., &c., and endorse it all by *irrefragable* testimony.

It has been said that perseverance can sometimes equal genius in producing results. With so much of natural advantage to present then, can we not add certainty to hope, in building up a rich future of development, and by well directed energy bring ourselves before the notice of the world at large as a country which offers advantages second to none, to the intending immigrant.

Cannot some scheme be elaborated whose main feature shall be that of securing to settlers of the right class, and before they leave old country homes, a carefully surveyed farm tract, partly cleared, with a plain but substantial farm house erected upon it ready for occupancy? At every centre in our country we number scores of wealthy men, retired from business, who haunt our money streets for investments and create new joint stock enterprises without end, only to experience a loss in turn, as our commerce becomes over-weighted with the load. Let profit be joined to patriotism. Loss can hardly ensue if capital, in the hands of an intelligent management, be earnestly applied to this highly important cause. The chief end aimed at in England, as well as in other countries in the past, by promoters of many colonization schemes, land companies, &c., has been to get as much money *in hand* from the emigrant as possible, and to turn quickly in each case, starting another venture at a distant place perhaps, but caring little as to the plight in which the settler, induced by their programmes, might find himself within a year, and far from home. Tracts of land have been taken up by these speculators who gauged the merits of the districts mainly by the facility through which these were acquired. Their victims have spread the story of disappointment, and resulting disaster into the older countries, until many a struggling toiler in their crowded boundaries, has become convinced that it is better to endure the ills with which he is familiar and which have a limit, after all, than to listen to enticements which are likely to lead him into quick and sudden ruin.

It is true that our great projected railways will, in time, work up a nucleus, here and there, of population, which without them, would not come to stay with any nation, but must we wait for this slow development? Why cannot a guaranteed provision for the worthier class of immigrant be secured to him *at once*, for a certain period after reaching our shores? It is those who fail for want of this that discourages others from coming. Why make the first year or two of an immigrant's existence among us, so hard that he gives up in despair? Why not extend to him as liberal a credit, in a degree at least, as one merchant extends to another whose business is likely to be desirable and profitable? There can be no *more* risk, if as much, provided we have energetic representatives in old country districts, who will take the pains to assure themselves that the proposing immigrant is a fit person in every way; that he is a *farmer*, steady, and vigorous in health, or that he is a woodsman by predilection, and would make a pioneer in our unreclaimed forest lands. To the farmer proper, it might be feasible to offer not only a plain homestead, ready for occupancy, but an outfit of tools and a selection of seed adapted to the land which he is to work; in brief, he should be as free from drawbacks and difficulties as possible, for he needs all the courage he can muster in coming into new surroundings. Every good farmer thus placed would bring more. If then, the traditional handicaps which have shackled the energies of countless settlers, the world over, are removed by humanitarian and politic measures for their protection and welfare, what is there to prevent an annual passage to us of just the material we need? In the end this must benefit us morally in districts which might be given over to disorder, in other and irresponsible hands. Such an element of good would accrue to a commercial advantage at our centres, as well as in our back districts.

Pending the adoption of some naturally attractive and binding inducement to the immigrant, land schemes of greater or lesser variety of detail will undoubtedly be inaugurated, for at the present moment attention is being directed to our great North-West as it never was before, and good times are bringing out ideas which periods of commercial depression discourage. Among the first of the programmes in this connection, is that of a joint stock enterprise which, it is stated, will be put on foot at Toronto, and be known as the British Canadian Colonization Company (Limited), the promoters being some leading men. The capital of the Company is to be $1,000,000, divided into shares of $100 each. In the notice of application for a charter, the purposes for which incorporation is sought are set forth as follows :—To acquire by purchase, lease, or otherwise, lands in the Dominion ; to improve, sell, lease or otherwise dispose of the same, and to assist immigration and settlement upon lands in Canada ; with power to assist immigrants and settlers to colonize the lands of the Company by grants of lands, advances of money or otherwise, and to take security for such advances and assistance and for the balance of the price of lands sold by the Company, &c., &c.

Another scheme has been planned, also at Toronto, under the name of the " Temperance Colonization Society," this Company is to make a request to the Government during the session this year, for a grant of lands upon the South Saskatchewan. The Company claims that it has numerous applications from persons in Canada, Great Britain, New Zealand, the New England States, and some Western States, for farms. The Company engages to settle the district, which may be granted to them, within three years, but if not accomplished in five years, to allow the property to revert to Government without opposition. It is one of the objects of this

Company, to prevent the manufacture or sale of spiritous and malt liquors within the line of the settlement.

If such Companies will go *far enough* with their assistance to emigrants, they will find their programmes profitable in these days of general encouragement, while their security will not be imperilled.

There is little doubt but that our great enterprise, the Canadian Pacific Railway, is attracting in Europe great attention. It may be made to appeal closely to the *interests* of possible emigrants as well. We have in Britain an efficient emigration agent, Mr. St. John, who is said to be doing everything within his power to turn attention toward our almost limitless areas in the North-West, and with inducements, as they are, he is reported to be making good headway for Canada. It is likely, too, that his exertions will be seconded by the effect of the poor crop in the United Kingdom last year, and the discontent it created. It is, however, essential that agencies at *many* points be created, and filled by intelligent men who will, like Mr. St. John, be able to talk from the standpoint of a personal knowledge about Canada, present strong inducements, and win the confidence of the class we most need in Canada. Then, let every representation be *lived up to*, let no misunderstandings arise between our Government administrators and the people we invite to our domains, and if individual enterprise enters the field, let all competition be fair, and never react to the disadvantage of the settler, upon whom in years to come we shall learn to rely as a most valuable factor in our growth and importance.

The arrangements made by our Government with the enterprising Syndicate for the construction of the Canadian Pacific Railway, by means of its Company, aided by subsidies of land and money, places Government in a position to deal directly and finally with the question of the sale of Government lands in the North-West Territories. The following regulations went into force on and after January 1st, 1882, and give the conditions under which Companies may enter into the districts named, for the purpose of colonizing, the terms extended to capitalists who may desire to cultivate large farms, the conditions to, and rights of settlers, &c. :—

DOMINION LAND REGULATIONS.

The following regulations for the sale and settlement of Dominion lands in the Province of Manitoba and the North-West Territories shall, on and after the first day of January, 1882, be substituted for the regulations now in force, bearing date the twenty-fifth day of May last :—

1. The surveyed lands in Manitoba and the North-West Territories shall, for the purposes of these regulations, be classified as follows :—

Class A.—Lands within twenty-four miles of the main line or any branch of the Canadian Pacific Railway, on either side thereof.

Class B.—Lands within twelve miles, on either side, of any projected line of railway (other than the Canadian Pacific Railway), approved by Order-in-Council, published in the *Canada Gazette.*

Class C.—Lands south of the main line of the Canadian Pacific Railway not included in Class A or B.

Class D.—Lands other than those in Classes A, B and C.

2. The even-numbered sections in all the foregoing classes are to be held exclusively for homesteads and pre-emptions.

a. Except in Class D where they may be affected by colonization agreements as hereinafter provided.

b. Except where it may be necessary, out of them, to provide wood lots for settlers.

c. Except in cases where the Minister of the Interior, under provisions of the Dominion Lands Acts, may deem it expedient to withdraw certain lands, and sell them at public auction or otherwise deal with them as the Governor-in-Council may direct.

3. The odd-numbered sections in Class A are reserved for the Canadian Pacific Railway Company.

4. The odd-numbered sections in Classes B and C shall be for sale at $2.50 per acre, payable at time of sale :

a. Except where they have been or may be dealt with otherwise by the Governor-in-Council.

5. The odd-numbered sections in Class D shall be for sale at $2 per acre, payable at time of sale :

a. Except where they have been or may be dealt with otherwise by the Governor-in-Council.

b. Except lands affected by colonization agreements, as hereinafter provided.

6. Persons who, subsequent to survey, but before the issue of the Order-in-Council of 9th October, 1879, excluding odd-numbered sections from homestead entry, took possession of land in odd-numbered sections by residing on and cultivating the same, shall, if continuing so to occupy them, be permitted to obtain homestead and pre-emption entries as if they were on even-numbered sections.

Pre–Emptions.

7. The prices for pre-emption lots shall be as follows :—

For lands in Classes A, B and C, $2.50 per acre.

For lands in Class D, $2.00 per acre.

Payment shall be made in one sum at the end of three years from the date of entry, or at such earlier date as a settler may, under the provisions of the Dominion Lands Acts, obtain a patent for the homestead to which such pre-emption lot belongs.

Colonization.
Plan Number One.

8. Agreements may be entered into with any Company or person (hereinafter called the party) to colonize and settle tracts of land on the following conditions :—

a. The party applying must satisfy the Government of its good faith and ability to fulfil the stipulations contained in these regnlations.

b. The tract of land granted to any party shall be in Class D.

9. The odd-numbered sections within such tract may be sold to the party at $2 per acre, payable, one-fifth in cash at the time of entering into the contract, and the balance in four equal annual instalments from and after that time. The party shall also pay to the Government five cents per acre for the survey of the land purchased by it, the same to be payable in four equal annual instalments at the same time as the instalments of the purchase money. Interest at the rate of six per cent. per annum shall be charged on all past due instalments.

a. The party shall, within five years from the date of the contract, colonize its tract.

b. Such colonization shall consist in placing two settlers on homesteads on each even-numbered section, and also two settlers on each odd-numbered section.

c. The party may be secured for advances made to settlers on homesteads according to the provisions of the 10th section of the Act 44 Victoria, chap. 16. (The Act passed in 1881 to amend the Dominion Lands Acts.)

d. The homesteads of 160 acres shall be the property of the settler, and he shall have the right to purchase the pre-emption lot belonging to his homestead at $2 per acre, payable in one sum at the end of three years from the day of entry, or at such earlier date as he may under the provisions of the Dominion Lands Acts obtain a patent for his homestead.

e. When the settler on a homestead does not take up the pre-emption lot to which he has a right, the party may within three months after the settler's right has elapsed, purchase the same at $2 per acre, payable in cash at the time of purchase.

10. In consideration of having colonized its tract of land in the manner set forth in sub-section *b* of the last preceding clause, the party

shall be allowed a rebate of one-half of the original purchase-money of the odd-numbered sections in its tract.

a. During each of the five years covered by the contract an enumeration shall be made of the settlers placed by the party in its track, in accordance with sub-section *b* of clause 9 of these regulations, and for each *bona fide* settler so found therein a rebate of one hundred and twenty dollars shall be credited to the party ; but the sum so credited shall not, in the aggregate, at any time exceed one hundred and twenty dollars for each *bona fide* settler found within the tract, in accordance with the said sub-section, at the time of the latest enumeration.

b. On the expiration of five years an enumeration shall be made of the *bona fide* settlers on the tract, and if they are found to be as many in number and placed in the manner stipulated for in sub-section *b* of clause 9 of these regulations, a further and final rebate of forty dollars per settler shall be credited to the party, which sum, when added to those previously credited, will amount to one-half of the purchase money of the odd-numbered sections and reduce the price thereof to one dollar per acre. But if it should be found that the full number of settlers are not on the tract, or are not placed in conformity with sub-section *b* of clause 9 of these regulations, then, for each settler fewer than the required number, or not placed in conformity with the said sub-section, the party shall forfeit $160 of rebate.

c. If at any time during the existence of the contract the party shall have failed to perform any of the conditions thereof, the Governor-in-Council may cancel the sale of the land purchased by it, and deal with the party as may seem meet under the circumstances.

d. To be entitled to rebate the party shall furnish to the Minister of the Interior evidence that will satisfy him that the tract has been colonized and settled in accordance with sub-section *b* of clause 9 of these regulations.

Plan Number Two.

11. To encourage settlement by capitalists who may desire to cultivate larger farms than can be purchased where the regulations provide that two settlers shall be placed on each section (but without furnishing the number of settlers required to be placed within each township), agreements may be entered into with any company or person (hereinafter called the party) to colonize and settle tracts of land on the following conditions :—

a. The party applying must satisfy the Government of its good faith and ability to fulfil the stipulations contained in these regulations.

b. The tract of land granted to any party shall be in Class D.

c. All the land within the tract may be sold to the party at $2 per acre, payable in cash, at the time of entering into the contract. The party shall, at the same time, pay to the Government five cents per acre for the survey of the land purchased by it.

d. The party shall, within five years from the date of the contract, colonize the township or townships comprised within its tract.

e. Such colonization shall consist in placing sixty-four *bona fide* settlers within each township.

12. In consideration of having colonized its tract of land in the manner set forth in sub-section *e* of the last preceding clause, the party shall be allowed rebate of one-half of the original purchase money of its tract.

a. During each of the five years covered by the contract an enumeration shall be made of the settlers placed by the party in its tract, in accordance with sub-section *e* of clause 11 of these regulations, and for each *bona fide* settler so found therein a rebate of one hundred and twenty dollars shall be repaid to the party ; but the sums so repaid shall not, in the aggregate, at any time exceed one hundred and twenty dollars for each *bona fide* settler found within the tract, in accordance with the said sub-section at the time of the latest enumeration.

b. On the expiration of the five years an enumeration shall be made of the *bona fide* settlers placed by the party in its tract, and if they are found to be as many in number and placed in the manner stipulated for in sub-section *e* of clause 11 of these regulations, a further and final rebate of forty dollars per settler shall be repaid, which sum, when added to those previously repaid to the party, will amount to one-half of the purchase money of its tract and reduce the price thereof to one dollar per acre. But if it should be found that the full number of settlers required by these regulations are not on the tract, or are not placed in conformity with the said sub-section, then, for each settler fewer than the required number or not settled in conformity with the said sub-section, the party shall forfeit one hundred and sixty dollars of rebate.

c. To be entitled to rebate, the party shall furnish to the Minister of the Interior evidence that will satisfy him that the tract has been colonized and settled in accordance with sub-section *e* of clause 11 of these regulations.

OFFICIAL NOTICE.

13. The Government shall give notice in the *Canada Gazette* of all agreements entered into for the colonization and settlement of tracts of land under the foregoing plans in order that the public may respect the rights of the purchasers.

TIMBER FOR SETTLERS.

14. The Minister of the Interior may direct the reservation of any odd or even numbered section having timber upon it, to provide wood for homestead settlers ; and each such settler may, where the opportunity for so doing exists, purchase a wood lot, not exceeding twenty acres, at the price of $5 an acre in cash.

15. The Minister of the Interior may grant, under the provisions of the Dominion Lands Acts, licenses to cut timber on lands within surveyed townships. The lands covered by such licenses are hereby withdrawn from homestead and pre-emption entry and from sale.

Pasturage Lands.

16. Under the authority of the Act 44 Vic., chap. 16, leases of tracts for grazing purposes may be granted on the following conditions :—

a. Such leases to be for a period of not exceeding twenty-one years, and no single lease shall cover a greater area than 100,000 acres.

b. In surveyed territory, the land embraced by the lease shall be described in townships and sections. In unsurveyed territory, the party to whom a lease may be promised shall, before the issue of the lease, cause a survey of the tract to be made, at his own expense, by a Dominion Lands Surveyor, under instructions from the Surveyor-General ; and the plan and field notes of such survey shall be deposited on record in the Department of the Interior.

c. The lessee shall pay an annual rental at the rate of $10 for every 10,000 acres embraced by his lease, and shall, within three years from the granting of the lease, place on the tract one head of cattle for every ten acres of land embraced by the lease, and shall, during its term, maintain cattle thereon in at least that proportion.

d. After placing the prescribed number of cattle on the tract leased, the lessee may purchase land within his leasehold for a home, farm and *corral*, paying therefor $2 per acre in cash.

e. Failure to fulfil any of the conditions of his lease shall subject the lessee to forfeiture thereof.

17. When two or more parties apply for a grazing lease of the same land, tenders shall be invited, and the lease shall be granted to the party offering the highest premium therefor in addition to the rental. The said premium to be paid before the issue of the lease.

General Provisions.

18. Payments for land may be in cash, scrip, or police or military bounty warrants.

19. These regulations shall not apply to lands valuable for town plots, or to coal or other mineral lands, or to stone or marble quarries, or

to lands having water power thereon ; or to sections 11 or 29 in each Township, which are school lands, or sections 3 and 26, which belong to the Hudson's Bay Company.

By order,

LINDSAY RUSSELL,
Surveyor-General.

Department of the Interior,
Ottawa, 23rd December, 1881.

The policy adopted by the Canadian Pacific Railway Company is to sell land only to actual settlers, the question of settlement being determined, not by the erection of a shanty, which plan has in many cases, succeeded in covering the letter of agreement, but by honest breaking of the soil and immediate cultivation. The object is a sound one, as it is to bring the greater part of the sections under cultivation as rapidly as possible. The price of the land is clearly set forth—two dollars and fifty cents per acre. The payments, one-sixth cash, and the balance in five annual instalments. At the expiry of these and their regular adjustment, the owner's title will be handed to him with the property. The condition required from settlers are that all taxes, which may be levied as the country grows older, shall be met, that no wood other than that which is absolutely necessary to use for fuel, fencing, or erection of buildings, shall be cut, and that within four years, three-fourths of the land taken up by the settler shall be brought under cultivation, a rebate of one dollar and twenty-five cents per acre being allowed. If, however, the settler erects buildings and resides on the land for at least three years out of the four, then the bringing under cultivation of one-half the land purchased within four years, shall be considered a fulfilment of the conditions. This is a brief recapitulation of the terms offered, as to their chief points, and the policy is certainly well devised, for it is likely to discourage the attempts of pure *speculators* who would otherwise buy up tracts for the purpose of selling them again, but only those of means can do this, as they must break up and cultivate the soil within a given time. The policy presents advantages to the proposing settler as well, for he is by it, assured of the cultivation of the soil about him, wherever taken up, and the consequent increase in the value of his own landed interest.

The vast regions of our North-West, extending from Lake Superior to the Pacific Ocean, and averaging six hundred miles in width by two thousand miles in length, are adapted to the uses of the agriculturalist, and are capable of supporting an immense number of the human race. Every variety of soil and climate necessary for the production of valuable crops incident to the temperate zone, is here presented. The country also abounds in mineral deposits, is well watered, and through many districts, notably the Saskatchewan Valley, offers a grand home to the earnest settler. The yields of many sections in the " Prairie Province " of wheat, potatoes, hay, &c., have astonished old growers in other parts of the country, while as a stock-raising section it is unsurpassed, and hardly equalled except in certain of the blue grass regions of the States. The wheat yield of the Northwestern Province, for 1881, was over three million bushels, and its capacity has not as yet been tested to more than an infinitesimal degree. One hundred and sixty acres of good land can be purchased and acquired in perpetuity and upon easy terms in Manitoba, for £80 sterling. While in Great Britain, in good districts for farming, the same area of soil would cost over five times this in *bare rental*. The farmer of the North-West then, becomes a *proprietor* for an outlay of £80, and goes to work upon land which will yield him rich returns and quickly.

While Manitoba calls loudly to the younger and more sturdy man, the older districts of Canada also present many advantages to the middle-aged farmers who leave Great Britain for a larger field, and who have capital and experience. In fact, it is now probable that the ensuing season will see many of the younger men of Ontario emigrate in round numbers to the North-West, and leave more room, as well as easy terms, to the farmer who wishes to settle in already cleared and cultivated portions of Canada. Certain it is that our country presents attractions for all classes who propose to make their bread from the soil.

As has been urged, we cannot well afford to allow other countries to remain in ignorance of our advantages, nor of our plans and details for encouraging incoming settlers. There is, and always has been evidenced, too much lack of knowledge abroad as to our capacities and native strength, and in London, where much useful information about Canada and its prospects might be centred, we have been caricatured and misunderstood. As a contrast to the attacks by *London Truth* and other widely circulated English papers, upon our surroundings, enterprises, &c., it is pleasing to peruse an article like the following from *Vanity Fair*, January 28, 1882, which shews that at least, our greatest undertaking— the construction of the Canadian Pacific Railway—is getting to be understood in detail, and will not long, in English centres, lack the appreciation it deserves :—

" We have before us the prospectus and official memorandum of this Company ; and though there has been, as yet, no actual placing of the securities of the Company upon the London market, they are obtainable, as the prospectus informs us, at the agency of the Bank of Montreal here, where provision is also made for payment of interest. It is well-known that the Bank of Montreal has itself in Canada subscribed for a large amount of the Company's five per cent. land bonds, and now offers them for sale at par. As an evidence of value, where the case is best known, it is announced that the Canadian Government takes these bonds by way of deposit from English Insurance Companies doing business in Canada and obliged by law to deposit in the Colonial Exchequer certain security for the benefit of Canadian clients. The lands on which investors are asked to lend their money are the *much-heard-of* acres of the so-called Fertile Belt, lying between the new Prairie Province of Manitoba and the Rocky Mountains. The documents before us speaks highly of the agricultural capacity of the country, but not too highly, judging from the reports brought back by many independent witnesses from the scene of action, who have been over there during the past year.

" Care must be taken to distinguish these bonds from ordinary railway bonds secured by mortgage on a railroad. The road may be a success or a failure. These particular bonds are not dependent for their ultimate value on the financial success of the road. The concession in all comprises twenty-five millions of acres, and on it land bonds to the amount of twenty-five millions of dollars—or one dollar per acre, its value as wild lands—are to be issued. There is abundant evidence, however, that the road must be built, and will be built, west from Winnipeg, the capital of Manitoba, through a level and easily-traversed country, to go a distance of 800 miles, that is, to the limit of what, for present purposes, may be said to be the famous North-West wheat-growing district. This is the territory visited by the deputation of Scotch and English farmers in 1880, and since that time thoroughly explored and surveyed, and made the medium of immense transactions by Companies and individuals with a view to settlement at a much higher rate than one dollar per acre. Whether eventually its products come to Europe by way of Hudson's Bay —a project first broached in this journal several years ago—or by the highways on land and ocean now in use, good judges believe that a new granary is being opened for English consumers, of which it is almost impossible to exaggerate the magnitude and importance. That the lands offered as security by the Canadian Pacific Railway Company are good value may be inferred from one of the terms of their bargain with the Government—namely, that the whole twenty-five millions of acres constituting their land grant were to be *fit for settlement*. It is impossible to conceive therefore that they have chosen or accepted barren and indifferent lands, for great as it sounds in English ears, twenty-five millions of acres by no means represents the majority of fertile acres within the district in question.

" In considering these land bonds as an investment it should be carefully noted that at present we are not dealing with the railway as such, but merely with a Land Company. The prospects of the railway, we believe, are excellent, but once that part of the road is built and worked which passes through the territory in question, the alleged difficulties of construction in British Columbia, to the west of the Fertile Belt, the north of Lake Superior, and to the east of it, need not be noticed either for refutation or corroboration in connection with the land bonds. For what it is worth, the investors in these bonds will have, of course, the Company's covenant, and will so far be interested in its success ; but what they may implicitly depend upon is the actual and intrinsic value of the lands conveyed to trustees for their benefit. It is curious that in advance of any attempt on the part of the Company to float its land bonds on the London market, determined and organized opposition has been shown to them, with a view, no doubt, to keep them away, but professedly in the interest of the public. This is, indeed, extraordinary philanthrophy on the part of a self-elected Salvation Army, and would generally be taken as evidence of a self-interested motive on the part of the opponent; perhaps an American rival running on a little lower parallel of latitude, or perhaps an Anglo-Canadian line, with American connections, jealous of a road which will be a competitor for the carriage of cereals from and through the Province of Ontario to the sea-board and of European imports and immigrants the reverse way. It is not worth while discussing the how and the why of this little plot; but we say emphatically that, other things being equal, there is no reason why the British public should not support a road which will be a trans-continental highway on British soil from the Atlantic to the Pacific. London, at any rate, should not be made the arena for American intrigue against what is in one sense a great Imperial project. The building of this road was a condition of the Confederation, which included the Pacific Crown Colony of British Columbia, and was known to be so by the English Parliament which in 1867 passed the Act of Union. Subsequently Lord Carnarvon decided that Canada was obliged to go on at once with the construction of the road, and both parties in Canada are pledged to its completion. The Government of Canada has presented the Company with twenty-five millions of dollars in cash, the same number of acres, and more than the same number of additional millions of dollars in the shape of 500 miles of road completed by the Government through the most difficult and least profitable parts to be traversed. The Company therefore has a considerable bonus to start with, besides a proprietary whose own capital is understood to be large. A fact in favour of the Company is that the Bank of Montreal should have taken a large quantity of the land bonds. There are few stabler financial institutions than this, and only two or three banks in the world with a larger paid-up capital and reserve. Its shares are at a premium of 100 per cent., and very many of them are held in this country."

Referring to the opposition early met with in the floating of the Company's bonds upon the London market, it may be said that the endeavour *did* meet with opposition, and it is believed that this was created by parties who were led, *through interest*, to assume a hostile attitude. To no appreciable extent can this influence the minds of proposing emigrants, as it is only the outcome of individual and limited attempts at discouragement, and as such can carry no weight.

In the competition for emigrants between the powers upon this continent, Mexico is coming into considerable notice. With a salubrious climate, good soil, rich mining interests and under a Republican form of Government, Mexico must become a rival, to a certain extent, of all other countries. Still, her geographical position, the possibility of her soil becoming the arena of political struggles with revolutionary effect, and the lawless character of many of those who have from time to time found an asylum within her boundaries, will naturally deter many of the old worlds denizens from settling within Mexican domains. It has been suggested in former pages, however, that our Government might with success, consider the practicability of introducing into its plan of immigration inducements, some new features which, would enlist the closer attention of European middle classes, and it may be in order here to place before readers some of the chief features of the Mexican scheme.

That Government, is authorised by Statute, to effect colonization by direct action, or by contracts with foreign or native companies under certain stipulations. The Government can allow to companies a subvention for each family established in the country, or a smaller one for each family landed at any port in its country ; to make advances of amounts not exceeding fifty per cent of the subvention ; to sell lands appropriate for colonisation at moderate prices, payable in instalments ; *the payments of the instalments only beginning two years after the colonist has built his homestead ;* to grant a bonus to each emigrant family, and to exempt from all port dues all vessels bringing to the Mexican shore, ten or more emigrant families ; and to allow a bonus for each native family settled in one of the emigrant colonies. The companies contracting . with the Government secure the latter by guarantees. All colonists or settlers are guaranteed Mexican Citizenship when naturalized ; but are exempted from military service and all taxes save those of municipal creation. They are also made advances on the ontlay of transportation, and subsistence for one year after they are settled, and they are finally permitted to *import free all necessary implements, machinery, &c.* All these privileges the Mexican colonist is promised for a period of *twenty-five years.*

As has been remarked, however, our northern country presents a better promise of peace, as well as a much greater degree of civilization, and these advantages must always be considered as paramount by the better class' of immigrants. In furthering any scheme of immigration which may set toward our shores, another auxiliary is also necessary, *i.e.* some plan of publication in which the necessary information is given the proposing immigrant, as to the condition and prospects of the land in which he is going to settle.

Attempts of various degrees of detail have been made to cover this need, but it is seldom that any is official, and properly or periodically published. The conditions going to make up the whole of each section should be carefully stated, for it should be borne in mind that many coming to us to till our soil, are not over-intelligent, and need plain and unvarnished directions and statements before they can choose their locations. Any form of publication which is likely to bewilder the ignorant will defeat, in a great degree, all other endeavours to secure their settling among us. Misapprehension and resulting disappointment should be sedulously guarded against. The emigrant has to place great confidence in our statements before he quits his native shores, and for humanity's sake, if for nothing else, we should see to it that our claims and information are laid before him in clear and incontrovertible form and detail.

A system of official and regular advices, covering the points of each district open for immigration purposes, can easily be established. Indefinite information, or highly-coloured claims, will only divert the possible settler's attention, and fail to enlist his inclinations. But if once we take the front, and by the exercise of common care and honesty, become known as reliable and safe authorities in these matters, we may rest assured of the annual attention of thousands upon older soils, who are clamouring for light by which they can be guided.

Allusion has been made to our slow growth in population. The lately taken census shews that since 1871 we have added only some six hundred and sixty-four thousand souls. The rate of increase is then only some eighteen per cent. against an increase of thirty per cent. for the United States. But even here there is room for some comfort, for during the decade we have seen such unexampled shrinkage in business interests, as has made it simply a natural impossibility to keep many of our people with us. During the years of stagnation many have been forced to leave, many French-Canadians going to swell their colonies in the New England States, while numbers of young men have found business engagements elsewhere. It is probable that halfway in the decade,—1875, we could have numbered as large a population as we did five years later, so with better commercial prospects, we should naturally show more gain immediately. It may be argued that the United States have also passed through a period of depression during the same time, but it is easily seen that the smaller country must always show a greater proportion of loss if its manufacturing industries, through inadequate protection, are not kept fairly up. Its resources are not equal to those of a larger country, for all parts of it are affected simultaneously, its interests are closely interlaced, and no district within its borders rallies independently of the others.

Taken all in all, there is room for congratulation that Canada, during the past ten years, has not only held her own, but increased her population. Every city shows some gain, the percentages being about as follows :—Toronto, 55 ; Hamilton, 34 ; Montreal, 31 ; Ottawa, 27 ; London, 25 ; Halifax, 22 ; Kingston, 14 ; Quebec and St. John showing the lowest proportions, the former counting 4½, and the latter 9 per cent. gain.

The French-Canadian does not appear to shake off his nationality, even though he remain in the States for years. In this he presents a difference to the average settler there, who, coming from other countries, soon learns to assimilate with his surroundings, and often becomes prominent in the politics as well as in many of the movements about him. Thus it may be urged and soundly, that he leaves Canada only because he is forced to do so through temporary exigencies, but will return when he is protected by new life in our own industries.

Representatives of all nations find in Canada a peaceful, permanent home. They can and do acquire more individual importance, proportionately, than is possible in most other countries. Those who remain here longest are the most enthusiastic in their allegiance to the conditions under which they have lived. There are more wealthy men in our cities than can be found, *pro rata*, in most centres in other lands, and nothing will tie a man more closely to a country, than the fact that he has benefitted himself by locating there.

In writing this sketch it has been the aim of the author to recapitulate, as clearly as possible, the chief advantages—natural and otherwise—which we as a people can lay claim to ; contrasting these with the drawbacks which are also features of our position and make up.

To this end, attention has been directed to our slow growth in the past, and, per contra, to the inducements we naturally present for its more rapid increase. Suggestions have also been made with the hope that their earnest advocacy may add, in effect, to our natural attractions. Reference has also been had to the geographical disabilities under which our country may be said to have laboured, in connection with its juxtaposition to the United States, its want of people and wealth, in order to compete with Great Britain's manufacturing power and thus conserve important interests here ; but we find good reason for the hope and even *confident belief*, that these drawbacks will be offset, for with new thousands crossing our borders and finding homes among us, new ideas and energy to work them out will also come. Even at present, in many manufacturing industries, we are using the best mechanical appliances and competing with other nations in style and finish. Our scattered distribution of population has been pointed out, yet the remedy exists ; *we must become better known to the outside world*. A knowledge of our liberal institutions, our freedom, our growing commercial importance and our morality, should be disseminated far more widely than ever before, and well directed effort to this end will surely be followed by gain to Canada.

In addition to those already cited, there are a few *internal* causes which, to some extent, affect our complete mutual co-operation, and hinder us from acting as a unit in advancing our common interests in a perfect manner. The French-Canadian, in some degree, isolates himself too much from other nationalities, and where this trait is too prominent, it must contract the sphere of his usefulness to his country. Again, many Canadians who were born upon old country soil, are inclined to belittle the land of their adoption, and do not express the pride they ought to feel in the liberty, and advantages they enjoy as dwellers in the Dominion. As time goes on, however, it is probable that reserve and prejudices, insular and otherwise, will be worn off by the attrition which larger populations and increased commercial interests always cause, then, no obstacle can remain in the path of our country's progress.

Outlook for Trade, Possibilities, &c.

At no time in the history of Canada has the outlook for business promised so much to her merchants as it does to-day.   Within the old-time boundaries of trade we are full of health.   Uncertainties have given place to gains of legitimate character, while casualties and resulting loss have ceased to be attendant drawbacks to the situation.

Here in our oldest, most closely competed districts, confidence is restored, tradesmen and producers are not so disproportionate in point of numbers as before, old liabilities are cleared away, and even should one bad crop ensue, it could not, in an appreciable degree, disturb the existing sense of soundness, and faith in the future.   We are in a commercial position to which the late conditions of uncertainty are strangers, and these must so remain until in the course of time we once more create an abnormal, unnecessary weight of mercantile interests.

To-day, however, a wide scope for action presents itself to every enterprising merchant.   The profitable expansion of general business is not only possible, but very sure of realization.   Ten years ago we had not the knowledge of our country's capacity, which we possess to-day. Neglected districts, through commendable enterprise have been explored, and are being developed at a rate which is attracting attention abroad. We have not properly learned, nor made known our natural advantages in the past, but are beginning, and more than beginning to repair lost time in these respects.   Endeavours to this end, however, must be *maintained*, spasmodic effort counts for nothing.   Each season should find us prominent before Old World eyes, with our advantages listed in a conspicuous manner.   It is probable that all this will be given more attention by the proper authorities, and that private enterprise will steadily turn in this direction.   With energy then, our newer lands will become the source of added wealth and importance to our country.   With well directed effort here, and commercial prosperity in our older districts, a volume of commerce must result, which shall be wonderful, yet natural in its growth and permanency.

In support of these statements and predictions, it is but natural that the reader should ask for the course of reasoning by which they are arrived at. In turn, he is asked to consider the significance of our progress in the North-West, as well as the probable extension of commerce into other countries alluded to in the later pages of this sketch.

Having then, left our most closely populated districts in the enjoyment of prosperity, and immunity from serious losses by bad debts, we direct our attention to the North-West. This portion of our possessions may be said to have been, for half a century, forgotten. It must, however, through natural conditions, become an important factor in our growth, and because so long ignored may develop all the more rapidly.

The country presents great natural advantages both to the farmer and to the stock-raiser. The crop of wheat grain last year was about 3,000,000 bushels, and this was achieved by only a very sparse farming community. With even a moderate accession of farming immigrants during the coming season, this crop will be doubled, while new stakes in the country will be created, and the producing interest maintained.

Railway communication will shortly be brought to such a stage of development as to encourage and retain a new tide of settlers. The Canadian Pacific Railway Company promise, it is said, to build during 1882 a line of road five hundred miles in length, west from Winnipeg. The Pembina Mountain branch—south of the regular through line, is to be completed by Fall. The Sault St. Marie branch of some sixty miles of road will be located so as to connect with the international boundary, while the Thunder Bay branch will ere long be thrown open to the carrying interest. The people of Southern Manitoba will also have the South Western and other roads now being projected—to use for transportation of crops.

It has even been proposed to build a line from Lake Winnipeg to Hudson's Bay, and information is now being obtained as to the practicability of the scheme. It has, however, considerable opposition in so far as adverse argument goes, the opposants contending that the navigation of Hudson's Bay must be attended with great difficulties, and can hardly be depended upon as an outlet to Europe. A leading member of Parliament has asked for papers and full information upon this matter, remarking at the same time as follows :—" I am aware that a number of gentlemen of prominence in Canada have had the construction of a railway, between Lake Winnipeg and Hudson Bay, under serious consideration. But there are supposed to be very serious difficulties in the way of navigating Hudson Bay. In the first place, the grain trans- ported by that route would not, it is said, be the grain of the current season, but of the season preceding ; and, in the next place, vessels of different construction from those ordinary employed would probably be required for a navigation which must be encumbered by a considerable quantity of ice. But my main reason for calling the attention of the Government to the matter, is to have ascertained what length of time that navigation really remains open. If, as is asserted by some, navigation is practicable for four months in the year, or thereabouts, this matter may be of considerable moment to Manitoba, but if it is practicable for only two months or six weeks, as some assert, then it appears to me it would be an idle waste of money to construct this railway. As the matter is one of interest to English shipowners as well as to the people of Canada, I would suggest to the Government the desirability of having a thorough exploration in the way I suggest." If this outlet can be successfully created, it will undoubtedly add to the growth of the North-West in a most material ratio.

Many questions have been raised as to the climate of our North-western Districts, and many to-day believe that it is rigorous in the extreme.

This is not the case. It has been found singularly salubrious in in many sections, and these its most fertile ones. In these there has been found a warm wave prevailing which has appeared and remained while grain and other crops were maturing. The further West we go, the more is this noticeable. It is positively denied that any crop has ever been frozen in the North-West which was put in the ground at the proper season and in properly broken land.

The cattle trade interest of our country can be rapidly advanced by the utilization of the extensive ranges of our North-West. The immense fodder grounds which these present are well adapted to the growing of stock which we can export, and whose merits will soon offset the prejudice in England against North-American meats. While our cattle trade has grown up from very small beginnings to a considerable size, it may be increased without limit almost. Already companies have been formed by prominent men to found in the Bow River and other sections, large ranches, upon which the growth of fine stock will be a speciality. In one or two cases, colonization features have also been incorporated with the primary object, and, judging from the prospectuses, and the well-known energy and influence of the promoters, their plans are well founded.

These then, are some of the conditions which promise for Manitoba an increased importance, and in every country such have underlain growth and prosperity. It now only remains for us to secure the attention of old country toilers and invite them to realize the benefits of a change to our vast fertile possessions. Furthermore, the eventual safety of our trading centres in this new country, *must depend upon the speed with which we build up producing colonies there.*

Winnipeg's growth has been remarkable, and it promises to eclipse in the coming season, the strides with which it went forward in 1881 —though the advance may be somewhat ephemeral. Over six thousand men will be needed in this city alone during the present year, to erect the buildings contracted for already. This requirement, together with the railway absorption of labour, will create a certain amount of competition for brain and muscle, and furnish the vendors of staples with a market. It must, however, be *supplemented* by a solid increase of the *producing* class, or the present nation of shopkeepers will fare hardly.

The impetus given to the growth of Winnipeg has been largely caused by speculation and the increase of trade interests. The first attraction must cease to exist in a short time, the second can only be maintained by a proportionate increase of producing and exporting strength. Brandon, Emerson, Morris, Portage la Prairie, Minnedosa, West Lynne, &c., are all places which are now in turn feeling the same impetus in a greater or lesser degree, and from the same causes. They must support themselves, and like Winnipeg, must eventually fall back upon the same source of elemental strength. Attention, however, has been so widely attracted to this land of promise, that more confidence is now felt in the future of its commercial centres—delusive though this confidence may prove if unsupported by other ground than that of *anticipated* immigration.

Some fear is expressed that, in view of the great exodus of people from Ontario into Manitoba, the former Province may become depopulated. A deputation, representing the Canada West Land Agency Company, has asked for Government aid in making Ontario better known to intending emigrants, and thus offset the drain of outgoing residents. As a result of the request it is probable that our agents abroad will be requested to insert in their circulars some notices in favour of Ontario, and thus draw attention to older farms and more thickly settled districts. If this be properly and systematically done, there is little fear of Ontario being deserted, for there is always a certain proportion of settlers who are able to effect purchases of farm property at reasonable rates, and who prefer to locate nearer centres, and among older surroundings. Beside this, it is the younger men chiefly who are thus leaving Ontario. These, in many cases, have not yet acquired large stakes or homesteads in their native Province, and do not leave gaps which older farmers would leave unclosed. Furthermore, these young men—when farmers—are just the material needed in the North-West. They will do far more to widen its importance than would older men who lack energy, and cannot adapt themselves to new circumstances.

The Government is meeting the requirements of the North-West in a fair manner, the estimates of probable expenditure for the next year having been increased to good proportions. Postal facilities will be enlarged, extra provision for the Mounted Police, and for the Indians, has been made, thus ensuring as much safety to settlers as is practicable. A fair sum, but still thought inadequate, is set apart for the encouragement of immigration, and altogether, more than one-half the total increased appropriations are on account of the North-West. The amounts which are thought necessary to apply to the opening up of the new country are stated as follows :—

Immigration	$180,941
Indians	249,062
Mounted Police	123,000
Dominion Lands	29,193
Post Offices	19,600
Total	$601,796

In former pages it has been shown that our exports and imports bear more healthy relative proportions to each other than ever before. Little attention should be paid to that class of writers who, during the past two years of improvement, have been invading the columns of our leading papers with long and sounding articles against the healthful effect of increased exportations. It is admitted that England may import many times more goods than she exports, yet still preserve a sound balance. Her immense *money wealth* enables her to do this. The interest account is in her favour, but there can be no comparison between the Kingdom and our sparsely settled country. Canada represents wealth at her centres, but outside these is comparatively poor. She is not yet a lending nation, but she is still a borrowing country, and so will remain for a considerable time. Having then her wealth to make, she must do it in the most natural and *only* manner. Her new tariff and growing inventive powers are sufficing to fill the needs of those who formerly were importers, in a large degree. She has been creating a name as a producer—slowly it may be, but surely ; and now her goods are wanted and can be relied upon, both in quality and quantity.

Our export total of last year was some $10,000,000 in excess of that of the preceding year. It was also greater than the amount of strictly dutiable goods imported. Our manufactures rose in proportion,

Owing to competition in carrying interests our wheat export fell off from the totals of 1880, but there may be found a remedy for this, perhaps by some such improvements as have been suggested in previous pages. Our barley exports, however, increased nearly $2,000,000 in value. Butter and cheese, live stock, furs, eggs, potatoes, peas, rye, lumber, &c., all show gratifying gains, while in our Maritime Districts, the export of canned lobsters, fresh and pickled mackerel, seal skins, &c., exhibit gains. Briefly, the exports are the largest ever recorded, and the effect of this must be highly beneficial to the country at large.

While we annually send the bulk of our products to England, we are also widening the avenues of trade with other countries. A reasonable amount of attention to the further enlargement of these outlets will, if continued but a very few seasons, be very beneficial, and must repay the merchants who extend it.

To France we sent last year $606,586 worth of forest products, $40,284 of agricultural products, and nearly $16,000 in value of fish, mining products, &c. In return we imported from France only $1,000,000 in excess of our exports to her, a seemingly small difference when it is considered that her wines, brandies, cordials, &c., are bought by every country in large proportion; and that Church ornaments, religious books, &c., are, owing to the similarities of religion and tastes, so much in demand in the Province of Quebec. A good purpose will be served and our advancement become more fully recognized in that country when we have an intelligent representative in trade interests there. It is said to be the intention of the Quebec Provincial Government to appoint such an agent, and it is possible that the Dominion Government may also decide to represent our country generally in the same manner.

With Germany our export trade shews an increase, and it is noticeable that the goods exported were of general character. The mine, fisheries, forests, fields, animals, manufactures, &c., were all represented. The imports from this country are larger in proportion than from France, the figures being for last year $934,000 of imports against $84,932 exports. These proportions are, with those between us and France, likely to be changed more greatly in our favour, for the German Department of Commerce has authorized the collection of Canadian products in detail for the Berlin Museum of Foreign wares, and thus will naturally acquaint us better with each other. At present we naturally import largely from this old country, as it furnishes us with raw sheep skins, hops, glass goods, gold and silver leaf, hosiery, drugs, toys, pipes, &c., &c. These goods all have some special adaptability to our wants, and as German goods, meet with a ready sale all over the world.

Brazil also opens up inducements to our manufacturers, produce merchants and others. That country wants so many of our goods that the only wonder is, we have not for years done more with her. A new line of fine steamers leaving Rio Janeiro will call at Canadian ports during the coming season, and there is now every indication that our trade with South America will grow. The following letter to the *Monetary Times* was written early in the present year by Mr. Wm. Darley Bentley, Brazilian Consul at Montreal, and explains the situation forcibly :—

SIR,—I have read with great interest the letters on this trade which have appeared in your paper, and though it is not my wish or intention to mix in a controversy on the subject, I feel sure you will give me space for a few remarks, knowing how much I have the development of this trade at heart.

Without reference to the letters in question, I wish to say that from my own personal observation I am clearly of opinion that there are all the elements of a good trade between the Dominion and Brazil, and that these must be matured and developed by direct communication, and I ground my belief in the broad fact which cannot be disputed, that each country produces what the other requires.

It is perfectly plain that Canada consumes coffee, sugar, tapioca, tobacco, cotton, wool, hides, hair, drugs, dyes, India rubber, &c., &c., and it is equally plain that Brazil produces these. Why then should they not come direct, without the intervention of England or the States ?

Again it is a fact that Brazil consumes flour, butter, cheese, lard, bacon, hams, codfish, lumber, agricultural implements, and a hundred and one other articles which are all produced and manufactured in Canada. Again I ask, why should this not go to Brazil? And the only answer is, " we had no direct communication," we did not know the markets," &c. This is now altered. The communication is there and it only requires energy and common sense to make a lasting and profitable trade.

Some persons say, why have not the Americans succeeded with all their endeavours? I can easily tell you why : They have never gone the right away about it ! And it is with a view of enabling the Canadian to avoid their errors that I am induced to write this letter.

The error the American manufacturers have made, not only in Brazil but in other foreign countries is this : They send the wrong man to these countries to represent them. They send a man who firstly knows nothing of the language or of any other language except English (and that very often imperfectly) ; he knows nothing of the country to which he is going, and he knows nothing of the people, their manners, customs, &c. He is sent with a lot of samples, &c.; he bounces in and out of stores, as he would do at Chicago or San Francisco. He is generally clothed in a white duster and a broad brimmed hat or a straw hat. He knows no merchant to whom to refer as to either his position or the position of those whom he represents. He gets possibly a few orders, but not having calculated duties, &c., the manufacturer finds he cannot execute the orders at a profit, and declines to fill them, thus ignoring his paid agent. Can any one expect success in such circumstances? I am not drawing an imaginary picture ; these are facts and have over and over again been brought before the people of the United States by their worthy Consul General in Rio. I can, however, instance one firm in New York who have taken quite a different course, and what is the consequence ? They are now the largest exporters to Brazil in the United States, but they are the exception.

To obtain a footing in Brazil and a share of the trade, let me advise Canadians if they send agents down, to obtain the services of some man of good address, conversant with the language and of French also ; let him know something of the habits and customs of the country and the people ; let him be studiously polite (for the Brazilians are as polite as the French) and above all if he gets orders let it be understood that these orders are *executed* whether there be a loss or not ; if the agent has made a mistake let his employer lose rather than show bad faith. It is thus that English merchants have obtained their position and standing in every country of the world, and if the Canadian wishes to succeed, let him follow this example.

I do not propose to take up your valuable space by going into details on what or what not might be profitably sent to Brazil, but I will only say that if any of your readers desire information, I will only be too pleased to give it to them.

I am, Sir,

Your obedient servant,

WM. DARLEY BENTLEY,

Brazilian Consulate General,   Consul General.
Montreal, Jan. 17, 1882.

The importance of advertising ourselves in a practical manner to the rest of the world has been strongly urged in this work. Here, and finally, the author wishes to press this upon the attention of his readers. It has been well said that though Canadian merchants have sold largely to English and American buyers of our forest and agricultural products, the market thus obtained has been created rather by the necessities of the consumer than by the *enterprise of the producer.*

This is not as it ought to be ; moreover, it is a standing reproach to us. If we wish to be fortified with trade, let us make ourselves known where we can, and thus provide ourselves with outlet facilities, some of which may be always available. Thus when times grow bad with us, or become so, at some other point, we still have a way of realization paved for our interests. The apathy which has characterized us in the past in this connection, cannot well be illustrated more pointedly than by presenting the following figures. These shew the insignificant dimensions of our trade with South America for the past two years :—

	Imports.		*Exports.*
1880	$283,481		$789,940
1881	637,620		732,111

Now when it is remembered that these figures are not *one-ninetieth* part of our total exports or imports ; that Brazil produces staples which we must have, and that we produce merchandize which Brazil must buy, it certainly seems incredible that the outcome of mutual business is so small. Climate it is true, must be allowed for, flour and butter sent from Canada must be put up in different packages from those ordinarily used. Still all this is possible. The merchants of Canada can surely meet the requirements of the South American markets. Furthermore, we can now enter the field with flying colours, and by keeping good faith with Brazilian houses, can bind to us a trade not likely to be lessened or diverted.

A considerable business with Australia is also possible, and though it has not as yet been encouraged as it might have been, it will one day attract attention. Australia must have fish, furniture, boots and shoes, light manufactures of many kinds, and might become a large consumer of apples. Canada produces all these goods, yet has allowed England to supersede her in Australian markets. It is true that we have made attempts to open up and continue business with the country. But the goods we sent out were put up and assorted in more of an experimental than a practical manner. Styles of packages have to be considered, but it demands only a fair amount of inventive power to cover all these requirements. England's ling fish, though inferior to our cod, have long found a large market in Australia. But the trade was kept because the packages were right. With more enterprise we can enter many markets in which we have never been properly represented.

It is likely that Australia will grow rapidly in importance as a producer, and as a consequence must also be a large consumer. Australia is a rival of no mean significance to the United States, as a producer of gold, wheat and wool. Her wheat ranks very highly in London markets, while her wool clip is nearly always good, and commands good prices. Some idea of the rapid growth of the Colony may be had by glancing at the following facts. The country is not, politically, over forty years old. The City of Melbourne has grown from nothing in 1835 to a population of 300,000, and the country, generally, is now redeemed from the lawlessness which surrounded the earlier colonists. Like all other portions of the globe, which have been built up through the search for gold, Australia has had her reactionary periods. But these were experienced in her earlier years, when she had no superstructure of commerce to offset the varying phases and frequent lethargy of her mining interests. Now, the markets of the colony are based upon natural conditions, and the interchange of trade must be proportionate to her population and resources.

Thus we have before us, outlets for our products to different parts of the world, which may create profitable interchanges, and enlarge our commercial interests in no small degree. The countries named, as well as others, can be allied to us by close and agreeable bonds, our importance in trade centres will be felt, and when depressed at home, our overloaded business interests will feel the relief which may be established by our energy now.

The rates for money will naturally increase with the extensions of old and new interests, and in time the prices of our various securities will again become sensitive. The uses for money however, will be of such character as to enable these to pay the interest exacted, while the earnings of our incorporations must, in the absence of losses, conduce to the payment of such dividends as will keep quotations for our securities from serious relapse, and probably increase their market values for a considerable time. General causes for improvement in all staple interests, are now evident. These will prove for a time too strong to be visited by adverse affect. Speculation—outside a short lived continuation of it in our North-West—is not now rampant, and will not meet with the same encouragement which is lent it in more uncertain periods. There is ample employment for labor, and prices paid for it are satisfactory.

These are all necessary conditions to good trade, and they are aided by the fact that confidence and success beget a *continuance* of prosperity. Merchants are slow to believe that prosperous years must have endings. It is not natural for anyone to furl his sails before it is necessary, the *too common* tendency is to keep them hoisted, even when the traders ships, begin to thump on the first shoals of the coast of ruin.

Reasoning then upon the signs which observation makes patent to our eyes, we may expect no serious shock to credit in the immediate future. When trouble comes again it must be preceded by a change in the conditions we are now working under. Uneasiness and distrust will only grow where they have soil.

CLOSING PAGES.

The sterling merchants of the past half century, have found in Canada a field productive of solid gain in a measure far exceeding their early and most sanguine expectations. In acquiring their fortunes, they have not had to resort to speculation, but have simply put in use the old fundamental rules which always underlie success. Thus they have steadily grown up with the country, demonstrating through all their records the soundness of old time business rules and the *value of honesty*. There is now a future for the present generation of younger merchants to work out. What policy will they adopt?

The depression, with its gross overweight of mercantile interests, has passed away, leaving the commercial atmosphere clearer. There is now afforded to the earnest, worthy trader, an opportunity to make good the loss of time caused by the stagnant years of the last decade. It need discourage no earnest man to look ahead with confidence for the next few years, at least, and if any are prone to forecast trouble, let them remember that in good times their croakings and ill-timed forebodings only meet the discouragement they deserve, and in bad times only intensify existing evils.

The severest stress experienced during 1875, 1877 and 1879 was largely caused by the advent among us of many traders for whom there was no possible future, in so far as success was concerned. Interests were created in a day, in many cases being formed for the most transparent motives of working out a stake, which ought to have been promptly wound up months before. The evident unsoundness of many successions to businesses of poor character, and the continuations of interests whose props had deservedly failed to sustain the accumulated rottenness of years, all prolonged the depression, and created unnecessary distress among worthier traders.

The manipulation of many interests has changed in method, and often in general character from that practised fifty years ago. Competition has grown keener, and population has not kept pace in a proportionate degree with the business weight imposed upon it. Hence it is often said that a business man of the present day must expect to cope with more ingenuity, resource, and even sharpness, than fell to the lot of his father to contend against. That he must exercise more brain power, use more policy, and avoid the expression of his higher convictions of right and wrong modes and customs. Is this so? Why cannot new ideas be handled without distorting them and their method of application? Why should a merchant, for the sake of increasing a turnover—barren in results —interlace himself with interests which any ordinary mind can diagnose as weak and short-lived? The advantage is only temporary, but the example is most *demoralizing*.

Many are to be found who will argue that the strain upon the merchant of to-day is unavoidable, that the difference between the current *expenses* of a trader fifty years ago and a trader of this generation, creates for the latter an abnormal condition against which he must strive, that it is an encounter of wits for which all must be armed. But it is a strange phase of the puzzle—for such it is made out to be—that wits so sharpened by daily attrition, fail to cast a backward glance at *results*, and compare these with those of fifty years ago? What does the modern strain *end in?* Can any old and sterling merchant of a preceding generation, bring forward an experience of old days so sweepingly bitter in its outcome, as have been the disasters of the past twenty-five years? Trouble in old times was created by *exceptional* causes, was the result of political disturbances, serious conflagrations, poor crops, crude transportation facilities, &c., &c. These created great distress while they lasted, but not of the same character, nor of the same wearying duration as has been laid upon more modern eras.

Half a century ago trade conditions were more as they should be. *Then*, there was a more natural balance struck between *production* and *consumption*. It was part of the old time belief and business reasoning, that a certain proportion of the human race must develop the wealth laying dormant in the soil. Now, proportions have changed. An army of *middle men* are supported in every business centre. Young men seek starving clerkships, ignoring the independence they might enjoy as agriculturalists. They eventually swell the ranks of that forlorn hope—useless traders—whose numbers become sadly decimated before they reach the safe intrenchments of wealth and position.

Reckless trading *can* be discouraged, all communities are better off in the end where it ceases to be a feature. Capitalists who are looking for their cent. per cent., float schemes upon an overweighted business situation, and after securing a dividend at first, are forced to write off heavy shrinkages which preclude any further return, and end in the absorption of the capital which has become responsible. Men of small means waste years of fruitless toil in order to support the stake of an overdone business, into which they are enticed by the overgrown and cramped wholesaler. Banks lose money in turn, no class is exempt from loss, *all* must participate in the inevitable shrinkage and distress.

What is the use of playing this farce over and over again ? There can be no laudable pride or profit in it. *Chance* enterprises lack every element underlying legitimate traffic. Why create them then ? A country can sustain a certain proportion of banking and trading capital,—no more. Why load it then with new corporations and wholesaling concerns, which must live upon what older interests discard ? It is only where solid growth of population and manufacturing interests, with a general development, are features, that such expansion is warrantable. Certainly no good argument in its favour can lay where these conditions are absent. During the past decade our population was increased by a poor half million, and for the greater part of that time, our manufacturing industries languished through want of adequate protection. Yet, from 1872 to 1876, discounting institutions, and wholesale houses were added to the already sufficient number, in such proportion as could barely have lived upon *four times* the population increase.

Banks and credit dispensers generally, are now freed from the unsound and uncertain business of past days. The purgation has been attended with great wear and tear of brain and capital, but it is accomplished, and our legitimate institutions and merchants may well pride themselves upon the management which has brought them through seven years of terrible trials so well. These bankers and merchants enjoy the fullest confidence to-day, even as they did many years antecedent to the depression. They are emphatically the fittest, and so have survived. What a contrast their records present to those of that class who believed in a *chance* business. Starting in a bad time, with insufficient capital and uncertain trade connection, the latter argued that with push and modern adaptation of old rules they could conquer impossibilities. They reasoned that they could teach the older houses how the snail's pace might be exceeded, and years of time be saved in the race for wealth. It is but repeating an old story to recount the manner of their defeat and ruin, but they were slow to realize the falseness of their theories, and did much harm by attempting to remain in business after their first stoppage.

No similarity whatever existed between many houses born during the decade just past, and those of older records. While many of the commercial infants of 1872 to 1878 grew into instant notoriety, and became well advertised, it was all upon a basis as shifting as sand. The first head-wind set them aback, and no subsequent manipulation of their rickety crafts could possibly bring them into a safe port. The merchants who, all the way through the depression, went on as though there were no trouble, were those who kept ever before them, the rules of prudence and care which first laid the foundation of their fortunes. They were open to shrinkage, but this was largely owing to the pressure upon the business situation *of the new traders*. They did not, however, jeopardize what capital they had accumulated, and true to old maxims, kept down expenses, did not push business against their judgment, and quietly accepted the aggregate loss—which to them was a minimum,— through each dark year.

These were the houses whose conservatism shielded them from the drain of disproportionate interest outgo. The *others* found, in many cases, their interest totals exceeding all other expenses, and there are instances where they succumbed under *its* weight *alone*. Allusion has been made in previous pages to the banks which failed during the depression. It was owing to the reckless management of these, that the useless houses referred to, obtained *any* lease of life. It was these institutions who *renewed* the lease in the face of compounding interest losses, and despite the fact that capital was all gone. Cases are known of houses running almost entirely upon an inadequate special capital, which was lost before the end of the first term of the limited partnership, yet was re-registered for another term, the house discounting their special partner's paper for large additional sums, which were greatly in excess of his total worth. The bank knew this, yet it continued its advances, and discounted besides, regular presentations of the weakest paper which could be found in the country. Houses were *created* by such banks simply to *freshen up* the character of old assets, the new house taking over an old firm's responsibility, and going on with brazen front only to roll up liabilities upon which far less was paid than could have been got from the original wreck. Houses have been kept alive when it was clearly shown that their private expenditure, interest drain, and other outgoes could not possibly be met, even with a larger turnover than they had ever done. No consideration seems to have been given to the fact that increase of business—when possible with them—meant an increased percentage of losses. These houses were, from the first, working under palpable disadvantages, as compared with the older merchants. Their failures were assured from the start, as no one *sure* element of success was present in the composition of their so-called " firms."

Happily, both weakly managed discounting institutions, and most of the useless jobbing houses have had their day, and are now lost to our sight. Their brief careers, however, have carried with them experiences, which, in their dire effect, will dwell with many of the present generation for a lifetime. The lessons taught us by the deserved misfortunes of these concerns are plain, and come to us emphasized by their recent occurrence and painful exemplification. We see now, more distinctly than ever before, that sound business rules cannot be set at defiance. Now is our opportunity to reform any tendency we may consciously feel within ourselves, to depart from safe business conduct. Now we may inaugurate a commercial *morale*, which shall be stern in its unswerving efforts to defeat fraud, and to discourage incapacity, chance ventures, and recklessness. It is within our power to prevent, very largely, the recurrence of the distress experienced during the past decade. It may not be possible to avert periods of stagnation, but it *is* possible to prevent such intensity of suffering as has in the past fallen upon us.

Every observant business man, who has gone with us through the vicissitudes of the past ten years, has stored up an array of precedents by which alone success can be won, has armed himself with vivid illustrations of the rapid decline of unsound schemes, and has individually felt the adverse effect created by the departure of others from legitimate ground. Let him then lend his influence to discourage the trader who steps over the limit line of sound and honest traffic. We could have gone to no better school than the one we have attended, no merchant of past generations has ever had the same advantage which has come to us. Merchants of fifty years ago were not brought face to face with exigencies of the same significance, yet they learned and practised virtues, which, allied to *our* procedure, would have saved us in more modern days.

Shall knowledge, acquired at the cost of so much individual and collective sufferings, remain unapplied to our future situations? It is *capital* of the best quality, why ignore it when so hardly earned? It will be many years before some of our business men *can* forget the trials of the past, and side by side with the recollection, will stand the precedents they have learned for the treatment of unworthy risks. Credit must be checked if unsound characteristics appear. Business is not play, still less is it chance. Speculation cannot be wholly separated from it, but its dangerous points may be well weighed, and if a proposed transaction continues to look uncertain and hazy, after due consideration is given it, all thoughts of closing it should be dropped. The success with which many unsound ventures have been floated, is directly traceable to want of firmness in declining an obvious risk; for it is but a poor commentary upon modern intelligence to reason that the risk is not seen. When successfully manipulated, these schemes lead to the promotion of others, until stakes are created which *must* be bolstered up, or loss becomes assured at once. All this helps to bring about an unhealthy expansion, and whether the interest in question be promoted by a corporation, or upon individual account, the final result affects a country much the same. Each mistake in grasping at promised profits of unnatural proportions, narrows the ground basis of business safety, for it destroys *confidence*. Credulity, vanity, pride and avarice are played upon, until good times give place to bad, the superstructure of commerce topples to a fall, and the balance is again restored only at the cost of suffering and money.

There have been periods within the past forty years of commercial history, when, had it not been for the presence among us of old school merchants, all would have been a chaos of conflicting, struggling interests. Certain situations needed the sanitary influence which these men exerted, and few of us realize how much solid service they performed in forcing back the waves of distrust which nearly undermined all faith in everything. *We must educate men to take their places*, for they will not be with us long. Individual ability, coupled with sterling integrity, are requisites, which never were more essential to any situation than that of to-day. We have seen the prospects which stretch before us, the possibilities which may be reached if sound principles guide us, and we have been taught vivid lessons and precedents which must not, *cannot* be easily forgotten. Elevated conceptions of right and wrong will come with noble practices, while personal comforts, and all the *apanages* of a correct, yet humane course, will be won by earnest endeavour. The men who have "fed on the roses and lain in the lilies of life" cannot at once meet the exigencies of the times, cannot be accepted as guides, and must themselves reform their views, but there are others who *may* be followed, and new material can be created, which shall prove a balance-wheel in future times of trial.

There is every reason for all to take a part in the framing of a better record, which shall prove a valuable inheritance to our business successors. We owe this to the coming generation. Each step taken in honest, legitimate courses counts. Just, honourable, humane action does not pass unheeded, all carry their lessons, and unite in creating confidence and inner satisfaction.

Growth & Fostering of Trade, &c., Addenda.

On the afternoon of March 14th, 1882, the supplemental report of the Factory Commission was presented to the House by Sir Leonard Tilley. It reads as follows :—

To the Hon. the Minister of Finance :—

In accordance with your letter of instruction, we have the honour to submit for your information the following supplementary report, containing the figures with reference to the state of wages, prices of goods, new factories and increased number of hands in the old established factories, since the fall of 1878. It will be observed by the figures that there has been a general increase in the number of hands employed in every branch of the manufacturing industries, but that the glass, cotton, woolen, and organ and piano works show the largest proportionate increase. It must, of course, be understood that the list of manufactories mentioned does not represent the whole of factories which have been started in the Dominion during the past three years. The ninety-six alluded to are simply those which have come under our observation during the course of the investigation. There are others located at places which we did not visit, and we have reason to believe there are some others in places which were visited by us. In our visits to the various places we found many buildings in course of construction to be used as factories. Amongst others we may mention that cotton factories are being erected in each of the Provinces. A large factory was about completed at Coaticook, to be used as a beet sugar works during a portion of the year, and in refining cane sugar when the crop of beets had been worked up. A very fine brick building was just completed at Campbellford, and is now in full running order, giving employment to 125 hands in the manufacture of woolen goods. We found in Nova

Scotia that the coal miners were doing a satisfactory business, the managers and miners feeling satisfied that their interests were being carefully considered by the Government. In connection with this we may say that Nova Scotia coal is being used by manufacturers along the line of the Grand Trunk Railway as far West as Cobourg and Guelph. The coal is said by those who use it to be a more economical fuel than any which they had previously used. Some conversation was had with the proprietor of a foundry at Charlottetown, who was greatly enlarging his premises, and he reported that orders for machinery to be used in manufacturing industries were coming in faster than he was able to supply the demand. The new factories are scattered over the whole section covered by our tour, each Province participating in the general revival of trade. The number of new factories is as nearly as possible one-fifth of the whole, so that 20 per cent. of the works visited were started since September, 1878. We were unable to get the increased number of hands in all the older factories visited, but we have ascertained the increase in a sufficient number of cases to give a basis. The table on page 6 will be found approximately correct.

We have the honour to be,

Your obedient servants,

WM. LUKES,

A. H. BLAKELY.

A detailed statement is then given of the new factories started under the present tariff. It is shown that ninety-six manufacturing enterprises have been developed since 1879, and that these give employment to over seven thousand operatives. The increase of labour being as follows :— In foundries, about 14 per cent. ; in furniture factories, 20 per cent. ; in boots and shoes, 11 per cent. ; in glass and pottery, 25 per cent. ; in organ and piano works, 28 per cent. ; in wool and knitting factories, 19 per cent. ; in tobacco and cigars, 7 per cent. ; clothing factories, 14 per cent. ; cotton factories, 30 per cent. ; rope, flax and brush factories, 11 per cent. ; in paper manufactories, 10 per cent. ; in general miscellaneous manufactures, 23 per cent.

Comparing the wages ratio between 1879 and 1882, it is shown that the changes are about as follows :—

Number of Factories where wages have remained the same.. 35
Factories started since January, 1879. and made no change.. 50
Factories showing increase of 35 per cent...................... 3
Factories   "   "   " 33 per cent...................... 2
Factories   "   "   " 30 per cent...................... 9
Factories   "   "   " 25 per cent...................... 21
Factories   "   "   " 20 per cent...................... 42
Factories   "   "   " 17½ per cent...................... 1
Factories   "   "   " 15 per cent...................... 66
Factories   "   "   " 12½ per cent...................... 5
Factories   "   "   " 10 per cent...................... 93
Factories   "   "   " 8 per cent...................... 4
Factories   "   "   " 5 per cent...................... 31
State of wages not ascertained.................................. 4
Factories showing decrease : none.

Insolvent Act, &c., Addenda.

While it was decided by Government, that no general Bill to create a new *general* Insolvency Act should be legislated upon in the Session of 1882, a Bill was introduced by Sir Alex. Campbell respecting Incorporated Companies—such as Banks, Insurance and Trading Companies. The main features covered by the Bill being the conditions upon which such Companies should be declared insolvent, proceedings for winding up, and general provisions affecting the handling of such incorporate estates. Copies of this Bill were distributed February 25th, 1882, and its provisions read as follows :—

The Bill declares that a Company shall be deemed insolvent—

(*a*) If it is unable to pay its debts as they become due ;

(*b*) If it calls a meeting of its creditors for the purpose of compounding with them ;

(*c*) If it exhibits a statement showing its inability to meet its liabilities ;

(*d*) If it has otherwise acknowledged its insolvency ;

(*e*) If it assigns, removes or disposes of, or is about or attempts to assign, remove or dispose of, any of its property with intent to defraud, defeat or delay its creditors or any of them.

A Company is deemed to be unable to pay its debts as they become due whenever a creditor in a sum exceeding two hundred dollars then due has served a demand in writing on the Company for the same, and when the Company has for a specified time thereafter failed to pay such debt and compound for the same to the satisfaction of the creditor ; such specified time to be ninety days in the case of a Bank, sixty days in that of an Insurance Company, and thirty days in that of a Trading Corporation.

PROCEEDINGS FOR WINDING UP.

When a Company becomes insolvent, a creditor for the sum of two hundred dollars may, after four days' notice of the application to the Company, apply by petition to the Court in the Province where the head office of the Company is situated, or if there be no head office in Canada, then in the Province where its chief place or one of its chief places of business is situated, for an order that the business of the Company be wound up. The Court may make the order applied for, may dismiss the petition with or without costs, may adjourn the hearing conditionally or unconditionally, or make any interim or other order that it deems just.

If the Company oppose the application, on the ground that it has not become insolvent within the meaning of the Act, the Court may appoint an accountant or other person to enquire into the affairs of the Company and report within thirty days, whereupon the Court must either refuse the application or make the winding up order without unnecessary delay. The Company from the making of the winding up order must cease to carry on its business. When the winding up order is made, no suit, action, or other proceeding shall be proceeded with or commenced against the Company except with leave of the Court and subject to such terms as the Court may impose. The Court may, as to all matters relating to the winding up, have regard to the wishes of the creditors or contributories, as proved to it by any sufficient evidence, and may, if it thinks it expedient, direct meetings of the creditors or contributories to be summoned, held, and conducted in such manner as the Court directs, for the purpose of ascertaining their wishes, and may appoint a person to act as Chairman of any such meeting, and to report the result of such meeting to the Court; in the case of creditors, regard is to be had to the value of the debts due to each creditor, and in the case of contributories to the number of votes conferred on each contributory by the regulations of the Company.

LIQUIDATORS.

The winding up order must appoint a liquidator or more than one liquidator of the estate. An Incorporated Company may be appointed liquidator to the goods and effects of a Company under this Act, and it may act through one or more of its principal officers, to be appointed by the Court. The Court may also determine whether any and what security is to be given by a liquidator on his appointment. If at any time there be no liquidator, all the property of the Company shall be deemed to be in the custody of the Court. The liquidator is to be paid such remuneration, by way of percentage or otherwise, as the Court directs, and upon the appointment of a liquidator all the powers of the directors cease. The liquidator is subject to the summary jurisdiction of the Court, in the same manner and to the same extent as the ordinary officers of the Court. The liquidator must, within thirty days after the date of the final winding up of the business of the Company, deposit in the bank appointed or named, as hereinbefore provided for, any other money belonging to the estate then in his hands not required for any other purpose authorized by this Act, with a sworn statement and account of such money, and that the same is all he has in his hands ; he is subject to a penalty not exceeding ten dollars for every day on which he neglects or delays such payment ; he is a debtor to Her Majesty for such money, and may be compelled as such to account for and pay over the same.

CONTRIBUTORIES.

Every shareholder or member of the Company or his representative, is liable to contribute the amount unpaid on his shares of the capital, or on his liability to the Company or to its members or creditors, as the case may be, under the Act, charter or instrument of incorporation of the Company ; and the amount which he is liable to contribute is deemed assets to the Company, and is a debt due to the Company payable as may be directed or appointed under this Act. The Court is to adjust the rights of the contributories among themselves, and distribute any surplus that may remain among the parties entitled therein.

CREDITORS' CLAIMS.

The property of the Company must be applied in satisfaction of its liabilities and the charges incurred in winding up its affairs ; and unless it is otherwise provided by the Act, charter or instrument of incorporation, any balance remaining must be distributed according to their rights and interests in the Company. The Court may fix a day within which creditors are to send in their claims, aud after due notice of the same has been given, the liquidator is at liberty to distribute the assets of the Company, or any part thereof, amongst the parties entitled thereto, having regard to the claims of which the liquidator has then notice ; and the liquidator is not liable for the assets or any part thereof so distributed to any person of whose claim the liquidator had not notice at the time of distributing the said assets or a part thereof, as the case may be.

FRAUDULENT PREFERENCES.

All gratuitous contracts or conveyances or contracts without consideration or with a merely nominal consideration respecting either real or personal estate made by a Company with respect to whose business a winding up order under this Act is afterwards made, with or to any person whatsoever, whether such person be its creditor or not, within three months next preceding the commencement of the winding up or at any time afterwards ; and all contracts by which creditors are injured, obstructed or delayed made by a Company unable to meet its engagements and with respect to whose business a winding up order under this Act is afterwards made, with a person knowing such inability, or having probable cause for believing such inability to exist, or after such inability is public and notorious whether such person be its creditor or not,—are presumed to be made with intent to defraud its creditors.

OTHER PROVISIONS.

All dividends deposited in a bank and remaining unclaimed at the time of the final winding up of the business of the Company, are to be left for three years in the bank where they are deposited, and if still unclaimed, are then to be paid over by such bank, with interest accrued thereon, to the Receiver-General of Canada, and, if afterwards duly claimed, are to be paid over to the persons entitled thereto.

All costs, charges, and expenses properly incurred in the winding up of a Company, including the remuneration of the liquidator, are payable out of the assets of the Company in priority to all other claims.

Where a winding up order is made, if it appear in the course of such winding up that any past or present director, manager, officer or member of such Company has been guilty of any offence in relation to the Company for which he is criminally responsible, the Court may, on the application of any person interested in such winding up, or of its own motion, direct the liquidator to institute and conduct a prosecution or prosecutions for such offence, and may order the costs and expenses to be paid out of the assets of the Company.

For Banks Only.

It is the duty of the liquidator to ascertain as nearly as may be the amount of notes of the bank intended for circulation and actually outstanding, and to reserve until the expiration of at least two years after the date of the winding up order, or until the last dividend, in case that it is not made till after the expiration of the said time, dividends on such part of the said amount in respect of which claims may not be fyled ; and if claims have not been fyled and dividends applied for in respect of any part of the said amount before the period herein limited, the dividends so reserved are to form the last, or part of the last dividend.

At the time of going to press with this book, the Bill had not been legislated upon.

LUMBER ADDENDA.

Inquiries made at end of February, 1882, show that the sawn stuff at Ottawa has nearly all been disposed of, that sawyers now know where they stand, and have, almost without exception, done well as regards marginal profits.

For the ensuing season, an allowance will have to be made in quoting prices. An advance of 20 per cent. has been made in shantymen's wages, 25 per cent. in drivers, and 15 per cent. in mill hands pay. In pork, for supplies, an advance of $5 per barrel, besides advances of less amount in other staples have also been experienced.

Snow has fallen in sufficient quantities to admit of drawing in the woods, but unless March and April contribute a seasonable quantity, the prospect is that the rivers will again be low at the start, and this year's cut will not be got to mill except in a small proportion.

The estimated cut is nearly up to the actual cut of last year. The cost in the mill, of last year's logs left over, and putting the loss in interest against the increased cost of this year's cut, will be about 18 per cent. less than the latter.

The increased cost of sawn lumber, as compared with last year, will be about 20 per cent., f. o. b., at Ottawa, or an average of about $2 per thousand feet all round.

There is little or no unsold sawn lumber at Ottawa. American and other buyers are feeling their way, and a few sales have been made for future delivery at good prices. Sawyers are hopeful, and believe there will be a demand for all they can produce, at paying prices.

Recent advices from the Western States, indicate that the lumber of the future is certain to cost the consumer more money than it has been bought for during the past season. A large tract, five miles from any stream, in the Menomenee region, has been sold at five times what it would have brought only two years ago. Capitalists are making speculative purchases for years ahead, particularly in pine tracts, and these have rapidly advanced in quoted values.

Dry Goods, Clothing, &c., Addenda.

See also Dry Goods, Cotton, Silk & Woolen Manufacturing Interests.

Among the staples usually turned over by the clothing manufacturers are English Pilots, Presidents, Naps, Tweeds, &c. The importations in this line are small, probably not over 10 per cent. of material, &c., but some cheap suits, low priced pea-jacket reefers, or wear for fishermen, are brought out and still sold in the Lower ports.

The chief distress which has been experienced through the depression in this interest, has been felt by houses that were not well managed, and whose stocks were not kept close and free from old makes, but generally speaking, our legitimate houses have made money steadily through even the hardest years. The trade may, in time, become overdone, but the outlook for it is good, and as our commercial interests extend into the newer sections of the country, there must be an outlet for an increasing production of clothing.

Our woolen cloth manufacturers may be said to have worked through the depression, and against many drawbacks, in a most creditable manner. Only a few of the smaller, weaker, and more unimportant factories having got into trouble, as a rule. It must be said, however, that those factories who more than held their own during the darker years, were very few in number. During 1880 and 1881, however, they were quick to catch the impetus which general trade experienced, and are now making better returns.

Our city cloth houses, doing anything of a general business, suffered heavy losses from 1875 to 1881, in most cases. These were not only caused by the making of bad debts, but by shrinkage and depreciation of stock. Those who adopted the policy of a safer mode of selling, lost by depreciation, and general results were unsatisfactory. During 1881, however, these conditions experienced a notable change, values had become steadier, and bad debts very few, while the turnover of business increased in some cases, fifty to one hundred per cent., as compared with 1877.

COTTON MANUFACTURING ADDENDA.

Since the writing of our main sketch was completed, it has been decided by several of our larger cotton manufacturing companies to make important extensions and additions to their present facilities, the operations of the past year warranting a largely increased output. At the annual meeting of the Montreal Cotton Company, it was resolved to increase their capital stock from $500,000 to $1,000,000, and to make such additions to their mills at Valleyfield as will admit of the doubling of their present capacity. A new building, 250 feet long, by 100 feet wide, and five stories high, will be put up during the present summer. The space thus afforded will permit of their running twice the number of spindles at present in operation, namely, 31,000, but it is not the intention to utilize the whole space at present. It is probable that in the near future the Company will make some additions to the lines of goods now being made, viz., shirtings and shoe drills, when all the space afforded by the extension will be necessary.

The shareholders of the Merchants Manufacturing Company, whose new mills at St. Henri, a suburb of Montreal, have just been completed, at their annual meeting recently held, instructed the directors to apply for amendments to their charter, authorizing the increase of their capital from $400,000 to $1,000,000. This increase of capital is a preliminary to important contemplated extensions, but the exact shape that the enlargement may take has not yet been finally decided upon.

The Canada Cotton Manufacturing Company, one of the oldest companies engaged in this industry, has also lately increased its capital by the issue of 1,250 new shares of $100. This new capital of $125,000 is to be devoted to the extension of the mill and the purchase of additional machinery.

Outlook for Trade, &c., Addenda.

———•———

Just before going to press with this work, it has been pretty well ascertained that the prospect for at least, a moderate influx of immigrants to our North-West is good. Our agents in Liverpool and London appear confident that opinion is setting strongly in favour of our country, while others just returned from the old country confirm this, saying that general attention is being directed to Manitoba, and that many earnest inquiries are being daily made. Intimations from good sources have been received, to the effect that some 20,000 emigrants have already secured passage by the earlier spring vessels bound to our ports. Advices from the booking agents in Norway and Sweden state that owing to the mild winter, navigation of the North Sea will be practicable at least a month sooner than it was last year, and that emigrants will consequently leave its ports for North America earlier than heretofore. The leading shipping agents predict a larger volume of proposing settlers, and state that their general destination appears to be the Red River Valley, this section having been well endorsed by Scandinavian farmers who have returned from it to spend the winter at home.

Additional colonization schemes are being formed within our older sections, and while these may take a certain number of people from Ontario and Quebec, these will be young men well calculated to develop the North-West, and by their energy maintain the spirit of enterprise now so evident.

A Company, in which several prominent, earnest men of Montreal are interested, propose to follow up an idea similar to that already suggested in this work, *i. e.*, extending assistance to the settler, upon his arrival, by providing him with a dwelling, helping him to stock and till his land, &c. All honour to such enterprise; if carried out, it will effect its objects when other plans fail. A Press Colonization scheme is also proposed ; others will follow, and our North-West become thoroughly known—to its advantage.

It is the intention of the Government to establish a means of collecting the chief statistics appertaining to the North-West. If this be done as a branch of the Department of Agriculture, it can, and probably will, assume the form of an annual report, and will exercise a certain influence in our behalf abroad. It is also announced, as the intention of our Government, to erect a new and commodious building at Winnipeg for the temporary shelter of immigrants. This is another move in the right direction. The building is to be ready about the middle of April.

Two petitions, respecting the proposed railway from Winnipeg to Hudson's Bay, have been submitted to Government. It is understood that one of these proposed Companies have had the location of their line approved of. The Lake Superior and James' Bay Railway Company's Bill is meeting with favour, and is likely to be passed, it is thought. The powers asked by the Company, are for the construction of a railway from Michipicoton, on the North-Eastern coast of Lake Superior, to Moose Factory, on James' Bay. Other Bills for new roads and re-construction, or extension of others, are being debated upon in Parliament, with fair prospects of being ratified. The needs of the carrying interest in the North-West are thus likely to be covered, and the inducements to emigrants are becoming stronger. If now, some plan is adopted by the promoters of colonization schemes, whereby the stranger immigrant may be made more independent and free in his start, by having a small house to locate in, all may work well. A *shelter*, no matter how cheap, is *the* requisite upon his arrival. If it be provided, this will keep him in heart, and aid him materially in becoming of early use to himself and to our country.

There will, doubtless, be re-action, losses and disappointment, experienced in property speculation at certain proposed centres in the North-West. At some points, future *cities* have been laid out, leading business streets—to be—indicated, and lots sold in these at foot front figures, where now only exist a few small, cheap buildings to mark the coming city's site. In some cases, a proposed *town* has thus been sold, the area devoted to the sales covering land by the square mile. One piece of land is made to pay a profit to a half dozen operators, not one of these profits being based upon intrinsic worth at present, or in a future near enough to warrant the figures. Now, all this can have but one result. No likely or even possible settlement can be created which will keep pace with the ideas thus recklessly circulated, and by many, foolishly adopted. It is a *gold fever* growth of values, in a country where gold *mines* are conspicuous by their absence. It is attended by the wildness so characteristic of speculation in new lands, and holders at its end, must submit to the inevitable re-action and very slow recovery always experienced under. like conditions.

It is, doubtless, well ordered that those who forsake legitimate trade, to yield to the demon of speculation in new and undeveloped land, shall experience some disappointment. They do the country no good, they are the first to lay it under a cloud. The reports of their earlier gains draw others to the scene, where later on they cannot even obtain a subsistence. Being non-producers, they swell the overfilled ranks of tradesmen, who in turn must await the influx of population to secure the gains, which at first, seemed certain of a speedy realization.

Apart from this one drawback, this inordinate craving for ephemeral acquisitions, the future growth and importance of Manitoba is heralded by fair promises. Her snug crop of wheat last year ought easily to be doubled, and with profit to the farmer, for the fertility of much of the soil is such, that grain can be raised at far less expense than in Eastern districts, while new transportation facilities will be added to carry it.

Not only are these favouring conditions present, but Manitoba wheat has already won a name for itself; the quality of the grain is better than in most countries, and is likely to be brought to a higher standard still, the hard floury Scotch Fyfe seed being now largely introduced.

GEOLOGICAL SURVEY REPORT, 1879-1880.

The following interesting report is condensed and published by the Montreal *Gazette*, March 16, 1882 :—

The work of the officers of the Survey during the season of 1880 embraced explorations and surveys in the ·Northwest Territories, the Souris River coal fields, the Hudson's Bay Basin, Manitoba, in New Brunswick, Nova Scotia and the Magdalen Islands. No field work was done during the season in British Columbia. Dr. G. M. Dawson was absent in Europe during part of the summer, attending the meeting of the British Association. The rest of the year, when not engaged in correspondence and other duties, he devoted to the preparation of his report of the Peace River explorations of 1879 and of the map which accompanies it. This map is all that is known of a region about 130,000 square miles in extent, from the Pacific Ocean to the 112 meridian from the 45th to the 57th degree of north latitude. The report and map together supply the most trustworthy information concerning that vast and interesting region. The expedition took up a period of seven months (from May 8 to December 9), its object being to learn all that could be learned of the physical features and economic importance of the country passed through. It deals in succession with the coast region (including the islands), its harbors, forests, mountains and rivers and climate ; the Skeena River region, its vegetation and climate ; Indian population of the Skeena region ; the lakes and mountains of Northern British Columbia, and the soil, production, climate and temperature of the regions around them ; the Lower Forks of Pine River to Dunvegan ; the Grande Prairie and Descent of Smoky River ; the country between Dunvegan and the Athabasca River : the Athabasca River from Drift-pile Camp to Lesser Slave River, and from there to Athabasca Landing, and on to Edmonton ; the country from the confluence of the Smoky and Peace Rivers, by the north side of Lesser Slave Lake to Old Fort Assiniboine and Edmonton ; the region along the Athabasca from the "Landing" to Riviere La Biche and thence to Victoria on the Saskatchewan. These descriptions are followed by a sketch of the geology of the region between the 54th and the 57th parallels, from the Pacific Coast to Edmonton. Of the Omenica gold district, Dr. Dawson says :—"The main points which seem to bear on the possible future of the district are as follow :—(1) The existence of rich deposit of gold and the possibility that, with greater facility of access, the known area covered by these would be increased and that it would become possible to work those of a lower grade. (2.) The occurrence of pellets of native silver or amalgam in association with the gold. It may not be found possible to trace this material to veins of workable dimensions, but its presence seems in some degree to show the general argentiferous character of the district. (3.) The chief promise of future importance as a mining centre seems to lie, however, in the fact that highly argentiferous galena occurs in some abundance, and, it is reported, in well-defined, wide veins. These it is impossible at present to utilize, owing to the cost of labour and carriage." Some of the most important veins are in the vicinity of a stream called Boulder Creek. One, known as the Arctic Circle vein, is said to be about 20 feet wide and to show about four feet of highly metalliferous ore. An adjoining claim shows a vein eight feet wide of nearly pure galena. The Arctic Circle vein yielded, by one analysis, silver equal to 42.2 oz. per ton of 20 cwt. ; by another, 40.81 oz., with trace of gold. Pig lead would contain about 50 oz. to the ton. Two assays of specimens of ore from a deposit known as the "Mammoth Ledge," yielded the following results :—Gold, per ton, 1-10 oz., $2.06 ; silver, per ton, 32 4-10 oz—$41.80. Clean galena would assay $131.85. Dr. Dawson mentions it as a point of considerable importance that in both the horizons characterized by sandstones in the Peace River district, coal occurs, showing that the carboniferous character of the rocks is not confined to a single series of beds. This, he adds, probably confirms the view advanced by Dr. Hector, and supported by Mr. Selwyn for the Saskatchewan country, as to the existence of a coal-bearing horizon in the cretaceous of that region in addition to that of the Tertiary or Laramie age. There can be little doubt that beds of a workable character exist in the region between Athabasca and Peace Rivers, and will be found by further search. A bed of coal, reported to be eight feet in thickness, occurs near the projected railway crossing of the North Pembina River, while between Fort Edmonton and the mouth of the Brazeau River, on the Saskatchewan, a seam of coal from fifteen to twenty feet thickness was discovered by Mr. Selwyn in 1873, and other thick seams are reported on the Upper Brazeau. While neither that of the North Pembina nor that of the Saskatchewan can be classed as true bituminous coals, they are still fuels of great value. Appended to Dr. G. M. Dawson's report are a list of plants collected in the northern part of British Columbia and the Peace River country in 1879, meteorological observations over the same area and from Edmonton to Manitoba (June 7 to November 28, 1879), a note on the latitudes and longitudes used in preparing a map of the region from the Pacific coast to Edmonton, and a note on the distribution of some of the more important trees of British Columbia.

In March, 1880, it was decided to obtain more precise information respecting the Tertiary lignite-coal seams of the Souris River, and, for this purpose, a contract was made with Messrs. McGarvey & Highman, of Petrolia, Ont., to undertake borings in the Souris River Valley. The work began seven miles east from Roche Percee on the 12th of July, and was finished on the 6th of October, 1880. The results of these bores in the Souris Valley, Moose Mountain Creek, South Antler Creek and Turtle Mountain, to the respective depths of 295, 155, 155 and 200 feet, are given in Mr. Selwyn's report. In the first of these (the Souris River), when a depth of 273 feet was reached, a seam of lignite was struck, and found to extend down for 6 feet 1 inch, when it ended in clay as above. In the second boring (Moose Mountain Creek) the lignite-bearing Tertiary formation was not reached, though at 83 feet deep a small, apparently drifted fragment of lignite was met with. Owing to the constant falling in of the sides, the strata passed through in the third boring (South Antler Creek) could not be very accurately described. In the fourth, also, no lignite was encountered, nor could it be said whether the formation which contained it had been reached. The account of these borings is accompanied by a description of the topographical features of the country where they were made. Appended to it is Dr. G. M. Dawson's report, first published in 1874, of his examination of the same district in connection with the International Boundary survey.

Dr. Robert Bell, with Mr. Cochrane as assistant and Messrs. Nelson and Langford as volunteers, continued his explorations in the Hudson's Bay Basin. Dr. Bell reached Winnipeg on the 16th of June, and from there made his way to Norway House and York Factory, making geological and general notes on the route. On September 13th he sailed from that place in the "Ocean Nymph," 320 tons, belonging to the Hudson's Bay Company, to England, the Bishop of Moosonee being also on board. The notes of the voyage are exceedingly interesting, not only for the opportunities of observing the character of both shores, but also in connection with the employment of this route between Europe and the North-West, in the near future, for general traffic. Sailing vessels, Dr. Bell says, are at a disadvantage in such a trip. The captain told him that the drift ice encountered was much worse than what he had met on his passage from Europe, a statement which surprised the hearer, as he had passed through much more formidable blocks in going in a steamer from St. John's, Newfoundland, to Halifax. The weather on the whole was very pleasant, and the Bishop held services on the open deck. In one day they made 184 knots, from noon to noon, but that was the best run of the voyage. Over a great part of the Hudson's Bay region, there is a temperate climate and large tracts of land are fertile. The bay averages about seventy fathoms in depth, the bottom appearing to consist everywhere of boulder clay and mud. Of the rivers that run into the bay about thirty are of considerable magnitude. Few of them afford uninterrupted navigation for large vessels to any great distance from the coast. During the season of high water, shallow draft steamers might ascend the Moose and two of its branches for more than 100 miles. Hayes River and two of its branches might also, apparently, be navigated in spring 140 miles inland, and the Albany for nearly 250 miles, while large steamers might ascend the Nelson for 70 or 80 miles from the open sea. The latter is the only muddy-water river entering Hudson's Bay. Most of the others have a slight brownish tinge, but their waters are quite wholesome and contain but small quantities of foreign matter. The only harbours are those formed by the mouths of rivers, and none of them, except Churchill Harbour, can be entered by vessels drawing more than ten or eleven feet, and by those only at high water. The Nelson may form an exception, as, though most of its estuary becomes dry at low tide, a channel runs through it near the centre, as far as the head of tide-water. In sounding this channel, although an average depth of about two fathoms at low water was found, continuous soundings throughout might have shown interruptions or shallower water in some places. If a certain shallow section, about two miles in length, were deepened, steamers coming in from sea might enter this part of the river and find good shelter or proceed up stream to the lowest limestone rapid. The engineer of the Nelson Valley Company has pronounced the route (as far as he located the line), from Winnipeg to Churchill, to be an easy and inexpensive one for a railway. The survey has since been continued. As a route for emigrants, Dr. Bell speaks highly of that by Hudson's Bay. The whole report is one of great interest, and we shall take another opportunity of laying its leading features before our readers.

In the Province of Quebec, explorations were continued by Mr. Vennor in the Counties of Terrebonne, Montcalm and Joliette, embracing about 900 square miles. Some details of interest in connection with the distribution of the bands of crystalline limestone and the labradorite rocks were ascertained. Promising deposits of iron were discovered at a number of new points, at one of which, near St. Jerome, a considerable amount of work has been done by a United States Company with a view to its development. Mr. Selwyn says, that if Mr. Vennor's determinations as to the bands of limestone on the western side of the labradorite area are correct, they prove conclusively the correctness of his own opinion that " the labradorite or Norian rocks of Hunt do not constitute an unconformable upper Laurentian formation, but occur in part as unstratified intrusive masses, and in part as stratifications with the orthoclase greisses, quartzites and limestones of the Laurentian system, as developed in the Grenville region and mapped by Sir W. Logan."

To the east of the region examined by Mr. Vennor an area of 1,600 to 1,700 miles was examined by Mr. Ord and Mr. McConnell, in the Counties of Berthier, Maskinonge and St. Maurice, and 350 miles of road, not shown on any existing plan, were measured by pacing. Mr. Webster made explorations over a large area of about 3,000 square miles on the south side of the St. Lawrence, extending from Lake Memphremagog northward, and north-eastward along the New Hampshire and Maine boundaries. The whole of this region is auriferous, but it had hitherto been, to a great extent, unexamined. Another season's work will be required to correctly lay down the distribution of the formations. Mr. Selwyn holds that the granites which occur over this area, the greater part of which is occupied by strata of Silurian age, are not, as generally supposed, intrusive, but completely metamorphosed portions of the strata surrounding them.

In New Brunswick the work was continued by Messrs. Ells and Broad, and that in Nova Scotia by Mr. Fletcher. In the former Province a good deal of road surveying and river exploration was accomplished, and in the latter, the Richmond and Port Hood coal fields were explored and the courses of several rivers traced.

In Palæontology, the examination of the fossil plants of the carboniferous rocks of Canada, in the Survey's collection, commenced in 1879, has been concluded, and several other collections have been examined.

The work of Messrs. Weston and Willemot in the Museum consisted largely in preparation for removal. The laboratory work included analysis of lignite from the North-West Territory and British Columbia, of iron, copper and manganese ores, of graphite rock, gold and silver assays, and miscellaneous examinations of mineral water, &c.

Twenty volumes have been added by purchase to the library, and 152 books, pamphlets and maps, presented during the year ; 745 copies of the Survey's publications have been distributed from the Montreal office, besides those sent out from the Department at Ottawa.

One thousand one hundred and eighty-three names were registered on the visitors' book—447 fewer than in 1879. The falling off was probably due to the expectation of an earlier removal. The Survey staff now consists of 1 chief officer, 4 first class, 8 senior second class, 5 junior second class, 2 third class. This is according to the classification of the Civil Service Act. Mr. James Richardson and Mr. Robert Barlow have retired under the superannuation provisions of the same Act.

The following figures show the costs of the various surveys :—

Souris River borings.....	$1,204 30
Hudson's Bay Basin..	1,945 35
(Quebec) Mr. Vennor's....................................	909 43
Messrs. Ord and McConnell.............................	728 35
Mr. Ells (New Brunswick).................................	926 74
Mr. Broad (New Brunswick).............................	517 94
Mr. Fletcher (Nova Scotia).............................	1,259 31

The report has a good many interesting illustrations.

The Director complains that, although the cost of publishing the results of the labours of the corps, and likewise the salaries of the staff, are annually increasing, no increase has yet been made in the annual appropriation for the work.